This story is dedicated to my father, Lloyd C. Little, who instilled in me not only an interest in history, but also a love of reading and an open mind.

CONFLICT IN THE NORTH

DANIEL L. LITTLE

iUNIVERSE, INC.
NEW YORK BLOOMINGTON

Conflict In The North

iUniverse books may be ordered through booksellers or by contacting:

iUniverse
1663 Liberty Drive
Bloomington, IN 47403
www.iuniverse.com
1-800-Authors (1-800-288-4677)

Because of the dynamic nature of the Internet, any Web addresses or links contained in this book may have changed since publication and may no longer be valid. The views expressed in this work are solely those of the author and do not necessarily reflect the views of the publisher, and the publisher hereby disclaims any responsibility for them.

ISBN: 978-1-4401-7674-6 (sc)
ISBN: 978-1-4401-7675-3 (ebk)

Printed in the United States of America

iUniverse rev. date: 10/13/2009

PART I

A SOVEREIGNTY VIOLATED

Lieutenant Colonel Christopher Sardoucy could not help gazing at the curvature of the earth from the lofty height he was flying. The forty-two year old United States Air Force pilot was cruising at an altitude of forty-eight thousand feet; well below the realms his big jet regularly prowled. Today's mission profile however, required a closer than usual look at the target. Chris enjoyed these flights. The restrictions placed on his flying activities as base commander were frustrating – limited as they were to flights within five hundred miles of the North American continent, but at least that allowed him to scrape up a few hours now and then in this monster of an airplane. His helmet, almost identical to those worn by NASA's astronauts and the small, confined cockpit, did not allow him much latitude for surveying the world passing below. Ironically, the aircraft he was flying had been designed specifically to do just that.

The Lockheed SR-71 Blackbird was huge. Huge, sleek, and black. Nothing marred the non-reflective, monochromatic paint except for the few markings required by the ground crew tasked with servicing the machine. The aircraft's serial number, painted in red on the outside of its twin vertical stabilizers, was the only visible identification from beyond fifty feet. No national insignia marred the expansive surface of the wings or fuselage which smoothly blended together, giving the aircraft its unique aerodynamic shape. Seen from the ground, it appeared to be something from outer space, and flew almost that high.

A smoothly flared bulge through the center of each wing housed the aircraft's two gigantic Pratt and Whitney JT11D turbojet engines. Their maximum thrust was classified, as was most everything else housed within the Blackbird's cavernous fuselage. At the moment, Chris had the throttles set to only sixty percent, which still allowed the JT11's to effortlessly push the aircraft through the atmosphere at just over Mach One. The data plate on the canopy rail to his left indicated this as the prescribed airspeed for the multiple cameras mounted in the belly of the aircraft to operate properly at this altitude. The low power setting was a testament to the Blackbird's potential top speed which was also top secret. The air crews often joked how when the first pilot retired from the recently formed reconnaissance squadron, they'd probably have to shoot him, as everything he did except for wiping his ass was classified to the highest levels.

Nestled inside the lower fuselage, where a weapons bay would have existed had this been the fighter interceptor originally envisioned by the Lockheed designers, a bank of rack mounted cameras of various types pointed downwards through openings in the fuselage. Like the cockpit, the cameras were heated or air conditioned, depending on the outside temperature, to a constant sixty-five degrees Fahrenheit. The heaters were running right now as the aircraft moved relatively slowly through the cool night air. When the SR-71 was tearing through the skies above the Soviet Union at Mach 3 plus however, the air conditioners ran steadily to prevent the cameras melting from the heat generated by the friction of the aircraft as it flew through the atmosphere.

Chris brought his gaze away from the panoramic view outside his cockpit and once again checked over his instruments, making sure the flight computer had him on course for the mission's photo shoot. Each of the film spools loaded into the cameras below him were worth a month's wages and he didn't want to land with endless feet of useless images for although he would be staying within the confines of the North American continent, this was definitely a tactical mission.

Had he been able to see directly below the aircraft, the colonel would have noted the moonlight reflecting on the surface of the ocean far below. Ahead, the reflected light disappeared, signifying the approaching land. A few moments later, right on cue, the cameras mounted within the black beast began whirring as the SR-71 crossed over the rugged landscape far below, rapidly leaving the frigid waters of the north Atlantic behind. Defensive systems lining the coastline he had just crossed were of no concern to Chris. He, like the other pilots of his squadron, believed themselves invincible to any defensive weapon while flying the high performance aircraft. 'Let the Ruskies try to shoot THIS f***** down!', was the squadron's unofficial slogan.

Glancing at the fuel gauges, Sardoucy allowed himself a moment to relax. Everything was going according to the mission profile and he would soon…a glint of reflected moonlight from outside the cockpit off to his right caught Chris' attention. Leaning over as far as he could within the confines of his space suit, he spotted a sleek silver shape holding formation just below and to the right of his aircraft.

"Damn! Damn those Canadians!" he roared out loud. If that jerk had been underneath while the cameras were running...

Seated in the comparatively spacious cockpit of his aircraft and holding formation low on the Blackbird's starboard side, Squadron Leader Benjamin Jones, RCAF, grinned broadly. He had just pulled over and up from beneath the American spy plane, after giving its cameras a nice overhead shot of the CF-101 Voodoo. Reaching down with his gloved hand to the radio controls on the right console, he switched channels and called over to the US Air Force pilot on the NORAD guard frequency.

"Blackbird niner five zero," he called, reading the numbers off the tail of the aircraft, "this is golf november four zero zero, do you copy on guard?"

Damn Canadian jet jocks! Chris fumed silently.

"Golf november four zero zero, this is niner five zero. Copy you on guard. I don't suppose you avoided my cameras this time?" Chris immediately regretted asking the question, knowing it was just what the guy flying the Voodoo wanted to hear.

"Cameras?" Ben was trying hard to sound innocent. "Oh I'm very sorry sir! I should have known that's what those square openings in the bottom of your fuselage were for!"

"That's just swell, Canuck!" Sardoucy pronounced 'Canuck' as though it were a swear word.

"Well, you know sir," Ben continued in a condescending voice. "If you would just file a flight plan with Canadian Air Traffic Control before you take off, this wouldn't happen and I could be back at my base watching the hockey game." He knew he was pushing it.

"Yeah, maybe next time!" Chris firewalled the throttles and started a turn that would bring him back to the reciprocal course for another photo run.

Ben watched amazed, as the sleek black aircraft quickly pulled away until it had disappeared into the darkness. Had it been any other type, he would have been tempted to kick in full afterburner and give chase but there was no point. The Blackbird would leave him and his Voodoo standing still.

And besides, he really DID want to get back and watch the game. The Montreal Canadians and his beloved Detroit Red Wings were going at it in the final game of the season tonight and that was a show not to be missed. Maybe, he thought, just maybe 1966 would be the year that Detroit broke the back of those arrogant Habs. Throttling back the Voodoo's J-57's, he began a lazy turn back to the south while dialling the radio channel back to his GCI intercept frequency.

"Sunflower this is golf november four zero zero. Target is identified as US Blackbird – tail number nine five zero. Request RTB."

The report would not come as a surprise to the ground controllers. They had been tracking the 'unknown' for some time and had assumed it to be another Blackbird on its way to Europe. When the aircraft had made an unexpected turn to the west and headed into Canadian airspace, Chatham had been alerted and Ben was sent up to investigate. The same thing had happened a few days previously and the talk around the Canadian base was that the Americans were having some sort of problem with their new spy plane causing the flights to abort and return to their base in the US.

"Four zero zero, roger on the Blackbird. You are cleared to descend into controlled airspace. Upon reaching level four five zero, contact Moncton center on three six eight point five." The ground control intercept officer who was controlling the flight from RCAF Station, St. Margarets, tracked the CF-101 carefully, ensuring its pilot would merge the big fighter smoothly into the commercial aircraft traffic transiting the area.

St Margarets was home to the 21st Radar Squadron, one of a string of Pinetree radar sites stretching across central Canada and parts of the northern United States from coast to coast. The radar stations served as NORAD's second line of defence against Soviet bombers trying to sneak over the pole, and the primary defence against any aircraft attempting to slip in along the Atlantic or Pacific coasts.

NORAD's first line of defence, far to the north, was composed of radar stations strung along the Arctic Circle. Commonly known as the Distant Early Warning or DEW line, they watched over the most likely route Soviet bombers would take to cross into Canada and the US. Following a warning from the DEW line, the men and women stationed at the Pinetree sites would track the incoming bombers and direct fighter aircraft from the Canadian and United States Air Forces into positions where they would be able to intercept and destroy the Soviet intruders.

Earlier this evening, a diligent radar operator at the Barrington, Nova Scotia, Pinetree site strategically located on a tip of land jutting into the Atlantic, had detected the unidentified aircraft on its flight east from the US mainland. She had watched as the small blip on her radar screen had made a turn to the north heading back towards Canadian airspace. The corporal had quickly instigated the process which culminated in the CF-101 Voodoo scrambling from RCAF Station Chatham, New Brunswick. Situated just south of the Miramichi River, the base was perfectly placed to cover the north - eastern reaches of Canada's defensive perimeter.

As the interceptor was taking off from the Chatham airfield, the young woman 'handed off' the unidentified aircraft to St. Margarets where the contact, already suspected by its altitude and speed to be one of the new SR-71's, had fallen under the direction of a ground control intercept (GCI) team stationed at the radar site just south of the Chatham air base.

Unlike the days of WW-II, when fighter aircraft were directed by a steady stream of voice commands easily intercepted by the enemy, communications between the interceptors and the Pinetree sites took place through a voiceless radio datalink. Information was transmitted from antennas located in remote, secure locations, to a small duel antenna mounted on the lower rear fuselage of the Voodoo. This invisible link allowed the team on the ground at St. Margarets to transmit the coordinates and speed of the intruder directly to the CF-101, where it appeared on a screen used by the radar intercept operator or 'Scope Wizard' seated in the fighter's rear cockpit.

The young man on the ground who had been following the 'blip' representing the unidentified aircraft had a pretty good idea who the intruder was from the information sent in from Barrington. The Soviets often practiced entering the Canadian ID Zones at low altitude, almost hugging the waves, but this aircraft was flying high and moving fast, the Blackbird's signature.

Those damn Americans were rapidly becoming as bad as the Russians and although they had been warned twice previously against surprise excursions into Canadian airspace, the Blackbird jocks seemed to think they owned the sky. The operator had smiled wryly as he noted the Voodoo which had just appeared on his scope. Typing quickly on the small keyboard built into the console in front of him, he'd relayed the course and speed of the intruder up the secure datalink to the interceptor. This would be an easy 'kill' for the Four Sixteen guys, he chuckled to himself.

The airman had read internal memos which had explained how the Canadian ambassador to the United States had warned Washington that the Royal Canadian Air Force would start intercepting their aircraft if they hadn't filed a proper flight plan or given prior notice of their intentions. That threat had apparently fallen on deaf ears.

Fine, the young airman had thought, watching the 'blips' merge as the Voodoo caught up with the 'unknown'. The Yanks would have to learn the hard way. Grabbing his clip board, he had noted the intercept details, while sitting back in his 'ring side' seat for the upcoming action. Not much else flying up there this evening, he'd observed. Everyone else must be home watching the hockey game. Or as he suspected in Ben's case, wishing they were.

High above New Brunswick, Ben descended rapidly into controlled airspace, causing chagrin for the controllers in the Moncton control center responsible for civilian air movements over eastern Canada. If he could get back to base in time, he would just manage to catch the last period of the hockey game.

"So what do you think, Cam?" Ben asked his weapons officer strapped in the ejection seat five feet behind him. "The Wings going to take the Cup tonight?"

"I don't know, sir," replied Flying Officer Camille LeBlanc, half heartedly. He wasn't as big a hockey fan as Ben was. "They're playing in Montreal tonight and the Canadians are a tough bunch on home ice."

Not having any duties at the moment, Cam was absent-mindedly gazing up at the Big Dipper through the large Plexiglas canopy that covered the pilot and radar intercept officer. The radar scope in front of him to the right - much smaller than the large area search unit on the ground at RCAF Station St. Margaret's - showed nothing flying in the airspace ahead of them and since they were now under the control of civilian ATC, he reached over and flicked the unit to 'Standby'.

The Voodoo's rear cockpit was quite spacious although cluttered with controls and switches for the radar and weapons systems, including the rotary weapons door a few feet beneath him. At the moment, a pair of Hughes Falcon missiles, the Voodoo's standard armament, clung to the door's launch rails. Cam was enamoured with the aircraft's various weapons systems. He liked to joke when Ben was getting too carried away with one of his intercept stories that without him, the pilot wouldn't be able to find his way onto the runway let alone actually locate anything in the air.

The two had become fast friends from the start, in spite of their obvious personality differences. Ben, the typical fighter pilot, was tall, handsome and outgoing - immediately becoming the focus of attention whenever he entered a room. Cam on the other hand was shorter with a slight paunch, sporting a full head of curly hair and a fair complexion; unusual for someone with his French-Canadian roots. More reserved, almost to the point of shyness, Cam also wore wings on his tunic, having earned them during his Air Cadet days while growing up in Moncton. In spite of that, he was perfectly happy riding in the 'back seat' with his 'toys'.

Known as Mutt and Jeff amongst the crews of Four Sixteen Squadron, they were without question the best intercept team on the base. The previous year at William Tell, the USAF/RCAF competition held annually in the United States, Ben and Cam had trounced the other Canadian teams and had very nearly taken the trophy. Unfortunately, a faulty rocket component had penalized them during one of their flights. Being caught red handed late the previous night 'zapping' one of the USAF's F-106 squadron leader's aircraft with full size RCAF roundels had not helped their cause much either.

'What a joy to see that Delta Dart proudly flying the Maple Leaf the next morning,' Ben would exclaim as he had told and retold the story.

"That's true," Ben replied, shaking Cam from his thoughts. "But man, I hope to hell Detroit takes the cup this year. I'm so tired of watching Belliveau waltzing around the Forum with it." Ben had been a rabid Detroit Red Wings fan for as long as he could remember and for just as long, had fostered a deep rooted hatred for the Montreal Canadians and their so called dynasty. Maybe 1966 would be the year the Wings pulled it off.

"Chatham tower, golf november four zero zero, on final."

"Golf november four zero zero, Chatham tower. You are cleared to land - runway two seven. Winds are two three seven at five knots - gusting to ten. Check the gear - both cables are up," announced the tower controller, pausing a moment before adding, "Chatham altimeter is two niner niner five."

"Roger - both cables up - gear down and locked – altimeter two niner niner five. Four zero zero."

The three men on duty in the control tower watched to the east for the first sign of the aircraft's landing lights. A few moments later, the powerful beams broke through the low cloud cover lingering over the base, appearing to stand still in the sky beyond the end of the runway. The illusion dispelled quickly as less than a minute later they caught a glint of runway lights reflected on the unpainted metal fuselage of the interceptor as it roared over the threshold and settled down to a perfect landing. Only a small puff of white smoke escaped around the main landing gear as the tires gently kissed the ground.

As the Voodoo sped down the runway, its braking chute streamed out from just below the tail, billowing open as it caught the rushing air. The sudden deceleration thrust the two men forward into their harnesses - the extra drag slowing the aircraft down until it had decelerated enough for Ben to lightly tap the brakes. Not one of the Voodoo's strong points, the pilots were diligently instructed to avoid using them at all until the heavy interceptor had slowed to less than twenty-five knots.

"Might as well get out and walk alongside at that point," Cam had commented one day when it appeared they would reach the end of the runway before the big jet had slowed enough to use the brakes.

"Four zero zero – next right. Contact ground on two eight nine point four. Have a nice evening."

"Two eight nine point four for ground, roger. Four zero zero." Ben reached down and switched the radio to the ground control frequency where another controller would guide him along the taxiways to his assigned parking spot.

"Ground, four zero zero is with you."

"Four zero zero, roger. Turn right on Bravo and you are cleared to the ramp. Oh, and Ben? The Canadians are ahead two to one...thought you'd want to know." The controller stifled a chuckle as the tower crew waited for the expected outburst.

"Damn! Damn those Canadians!"

Carefully manoeuvring the fighter along the ramp, he taxied the Voodoo up to the flight line and shut down the engines. Ground crew were at the side of the plane in moments, setting the boarding ladders in place as the canopy popped open. Plugging in an auxiliary power unit which would provide electricity to the various systems with the engines shut down, they scurried up the ladders, helping the aircrew disconnect themselves from the aircraft. Confirming the opened canopy was fully locked and at the same time that the engines had shut down within normal parameters, Ben unfastened the harness that had held him securely to the ejection seat and looked over his shoulder.

"Cam, would you mind…"

"Done sir."

Cam knew Ben would be hot tailing it for the squadron ready room to catch the end of the hockey game. Besides, from the sounds of things, he'd want to be on Ben's good side if Detroit lost tonight. A half hearted Toronto Maple Leafs fan, Cam wasn't following the playoffs this year…as usual. Ticking his way down the shutdown list, he reached over and set the weapons door to 'access' before unfastening his harness. He was rewarded with a dull whine from below the aircraft as the weapons door swung half open, exposing the Falcon missiles for the armourers.

Ben had quickly climbed out of the cockpit and slid down the boarding ladder, nearly running over a ground crewman as he skipped the bottom two rungs and bounded across the ramp to the alert lounge. It wasn't too late, he thought, hurriedly glancing at his watch. The third period hasn't started yet, and Gordie Howe will save the day. He had to!

Cam climbed down the ladder more slowly and stopped to chat with the ground crew who were checking over the aircraft. They shared a laugh about Ben and his team's Stanley Cup quest before discussing the intercept. Signing off on the log and maintenance books a few minutes later, LeBlanc commented how there had been no technical problems during the flight and even the perpetually cranky radar cooling system had worked like a dream.

Walking in the same direction Ben had taken, Cam stopped for a moment as he always did, and glanced back at the aircraft now sitting quietly beneath the floodlights. The CF-101 Voodoo's sleek lines were unbroken except for the pair of drop tanks hanging below the fuselage and even those were streamlined for supersonic flight. The weapons door, now half open, revealed a pair of Aim 4D Falcon missiles mounted on one side. Already, the armourers were preparing to remove the missiles from the aircraft before trucking them back to the weapons bunkers located on the south side of the base. An ingenious device, the weapons door could carry two of the heat seeking missiles, as well as a pair of deadly, nuclear armed AIR-2A Genie anti-aircraft rockets mounted on the opposite side.

Flying the '101 was a dream and the 'One-O-Wonders' as the pilots were nicknamed, all loved the powerful interceptor. Any of them would have preferred that Canada's ultra-sophisticated Avro Arrow had grown to fruition of course, but that was not to be. The Arrows were gone now – chopped up like so much scrap metal and sold as such. Rumours abounded that one had been spared the cutter's torch, but other than for a few parts and most of one cockpit, they were only that; rumours.

In 1959 the newly elected federal government, weary of the escalating costs attributed to national defence, had felt the advanced aircraft was becoming a huge financial burden for Canada. Already committed to a naval ship building program that was well over budget with no end in sight, the Prime Minister had made a very tough decision. Construction of the new destroyer escorts slipping down the ways on both coasts, was employing thousands of people in an assortment of well paying trades, but they were also soaking up a large portion of the defence budget in the process.

The army meanwhile, always the poor cousin when it came to defence spending, was starting to argue loudly that they were being completely left out of the budget once again, when in fact they had been the only part of Canada's military doing any REAL fighting since World War II.

The decision had finally been made quietly within the highest levels of government to scrap the Avro Arrow project. It had been a truly sad day in Canadian history, made more so by the federal government's seemingly insane decision to not only end the project, but also destroy the existing aircraft and everything else related to it from blueprints to models. No reasons had been made public for these actions, outside of the budget issues, and with the limited information coming from the Prime Minister's Office, the press had a field day with the story.

To fill the void left by the cancellation, the government had hurriedly acquired reconditioned USAF, F-101 Voodoo's knowing that the huge expanse of Canada's north could not be left to the few remaining squadrons of 'Clunks'. The venerable Avro CF-100 had been a fine interceptor when first introduced, but the straight winged aircraft was now long in the tooth and completely outclassed by the modern jet bombers flown by the Soviets. Adding to their embarrassment of sitting almost defenceless, sandwiched between the nuclear arsenals of the United States and the Soviet Union, the Canadian military had been convinced to invest in the nuclear armed Bomarc missiles which had turned out to be a dismal failure.

Accusations had flown through the media and airforce ranks. Everyone was blamed, from Crawford Gordon, the head of Avro Canada, to the United States government who was thought to have poisoned the Prime Minister with visions of useless and expensive interceptors sitting on the ground while Soviet missiles landed on Canadian soil. Neither of course, was the true story, but truth as always, was the first victim of history.

*   *   *

Ben flew through the doors of the squadron ready room and rushed breathlessly to his favourite chair which had been left empty by the others crowded around the television. The voice of Danny Gallivan calling the play by play action indicated that he was not too late.

"Where are we?" Ben called out to no one in particular.

"Third period's just started. Not lookin' good for Detroit though," answered Flight Lieutenant Jim Fougere. "Richard scored one within ten seconds of the puck hitting the ice."

"It's not over yet," muttered Ben, his eyes glued to the puck. Three quarters of an hour later however, it was over and as Ben watched Jean Beliveau proudly skating around the rink while holding the Stanley Cup high in the air, he had to admit that maybe, just maybe though, the Canadians really were a damn dynasty.

"Well that's that for another year," Jim announced. "Sorry Ben. How'd the intercept go?"

"Huh?" Ben was contemplating Jean Beliveau and the Stanley Cup strapped to his Voodoo's weapons door and had only half heard the question. "Good. Another Blackbird snooping around up north. You'd think those guys would learn by now. It's not like they're going to sneak in without our noticing."

"That's for sure," Jim agreed. "Why do you suppose the yanks have such a thing for northern Labrador anyway? That's the third intercept in that sector this week."

"I don't know, but this guy was really pissed off with us for covering his cameras. He hit the afterburners and really tore out. Seemed strange," he added. "They usually chat it up a bit before we go our separate ways."

Ben hadn't really given the intercept a lot of thought in his rush to get back in time to catch the end of the hockey game. Thinking back, he realized the Blackbird pilot really had seem perturbed, although the intercept had ended the same way most of them did. Perhaps the USAF had an exercise going on and Four Sixteen Squadron, not being informed, had messed it up somehow. Or, he considered, maybe the guy was just having a bad day. Perhaps his favourite team had just gotten trounced…again. Shit, Ben thought in disgust. I might as well be a Leafs fan!

* * *

A few hours later the stillness of night time hung over the base, occasionally interrupted by the sound of a Pratt & Whitney J-57 spooling up during a test run. Maintenance crews would work through the night making sure the squadron's aircraft were completely ready should the 'unimaginable' ever happen. The men and women performing the work knew that their jobs, no matter how unimportant they might seem, were crucial to making sure the day they seldom dared speak of would never come.

In one of the hangers on the base, a crew of 'Witch Doctors' was busy making sure all the systems on the Voodoo which had just been towed in to replace the earlier scrambled aircraft were functioning properly. Every piece of equipment on the interceptor had been gone over twice and a few of the more cantankerous ones, three times.

Four Sixteen Squadron prided itself on going from alert horn to airborne in less than five minutes and none of the Voodoo 'Witch Doctors' wanted to be responsible for missing that mark. An armourer crouched below the nose of the aircraft, fretting over the connections to the two Falcon air to air missiles attached to the racks on the rotating weapons door. They gave the Voodoo its medium range punch. Developed by Hughes, the company owned by the eccentric millionaire, they were now the standard air to air weapon for most Canadian and US interceptors.

The '101's long range punch was safely stored far across the airfield in underground bunkers guarded by American troops as part of the US-Canadian nuclear weapons agreement. The Douglas AIR-2 Genie rockets stored there seldom saw the light of day. Occasionally one or two were brought over to the flight line for the ground crews to practice with. They would carefully load them aboard one of the aircraft, supervised by armed guards which added to their tension. The practice was primarily to weed out any of the weapons loaders who might have problems working in close quarters with the nuclear armed rockets.

Corporal Graeme Johnson who was responsible for this particular aircraft, stood back and looked it over one more time. Last month, a Voodoo had scrambled with the power cable detached from the weapons door leaving the Falcon's inaccessible, and he was not about to let that ever happen on his shift. Satisfied that everything was okay with this bird, he signed the acceptance forms, confirmed the serial numbers on the weapons and gave the crew a 'thumbs up' before walking back to the maintenance hanger.

Already, the hanger crew was preparing another pair of Voodoos to replace the one he'd just left. It was a busy time at Four Sixteen Squadron. Between the Russians constantly testing the Canadian air defences and now the American Blackbirds on their unannounced intrusions, there was an awful lot of flying going on.

"Glad I'm not paying the fuel bills," he muttered to himself before greeting the crew bringing in the new aircraft.

A short distance away inside the alert hanger, two aircraft stood quietly in the cool night air. Their noses pointed to quick opening doors that lined up with a short taxiway leading directly to runway twenty seven. There, with very little engine run up, they would roar off into the air. A few maintenance crewmen tinkered around the aircraft, making sure that everything was as it should be. An identical scene played out on every NORAD base across Canada and the United States. The stresses on the men and woman tasked with keeping the men and machines ready were enormous, but they diligently carried on, motivated by the knowledge that what they were doing made a difference.

* * *

Six hours later, the morning sun was beginning its climb into the eastern sky above the runways at Chatham. The early light gave promise of a beautiful spring day and already a few hardy souls were out running along the base perimeter fence. Wing Commander John Tremaine had arrived at his office an hour earlier, looking over the reports from the previous night's intercepts. According to one of the reports, Ben had shadowed an SR-71 for a short time before the American had left him behind. The report also noted that his aircraft had probably been 'accidentally' photographed by the cameras mounted in the spy plane's underbelly. He smiled at the image of the silver interceptor slipping beneath the great black beast. The Canadians had nothing to hide and besides, at the range the images were taken, the Voodoo would be horribly out of focus.

Typical Ben, thought the commander of RCAF Station Chatham, tossing the report back into his 'in' box. Good thing the intercept happened BEFORE the end of the hockey game last night or his squadron leader might have shot the American aircraft down. John chuckled out loud imagining how THAT report would have read. Ben was going to be impossible to live with for a few days. Probably even worse when the rubber octopus his squadron mates had mailed to the proud Red Wings fan, arrived in his mailbox.

A knock on the door brought him back to the moment.

"Come!"

Ben walked in and stood quietly at attention in front of his CO's desk.

"At ease squadron leader. Sorry about the Wings – maybe next year. I was just going over your report. Looks like you had a busy evening."

"Yes sir." Ben stood at ease. "I caught the Blackbird at forty-eight thousand feet and tailed him for a few miles. Then I accidentally slid under the SR-71's fuselage into his camera range. Sorry about that sir." The look on Ben's face was anything but.

"You mentioned that the pilot seemed more perturbed than usual," John noted. "Anything in particular make you deem it necessary to state that in your report?"

"Just the way he said he'd have to refly his camera run, sir. And when he pulled away, he kicked in what had to be full afterburner."

"Maybe he just had a bad day, Ben."

"Yes, sir. That's what I thought at first. But there was something else…a gut feeling."

The wing commander understood when a fighter pilot spoke of his 'gut feeling'. Never something to be taken lightly, that 'feeling' was often the only thing which kept his pilots alive and Ben had better instincts than most of the men in the squadron.

"Okay Ben. I'll note that in my report as well. Maybe I can make a few phone calls and see what our neighbours to the south have going on." John paused for a moment, wondering who would be the best person to call and make an informal inquiry, before looking back up at Ben.

"You're dismissed squadron leader. Good work."

"Thank you sir," Ben replied, standing at attention and turning on his heels for the door.

Wing Commander Tremaine sat back and pondered his squadron leader's report. The SR-71 flights had been more frequent than usual in the past month, and why did the Americans steadfastly refuse to file their flight plans with Canadian ATC? One thing was certain - this game going on between the Canadian and American airforces had to stop. If for no other reason than the huge reserves of fuel being wasted by the squadrons.

Outside the window, the roar of jet engines signalled yet another scramble. There was no mistaking the rumble made by a pair of J-57s running at full throttle. Turning around in his chair, John watched the sleek silver shapes lift off the runway and turn sharply to the east, maintaining low altitude. Good, he thought. They're headed out to sea. Must be another Bear trying to sneak past the Canadian defence systems.

* * *

"Golf november flight, this is Sunflower. Bogie is angels nine, two hundred and thirty miles off your eleven o'clock. Climb to angels ten and I'll bring you in on the hook."

"Roger that Sunflower, climbing to angels ten."

The pilots pulled their interceptors into a steep climb, losing only a little speed in the short ascent. In the lead aircraft, Flight Lieutenant Jeffrey Talbot checked with his weapons officer.

"You got him Jack?"

Seated behind him, Flying Officer Jack Morrison had observed the intruder as it appeared at the top of his radar scope. It had not yet been picked up by the Voodoo's radar, which had nowhere near the power to 'paint' the target at this range, but had been placed there by one of the black boxes in the aircraft's nose which were steadily receiving data from the radar station at St. Margarets.

"I have him sir. He's well below mach - probably a Bear."

Jack referred to the four engine Tupolev TU-95 bomber. Codenamed 'Bear' by NATO, the huge aircraft had been in service for a few years with the Soviet airforce. Their answer to the American B-52 Stratofortress, its powerful jet engines turned huge counter-rotating propellers giving the sleek aircraft an impressive speed. This also made it perfect for harassment flights designed to test North America's aerial security.

"Thanks Jack." Squeezing the radio button, Jeffrey called over to his wingman. "Three nine eight, copy?"

"Roger. Loud and clear."

Flight Lieutenant Danny Brown was holding his Voodoo in close formation just off the right wing of Jeffrey's aircraft.

"What do you think? Squeeze play?"

"Sure!" His enthusiastic response exposing the kick he got out of performing the manoeuvre.

"Sunflower, this is golf november flight," Jeffrey radioed. "We will be conducting the intercept from here. Thanks for the assist."

"Roger - golf november flight taking over intercept."

"How far?" Jeffrey called into the intercom.

"Fifty miles. You'll be seeing him shortly," replied Jack, watching the small dot representing the TU-95 move closer to the center of his radar scope. He reached over to the right and switched the radar's range scale to '50', putting the dot back at the top of the screen and activating the Voodoo's own radar to track the intruder. Within seconds, the dot transformed from a clear, artificial indicator on the scope to a fuzzier, live contact.

"Danny, break left and take the port side. I'll come up his starboard side. Let's go out to forty miles so there's less chance he'll spot us both."

"Sounds good! Break in three...two...one..."

The two aircraft split sharply away from each other in a manoeuvre that would take them out and behind the Soviet aircraft. Once in position, the two pilots would go to full afterburner and streak in directly at the Bear's cockpit, crossing wingtips a few hundred yards in front of the Soviet pilots. It was an impressive manoeuvre and always alarming to the Bear's crew. Whichever of the two Voodoos they were watching bore in on them at high speed, they would be startled when the second one suddenly appeared directly in front of them out of nowhere.

"Beginning pass in three...two...one...burners on!" Long streaks of flame shot out the engine nozzles of the two aircraft as raw fuel was sprayed into the exhaust, shoving the crews back hard in their ejection seats. Struggling against the force, Danny aimed at a spot in front of the Bear's cockpit, while his weapons officer called off the range to both the Bear and Jeffrey's Voodoo to make sure they did not collide.

As planned, the two fighters crossed wingtips directly in front of the bomber's nose, causing the Bear's pilot to dive suddenly in order to avoid what he thought was an imminent collision.

"Damn! I bet he shit his pants!" Exclaimed Danny, pulling around to form up on Jeffrey's fighter.

"Great flying Brown!"

Slowing to match the Bear's airspeed, the Canadian pilots slid their aircraft into position on the bomber's port side. The usual waves were exchanged and pictures taken as the three aircraft held a tight formation.

The Russian pilot gave a smile with an enthusiastic 'thumbs up' to the Canadians. Probably a frustrated, fighter pilot wanna-be, thought Jeffrey. Waving back in return, Flight Lieutenant Talbot pulled up on the joystick and the two Voodoo pilots altered course for home.

Receiving clearance from Moncton Center, they landed in formation half an hour later after a few practice touch and goes. Dropping their drag chutes and popping the canopies while taxiing to the ramp, the pilots brought the two Voodoo's to a stop on the flight line, just as the alert horns went off.

"Going to be another busy one," Danny hollered to Jeffrey over the roar of jet engines as they climbed down from their fighters.

"You're right! Hey, I can't wait to see the pictures! Jack said he got one of the Bear's pilot giving us a 'thumbs up'!"

"That's great," Danny chuckled back. "Make a copy for me too!"

"Will do! See you in debrief!"

* * *

As the 'One-O-Wonders' walked across the Chatham tarmac to the debriefing room, a little more than eight hundred miles to the south west in one of the many small conference rooms that filled the CIA headquarters building in Langley, Virginia, images taken earlier by an SR-71 where being examined. The three occupants of the room spoke little. Two of them, hunched over a desk, were staring intently at a collage of photos spread out before them. The men were using illuminated magnification devices specially designed to examine reconnaissance photos.

Without looking up, one of them finally spoke. "Well, it certainly looks like a periscope and maybe an antennae as well. Is this the best we can do to sharpen up the image?"

"Yes," responded the older man to his right. "They didn't want to push it any further or we'd lose depth of field."

"Hmm..." The first man refocused his magnifying device and gazed again at the photo which had been taken by a Blackbird while flying high over the water.

"You can see they were just beginning to submerge. The stream of air bubbles from the sub's ballast tanks give that away," he noted, pointing the details out on the photo as he spoke. "Bet it's one of their nuclear ones."

"A minute later and we wouldn't have seen anything," the senior analyst agreed. "This is the third time a Red sub's been spotted in that quadrant this week."

"But why there?" the young man muttered aloud to no one in particular. He often spoke his thoughts out loud, a habit the other analyst found annoying. "What would the Russians be up to in that area? If monitoring the Pinetree sites is what they're after, the nearest one is hundreds of miles away."

"We don't know. John's team has been working the photos and they didn't find anything other than the submarine. The Blackbird's pilot had to make a second pass because of a Canadian aircraft intercepting him." He paused a moment to reflect on the Canadians interfering with their aircraft. This time it had been fortuitous. "That's how we got the sub – on the second run. The other photos from the previous pass don't show anything."

The older man spread four more photos on the desk and they settled down to examine the new images. These were of the coast line close to where the submarine had been spotted. From the altitude the images had been taken, the land appeared desolate and barren.

"No, you're right," Peter said, placing another photo under his magnifier. "I didn't see anything out of place either except for the submarine. Maybe he was just..." He stopped suddenly, bending closer to the table.

"What is it?"

"Look! Right here!" He pointed at a spot on the photo and moved aside. "Damn! I thought it was a shadow and nearly missed it!"

Sure enough, among a group of rocks close to the coast, a dark area stood out from the landscape. It was too square and monochromatic to be natural, almost as though someone had spread a tarp out to cover something..

"Hell, I didn't see it," the older man remarked, reminding himself that this was the very reason at least ten different people looked at every photo which came into their department. It was said the men and women who worked here had long given up their sanity to their obsession with reconnaissance photo interpretation.

"Well, it looks as though our Soviet friends are up to something in Labrador," Peter smiled. "Guess we'd better let the Canadians know."

"We won't be doing that Peter." The remark came from the third man in the room. He was older again than the other two and the door to his office down the corridor was marked by three letters - DCI. The two men looked up as one at the Director of the Central Intelligence Agency, puzzled, but knowing there must be a reason behind the decision. They both incorrectly supposed the Canadians must already know about their Russian visitors since these photos had been interpreted by someone else earlier in the day and the Canuks would certainly have been notified then.

"I need a report on your observations in thirty minutes, gentlemen."

* * *

Propping himself up, Squadron Leader Ben Jones looked over at the clock on his night stand for the fourth time in the past hour. The barely visible hands showed a little after 3:00am and he groaned quietly, realizing it would soon be time to get up and head over to the base. He had slept fitfully – more awake than asleep - rehashing the previous night's intercept again in his mind. Quietly turning over, he looked at his wife Joanne, who was still sound asleep. She would awake a couple of hours after he left to get their children's breakfast ready before sending them off to school.

In the past, Mrs. Jones had forced herself to rise early with her husband, but Ben had made it clear that with all she did looking after the kids as well as their home, he wanted her to take advantage of the extra sleep. He remembered with fondness the morning he had told his wife that she needed her beauty sleep. She had playfully tackled him, shoving him hard to the kitchen floor. The ensuing sprained wrist from their roughhousing had grounded him for a week.

Reaching over, he turned off the alarm. He would not be needing it as there would be no more sleep for him tonight. Quietly leaving the bedroom so as not to disturb his wife, Ben made his way to the kitchen where he put a pot of coffee on before heading to the shower.

Afterwards, as he was shaving, the nagging question which had kept him awake again wriggled its way into his mind. Why had the Blackbird jockey been so pissed off at him? Ben mentally ran through the intercept for the umpteenth time. Nothing else unusual had occurred at any point of the flight. Maybe the American pilot really was just having a bad day, as the boss had suggested. The altitude had been typical. They were out over the Labrador Sea, heading west when he had slipped underneath the huge black aircraft, blocking its sensors… the thought froze in place. That was it! All the previous intercepts he could recall had taken place much further north, or further off the coast as the SR-71s were either flying to or from the Soviet Union. Why had this one been coming in from Greenland heading in a westerly direction? The Blackbirds were based far to the south in Texas, which would have put the spy plane's pilot on a much more southerly heading if he was returning home from a mission over the USSR. It seemed obvious to Ben now that the American was not just flying over Canada, but had been taking pictures of something either in Labrador or just off the coast. He would have to check this theory out with the base commander later in the morning.

Pouring himself a cup of coffee, Ben quietly walked into the bedroom he shared with his wife. Joanne rolled over, mumbling something in her sleep before laying still again. He hoped she was having a happy dream. Soundlessly leaving the room, he briefly looked in on the kids who were also fast asleep. Taking a sip of coffee, he walked out the back door and sat on the step, letting the caffeine wake him up and breathing in the fresh, morning air. Above him, stars twinkled in the clear dark sky. A full moon, slowly setting in the south west, cast long, eerie shadows on the ground giving the backyard a surreal atmosphere.

The small PMQ occupied by the Jones family, just up the street from the base main entrance, stood among a row of similar buildings which made up the married quarters of RCAF Base Chatham. The neighbourhood was quiet and serene, the stillness broken only by a neighbourhood cat who padded over and climbed up the steps, looking up at the man sitting there. Ben rubbed the animal's chin, eliciting a purr from the cat before it skulked off in pursuit of more interesting game. Squadron Leader Jones cherished this time of the morning when everything was so peaceful and the Cold War seemed a million miles away.

Over on the base in maintenance hanger two, it was anything but.

* * *

"Damn it Frank! I've told you before! You can't be walking on the wings wearing those shoes!"

Flight Sergeant Josh Bernard was unhappy with the assorted black scuffs he'd discovered on the left wing of Voodoo oh six two. The short, muscular, Irish Catholic was glaring up at the corporal guilty of this act of disrespect to one of his airplanes and although a good four inches taller, the corporal was clearly intimidated by the tirade being directed at him.

"I'm sorry sarge. I wasn't thinking," he replied timidly. "I'm working a double shift again tonight."

"Well, try and keep focused, corporal," Josh replied, his voice softening somewhat.

He knew the Royal Canadian Air Force was working hard to retain men like Frank who seldom screwed up, while at the same time trying to entice new enlistments as the Cold War continued to heat up. The on-duty hours were murder, and the toll was evident in the faces of everyone on the base. The younger families coped as best they could, while developing a strong bond of friendship and support for each other.

The airforce had recently managed to recruit some good men, but keeping them, especially with the stress of constant alerts and endless overtime, not to mention the hell of Operational Readiness Inspections was another matter. The RCAF was doing all it could to improve life for the lower ranks, and the officers as well when it could, but improvements seemed to be taking a long time. To some men like the corporal, too long. He looked down and cursed silently for letting himself forget the shoes and disappointing his sergeant.

"And clean those scuff marks off! Squadron leader sees those and he'll have us both cleaning out burner cans," Josh added jokingly.

Josh Bernard would have never thought it himself, but it was men like him on bases all over North America who were managing to keep two airforces functioning smoothly in these trying times. He finished the checklist on the oh six two aircraft, signed off on it, and returned to his office.

A note on his desk informed him that his wife had called at ten the previous evening. It said the matter was not important. Good thing, he thought. She'd be fast asleep by now. He sat back for a moment in the well worn chair behind his desk and closing his eyes, rested them for a few minutes. Bernard was also working a double shift this night and he was looking forward to getting home before the kids left for school. Then he'd sleep for a few hours before getting up to spend some time with his wife - his 'second' wife - as she always addressed herself. His first wife or wives rather, were parked just outside the office in the cavernous hanger. Linda occasionally joked that if he gave HER as much attention as he did those damn planes, she'd be the happiest woman in the world. She was kidding, he knew. With their brood of seven children and another one in the hanger, she already was.

* * *

Four miles off the rugged coast of eastern Labrador, *HMCS Margaree's* knife-like bow sliced through the cold, choppy waters of the Labrador Sea. The destroyer's light grey paint was coated in a layer of moisture, making it glisten in the noon day sun. Her smooth, streamlined hull gave notice that she was a thoroughbred, designed for speed. The three hundred and sixty-six foot length was broken only by a large numeral '230' painted on her sides just below the bridge. The only other visible markings were a red maple leaf emblazoned on the outside of each of the destroyer's twin funnels.

Her original, triangular silhouette, once one of the most beautifully designed warships afloat, was now broken by the addition of an aircraft hanger. Added behind the ship's superstructure, the space had been built on to store the ship's new Sikorsky CHSS-2 Sea King helicopter. From the stern facing hanger doors, a large landing platform now extended aft over where the after Mk-33, 3" 50cal. gun turret had originally been positioned.

The navy engineers tasked with redesigning the ship had deemed the guns pretty much useless in this modern age of jet aircraft. The possible exception being to threaten small, unarmed adversaries. Those same engineers had also shown foresight by giving in to demands from the ship's crews, allowing the retention of the forward gun turret. Although the primary function of the *St Laurent* class destroyers was the detection and destruction of submarines, no self-respecting sailor would dare be seen at sea aboard a ship that did not carry a single gun mount.

One of the ship's original pair of Mk-10 Limbo anti-submarine mortar systems had also been removed in order to make room for the helicopter landing area. The remaining three-barrelled device, capable of tossing a two hundred pound depth bomb out to a range of eleven hundred yards, sat in a deep well incorporated into the ship's stern. The mortars had been the warship's primary anti-submarine weapon when *HMCS Margaree* had originally been launched in March of 1956, but now, ten years later, like the 3" gun turrets, they were considered a weapon of a bygone era. The new torpedo armed Sea King helicopter would be the ship's principal sub killing weapon now, or so the navy hoped.

When originally launched, the *St. Laurent* class destroyers were arguably the best anti-submarine warships afloat, continuing the reputation Canada's sailors had earned during the second world war as the best submarine hunters in the world. With the sleek ships being modified with not only the addition of a helicopter capability, but also a new variable depth sonar system hanging off the stern, the Canadian navy was remaining at the forefront of anti-submarine warfare technology.

Margaree's crew were continuing their post-refit workup with the new weapons as the destroyer, one of the first to be modified, steamed on her northern patrol. Although these waters were not likely to be harbouring Soviet submarines, the area was often used for training by the Canadian navy as it was well clear of commercial shipping lanes. The crew were standing their watches throughout the ship while the captain scanned the horizon from his position above the superstructure on the open bridge. He did not really expect to spot much in these obscure waters other than the odd whale, but he was thoroughly enjoying the view, except that is to the stern, which was now obstructed by the hanger structure.

The seas were relatively calm this bright, sunny day, and Lieutenant Commander Barry Delaney, *HMCS Margaree's* commanding officer, was pleased with not only the weather conditions, but also with a communication he had just received. The Montreal Canadians' win last night had brought a radio call from his life long friend and skipper of the Royal Canadian Navy aircraft carrier *Bonaventure*. Poor Dean, Barry thought with a grin, that'll teach him to bet against the Canadians.

Looking over the sides of the destroyer's open bridge, he saw the first signs of broken sheet ice flowing by in the ship's wake. A man wouldn't last long in that, he mused. Sailing north just off the coast of Labrador, the water wasn't going to get warmer anytime soon.

"Helm, slow to five knots," he ordered into the intercom to the sailor manning the ship's wheel inside the enclosed bridge a deck below. "Maintain present course."

"Aye, sir," came the sharp, slightly distorted response from the speaker behind him. "Slowing to five knots."

Barry cherished these sunny days of spring when he could command his ship from the open bridge and enjoy the invigorating, cool air. He felt cramped and even a little claustrophobic within the enclosed bridge below. It didn't bother him anywhere else on the ship, but sitting in his chair surrounded by the bridge crew…well, there was a lot more freedom up here in the brisk sea breeze.

"Sir, sonar reports a contact to the west." The petty officer standing behind him was wearing a headset connecting him to all stations on the destroyer. "No range estimate at this time."

"The west?" Delaney turned to look at the man. If they had been sailing much more to the west themselves, they'd be able to see the Labrador coast.

"Confirm that direction, petty officer. Go down there and see if they've lost their compass."

"Yes sir," the sailor responded, reaching for the ladder to the lower bridge. He wished the CO would stand his watch below where everyone was within voice range.

"No one runs a ship from up here anymore," he muttered quietly to himself while descending the ladder. Confirming the accuracy of the sonar report, he climbed again to the deck above and repeated the message to Commander Delaney.

"He must be one brave sub skipper. Helm, bring us left two niner zero degrees," Delaney ordered, thinking he would soon have to start asking for depth soundings if they closed much further on the coast. "Keep this speed."

"Left two nine zero degrees at present speed, aye sir," echoed the sailor manning the intercom on the bridge below. There it would be echoed again to the sailor manning the ship's helm. Could be worse, Barry thought. At least the modern electric intercom allowed easy communication with the men below instead of having to constantly shout into the dreaded voice tubes which had also been installed on the ship as a back up.

"Lieutenant," he called over to an officer looking out to sea on the port side of the bridge. "Take the helm. I'm going down to combat and see what they've got."

"Yes sir!" Lieutenant Henry Learner answered. Like his commanding officer, he too preferred to con the ship from the fresh air of the open bridge.

Commander Delaney quickly descended the ladder to the lower bridge and slipped through the dark curtain which covered an opening in the aft bulkhead. A short ladder led down to a darkened room where the ships radar and sonar sensors were monitored. This space, known as CCR, seemed to be continually shrinking as new capabilities were added to the warship. The dimly lit area was warm in spite of *Margaree's* ventilation system, heated by the hundreds of vacuum tubes contained within the various pieces of electrical equipment filling every nook and cranny. The ship's recent addition of the Sea King, had created the need for yet another console in CCR, for 'air', a miniature air traffic control center for the ship's helicopter.

The more sensible addition to *Margaree* in Commander Delaney's mind, had been the variable depth sonar or VDS mounted on the destroyer's newly reshaped stern. The device which resembled a stubby airplane, was attached to the ship through a long cable wound upon a huge winch, allowing it to be dropped into the water behind *Margaree*. Sonar transducers installed in the apparatus allowed the operators in the ship above to listen for submarines below the ocean's thermal planes, layers of different temperatures which occur naturally in the oceans. Submariners had long since learned that they could hide just below these temperature layers, hidden from a surface ship's sonar which would bounce off of rather then penetrate the invisible blanket of water.

Delaney wasn't so sure about the new Sea King helicopter sitting in its hanger aboard the ship. Since *HMCS Margaree* had been re-classed as a DDH last October, the large helicopter had only flown off the deck a few dozen times. Once, during very high seas, the pilot had brought the big Sea King in to land while the ship was being violently tossed about by huge waves. The 'bear trap' capture device had worked as advertised and hauled the aircraft down to the deck without incident. Barry had been extremely impressed with that exhibition, but was still sceptical as to how practical the helicopter would be in chasing down submarines. He constantly joked with the 'air' crew about taking his 'personal' helicopter ashore, rather than using one of the ship's boats.

The commander did have an open mind however, and was more than willing to let the 'flyboys' give it a try. Delaney was pondering that possibility now as he made his way to the far corner of the combat information center where his sonar operators sat at a pair of dimly lit consoles. Stepping over to the one currently manned by a leading seaman, he watched the large round screen as the sound waves flowed out from the sonar dome mounted on the bottom of the hull behind the ship's bow. Moments later, a tiny blip appeared on the left side of the screen. This close to land, the VDS was no help as there were no thermal planes in water this shallow.

"He must be awfully close to shore," Commander Delaney spoke softly, still managing to startle the young man seated in front of him who had been unaware of his presence.

"Yes sir," Leading Seaman Brent O'Hanlon responded, quickly regaining his composure. "I lost him twice in the beach noise, but he's moved further off shore now so he's a little clearer. Sounds like one of the new nuclear boats, sir."

"How can you tell, O'Hanlon?"

"Just the fact that I can hear him at all sir. At this distance, I don't think I'd have picked up a diesel boat running submerged on batteries." Brent paused silently for a moment. "Wait. I can make out his pumps. He's nuclear all right."

Barry was impressed with this young man. He was good and more importantly, showed confidence. That was an important quality in this game. A commander could not wait for his crew to decide what they thought might be going on around them and he certainly didn't have time to watch all of the sensors himself.

"Any guess who's, O'Hanlon?"

"Not yet. They all sound pretty much the same," he replied without taking his eyes off the scope. "If you want a guess, I'd say it's a Soviet 'Hen,' (he was referring to the trio of new Russian submarine classes, identified as the *Hotel, Echo*, and *November* by NATO) but I can't confirm her yet." Brent looked up, an expectant expression on his face. "Are you going to send the Sea King after it sir?" He was anxious to see how the new weapons system would work on the Russians.

Barry looked over to the 'air' console directly across the room. "Air! Do you think you can get that noisy monster of yours to leave the deck and go see what young Mr. O'Hanlon here has found?"

"Aye! Right away sir!"

"Good job O'Hanlon. Keep on him!"

Commander Delaney stepped over to the plotting table to check on how close they were to the rugged shores of Labrador and how much water was under the keel. Running the ship aground was a sure fire way to end his naval career and he was not about to let that happen.

On the flight deck, the Sea King's crew had unfastened the rotors and were unfolding them from their stowed position against the flat sides of the helicopter. A small group of curious sailors stood by to give assistance to the air crew if they requested it, but mostly they just wanted to watch the unfamiliar operation. Having spread the rotors and locked them in place, the flight crew climbed into the aircraft and slid the side door closed. Moments later, a high pitched whine emanated from the aircraft as the pilot started the jet turbines and the rotors began to move. After a brief engine run up, the helicopter slowly lifted from the flight deck. Gesturing at the noisy machine, one of the crew pointed to the Mk-44 torpedoes slung on either side of the helicopter. It was the first time they had seen weapons mounted to the aircraft.

The roar of jet engines and the beating of rotors threatened to deafen the crew members who watched in astonishment as the noisy contraption slid to starboard away from the ship. Dipping the helicopter's blunt nose before turning west just above the water's surface, the pilot headed in the direction of the submarine's last contact. Below in *Margaree's* CCR, the petty officer at the 'air' post announced to the CO that the Sea King was airborne.

"Sonar, give 'air' the current coordinates of the contact and let them know if you pick up any changes in the sub's course," Commander Delaney ordered.

"Aye sir. On the way." Brent scribbled down his estimate of the submarine's location and brought it over to the 'air' console, where the airman radioed the information up to the helicopter.

Brent returned to his scopes and watched the blip which represented what he suspected was a Russian submarine. An uncanny ability to compartmentalize his thoughts allowed him to imagine the Sea King approaching the location of the submarine while still gazing at the electronic representation of it in front of him. He had been patiently awaiting this moment since first seeing the helicopter landing aboard ship.

When he had returned to *HMCS Margaree* after a long leave the previous November, O'Hanlon had not been surprised to see the hanger structure added to the upper decks. He had been made aware of the changes which would mar the beautiful lines of his ship. *Margaree's* original single funnel had been replaced by two smaller ones on either side of the box-like structure that would house the ship's helicopter. Examining the large landing platform stretching aft from the hanger's doors, he had felt as others did, that perhaps the navy engineers had taken leave of their senses.

Seeing that one of the Limbo mounts had been removed to make room for the flight deck convinced him they really had gone too far. That had not been part of the original plan, but had come about as a weight trade off for the new VDS equipment. The Limbo mortar could lob a depth charge a good distance from the ship and with only one of the three-barrelled systems left, how the hell was he supposed to straddle a submarine and sink it? He supposed they could still destroy a sub on the surface - taking it out with the remaining 3"50 on the foredeck which was assuming of course that the other fellow would oblige them by surfacing within gun range.

Brent gave passing notice to the new red and white ensign fluttering from the stern pole. The redesigned Canadian flag had been reluctantly accepted by the army and air force and even less so by the navy. Heavily steeped in the traditions of the British Royal Navy which had given it birth, the RCN was fearful that the HMCS preceding their ship's names would be the next thing to go.

The Prime Minister was hard pressed to convince Canadian soldiers, sailors and airmen that the flag would give Canada a distinct identity, proving to the world that she had grown up and moved away from her British 'mother'. Brent had heard more than one old salt lament that maybe they should 'move away' from the Prime Minister instead.

An even harder sell for the new PM was the government's current move towards unification of the separate branches of Canada's armed services; a cost saving measure they claimed would allow the acquisition of more equipment in the future. Of this, Brent was sceptical. He could not comprehend a military force where all three branches wore the same green uniform. That simply defied logic.

While on leave, O'Hanlon had thought over his options and finally decided to make the navy a permanent career. Joining the senior service straight out of high school, the young man had striven relentlessly to reach his current rank of leading seaman. *HMCS Margaree* was his first posting and Brent was proud of her and his shipmates. He had no idea what had first attracted him to the sea. There was no family lineage pointing him to a career in the armed forces, let alone the navy. In fact, he'd only learned how to swim the previous summer. But the seas had stolen his heart. The ship's crew was like a big, rambunctious family to him and he cherished the bonds which had developed amongst his mates. They all shared a fierce pride in their ship, the CO and the navy, in about that order.

Their commanding officer knew he had the crew's respect, but only half their loyalty. The rest belonged to *Margaree*, a relationship which had existed between sailors and ships throughout the ages. Commander Delaney was considered a good type by the men he led and Brent instinctively liked the man. The CO had been hesitant about the upgrades to the ship when the engineers had gone over the changes with him and some of the crew, including O'Hanlon, and Delaney had failed to hide his misgivings about the helicopter, but had been willing to give it a chance. A few other officers had ended up sailing desks after making disparaging comments regarding the helicopters, the new flag and especially unification.

The political environment was changing fast, Brent had surmised after the meeting. All this talk of unification and God forbid, green uniforms! He had even heard the new destroyers being designed for the Canadian navy would be powered by gas turbines. Jet engines propelling a ship! With no steam, what would they use to power the ship's horn?

"Ivan, you are in for one hell of a surprise," the part of Brent's mind monitoring the submarine whispered to the small blip on the screen, as he circled it with his grease pencil and wrote in the time. His uniform might be green someday, but what he wore would make no difference to this or any other submarine. He'd still hunt it down and if necessary, kill it. To the men on surface ships, all submarines were treated as the enemy.

Aboard the Sea King, Flight Lieutenant Phillip Barkus looked ahead to the ragged coast and wondered what brand of submarine captain would be sailing submerged in these treacherously shallow waters. Behind him, the three members of his tactical crew were pouring over their equipment, anxious to prove the helicopter's abilities to the men back on board *Margaree*. They had been relentlessly tormented by the crew about their 'flying machine' with taunts about their ability to do anything about it if they actually did detect a sub.

"Bob, unlock the dipping sonar," Barkus called into the intercom. "We'll be over the target area in two minutes." They were just east of where O'Hanlon suspected the submarine was hiding and in order to get an exact fix, they would triangulate their bearings with those from the ship and pinpoint its exact position.

The Sea King crew would have never been able to communicate without their helmet mounted intercom system, blasted as they were by the roar of jet engines just above their heads, not to mention the constant slapping sound from the rotors as they pulled the heavy machine through the air.

"Sonar is ready sir! Starting to drop now!"

Phil glanced down at his instruments and noted they had reached the approximate spot where *Margaree's* sonar operator had indicated the submarine should be located.

"Man," he exclaimed. "We are REALLY close to shore!"

Manipulating the control stick, he brought the Sea King's forward motion to a halt and set the auto pilot to hold them at the present altitude and position. Fortunately there was very little wind today so 'dipping' would be a piece of cake.

"Let 'er go Bob!"

"Sonar head is in the water!" Bob announced while the other two members of the crew checked the displays looking for any sign from the Soviet submarine. At the left hand console, Petty Officer George Dorey focused intently on the sounds coming through his headset from the passive sonar transducers in the head. All he could hear were dull thunks as small fish bumped the sonar head and the distant roar of surf as the ocean pounded the nearby rocky shore. The water here was far too shallow for the passive sonar to be of much use.

"*Flapjack*, this is *Buttersquare*, we are going active," Bob radioed over to *Margaree* to warn her sonar operator before he started pinging with the powerful dipping sonar.

"*Buttersquare*, we copy that. *Flapjack* out."

Reaching up, George slid a small plastic cover aside and pressed the 'Active' button. A powerful sound wave emitted from the transducer in the sonar head and flowed out through the water in a circular pattern.

"You get anything, Ted?" George had to shout to the man seated right next to him to be heard above the noise from the turbines. Ted listened intently through the headphones, but there was no answering echo that would have indicated a submarine nearby.

"Nothing," he hollered back. He had removed his helmet with the intercom to use the headphones attached to the sonar suite. "Try it again."

George punched the button and once more listened intently for a return echo. He tried to relax, knowing that a heightened anxiety would affect his hearing.

Ted stiffened in his seat. There…barely…a faint but distinct echo reached his ears and he pointed to his headphone, daring not to speak as though the Russians could possibly hear him over the loud rumbling of the Sea King hovering just above the water's surface.

"Sir, I have him. Bring us left to course three zero five degrees. He's about five hundred yards out." Ted exclaimed, much louder this time. "That sonar guy back on the ship nailed him dead on!"

"On the way!" Phillip pulled back on the collective to lift the helicopter high enough so the dipping sonar hanging below them would clear the waves. This would save time as the Sea King could climb faster than the winch controlling the sonar's cable could haul it back up. Adjusting the controls he brought the craft to the new heading and covered the five hundred yards in a few moments where he again lowered the aircraft to its previous altitude and set the auto pilot.

Behind him, George hit the active button once again and this time was rewarded with an immediate echo as the sound wave crashed into the submarine's hull and reflected back to the sonar head.

"Got him! He's right beneath us! Can't be more than a hundred feet down!" Ted hollered out. Adjusting his helmet, he called over to *Margaree*.

"*Flapjack*, this is *Buttersquare*. Target is directly below us. Depth approximately one hundred feet. Requesting instructions."

The 'sparker' at the communications console looked up at Commander Delaney with an expectant expression.

"Ask him what the Ruskie's doing," Delaney commanded.

"*Buttersquare*, this is *Flapjack*. What is the submarine up to?"

"He's stopped at the moment," responded George. "Unless he's deaf, he knows we have him."

Mere moments passed before the next radio message came from the Canadian destroyer. "*Buttersquare*, you are clear to drop grenades over his position. Report any activity." The hand grenades dropped into the sea would alert the Soviet crew that the Canadians were aware of their presence. This was common practice and usually resulted in the 'found' submarine surfacing as the crew knew the ship sitting above them would either chase them down or wait them out until they had to surface and charge their batteries.

With the transition to nuclear powered submarines, this scenario was now reversed completely. It would now be the surface ship which would eventually have to break off the chase in order to refuel.

"Roger that *Flapjack*. Preparing to drop grenades now." Looking over his shoulder, Phillip confirmed the crew had heard the instructions and noted that Bob had yanked the pin on one of the old World War II grenades before dropping it out the opening in the door on the helicopter's port side.

"Got it!" Ted exclaimed. "It was close to the sub's location – wait, he's powering up!" He heard the unmistakable sounds of the nuclear power plant's coolant pumps increasing speed.

On *Margaree*, Brent O'Hanlon heard the noises as well. "Sir! Target is moving...fast!"

"What's his heading?" Delaney asked.

"East sir. He's going to pass right below us." Cold realization of what was about to happen hit Brent at the same time as his commanding officer. "Request permission to retrieve the VDS!"

The Soviet captain was using a tried and true tactic - head directly for the enemy ship to throw his sonar off with the close proximity. Unfortunately, this submarine's captain had not yet been briefed about the Canadian warship's new towed sonar system. That information had only just reached the Soviet Naval Command offices through KGB operatives.

"Granted! Make it smart!" Even as he gave his ok, Commander Delaney's knowledge of geometry told him *Margaree* would not be able to reel in the VDS in time.

"*Flapjack*, the target is heading right for you!" Ted's warning from the Sea King came too late.

Delaney punched the intercom button for the bridge on Brent's console and ordered 'all stop' before sounding the collision alarm.

Two minutes later, at close to twenty knots and a depth of just over one hundred and fifty feet, the *November* class nuclear submarine ploughed into the heavy cable connecting the VDS to the stern of *Margaree*. The thick steel line scraped over the boat's hull, and despite the massive stresses placed upon it, stayed intact until it struck the propeller guard, which held fast for a few moments before an improper weld allowed it to snap from the hull. The cable then became hopelessly entangled in the boat's port propeller before finally severing from the destroyer.

On *HMCS Margaree*, crewmembers hung on tightly to whatever they could as the ship's stern was abruptly swung to starboard and the destroyer heeled over hard before slowly righting herself and coming to a complete stop.

"All stations! Report damage!" Commander Delaney calmly ordered over the address system. He was not so much concerned about damage the collision between the submarine and the VDS might have caused *Margaree*; that would be slight. How the Soviet captain would react was the unanswered question. He might already be ordering his tubes flooded in preparation to firing on the destroyer. "Action stations! This is not a drill!"

To his right, a sailor mashed a red button on the bulkhead and loud horns erupted throughout the ship. Above the sound of sailors rushing to their posts, could be heard loud metallic clangs as water-tight doors were slammed shut and dogged down. Powerful pumps situated in a stern compartment forced filtered air into the destroyer's spaces, creating a positive pressure throughout the ship. This would keep radioactive fragments from entering, should *Margaree* have to sail through a radioactive fallout cloud in the event the unthinkable happened.

"Sir," Brent shouted loudly above the din. "Contact is now dead in the water about one thousand yards east. Mechanical thrashing sounds. I'd say he's caught in the VDS cable."

Brent could see the consternation on the captain's face. Obviously, this particular test of *Margaree's* new systems was not going well.

"Keep listening, O'Hanlon," Delaney ordered. "Inform me of ANY change."

"Aye, sir." Brent replied, not removing his gaze from the sonar display.

Aboard *Margaree's* Sea King, now hovering over the submarine's last known position, Ted listened for any sign of its plight. He could hear crashes and banging as the Russian crew cleaned up after their sudden stop. Anything not fastened down inside the submarine would have gone flying to the deck. Suddenly there was a loud mechanical screech followed by a terrible metallic crunching before everything went silent.

"*Flapjack*, this is *Buttersquare*," Ted knew what the noise had been. "He's caught the VDS cable around his props. He tried to move and something broke down there."

"Roger that *Buttersquare*. We have that here too. Stay on station and prepare to render assistance."

That would present a unique situation, Flight Lieutenant Barkus thought. He wasn't sure how a rescue of Soviet sailors should proceed. In his opinion, they were just as likely to shoot his aircraft down as consider it any kind of salvation.

"Ted," he called to the sonar operator. "Anything happening down there?"

"Nothing yet, sir. He's gone real quiet."

"Okay. Grab the rifle. Just in case."

An FN semi-automatic rifle was always carried on board for anything from scaring sharks to survival. Scanning the ocean, Phillip could see no sign of a periscope or antennas poking through the water's surface. Maybe the submarine was disabled and couldn't blow its tanks. Poor buggers if that were the case. Having toured the brand new *HMCS Ojibwa* in Halifax a few weeks ago, he had seen first hand that there was little likelihood of escaping the sub if anything went wrong while they were submerged.

* * *

Below the water's surface, chaos had ensued aboard *K-32* as the crew rushed to determine the extent of the damage caused by the collision. Some of the men's faces had shown utter fear at the scraping sound made by the cable passing along the hull and a few had momentarily panicked when the noise had changed to a grinding scream and the boat had swayed aimlessly before coming to an abrupt stop.

It was as if a giant hand had reached down into the water and held the submarine in place and just as suddenly, had released it, allowing the boat to move a short distance before it drifted to a stop. A quick thinking engineering officer had shut the reactor down, saving it from scramming. This left them temporarily powerless except for a small back-up battery until the nuclear power plant came back on line. Now past their initial fear, years of training kicked in and the crew went about their tasks with quiet determination.

K-32's captain discovered that even with full power from the reactor restored, the submarine's propellers were damaged to the extent that they were unable to supply any amount of propulsion. His sonar operators had informed him the Canadian warship was not moving and he suspected the destroyer's captain was now playing a game of cat and mouse with him, waiting for some reaction from the Soviets before deciding what to do with his prey. What was this device which had captured his submarine and left him unable to move? Perhaps a new weapon of some kind? He pondered the possibilities, never guessing that this had simply been an accident.

A hundred feet above him, the officers aboard *HMCS Margaree* faced a different dilemma as they speculated on the Soviet captain's next move.

* * *

"He'll probably surface and have divers go down to untangle the cable," Lieutenant Henry Learner offered. "I suspect that once he sees what's caught in his props, he'll try to bring the VDS aboard and take it back to the Soviet Union with him."

"Yes, and who could blame him?" Barry responded. He leaned back in his chair, fingers interlaced tightly behind his head as he always did when faced with a difficult dilemma. They had never covered THIS scenario during war games back in Halifax.

From behind the small desk, the only piece of furniture in the cramped office, Lieutenant Commander Delaney surveyed the men occupying his quarters. Sitting stiffly but silently next to the XO, Sub Lieutenant Joe Brannigan, was trying to relax. He had spent the past half hour in constant contact with the teams manning the ship's weapons and so far, everything was working flawlessly.

"You've been awfully quiet, Joe," Henry remarked, looking over at the officer who appeared in deep thought.

"I don't have much more to add," he replied. "All weapons systems are functional and we're ready. I realize our position and if need be, we'll get the job done."

None of the three men seated in the room were prepared to discuss out loud what that 'job' would be. They were however, all thinking about it. For now, they were content to wait out the answer from Canadian navy headquarters in Halifax. They realize that the message sent there ten minutes earlier by Commander Delaney would be causing mayhem amongst the admirals. Meanwhile, on a lighter note, a cartoon of Delany holding onto a huge fishing rod with a snarling submarine caught fast on the line and his smiling mouth exclaiming 'VDS bait!', was already making the rounds throughout the ship.

A sharp rap on the door made all three men jump a little.

"Enter!" Delaney shouted.

"Sir," spoke a petty officer as he walked hesitantly into the room, "message from Halifax."

"Thank you, petty officer."

Barry stood, reaching for the folded piece of paper. He noted the seal and 'Secret' stamp on the side proffered to him. Remaining on his feet, he broke the paper seal and unfolded the note while the others watched his face for any sign of the message's contents. They saw the answer reflected in his downcast eyes.

"We sink her…"

There was a period of silence broken by Lieutenant Henry Learner who quietly muttered one word -

"Shit."

"No point in putting this off, gentleman. Joe, have your men ready on the Limbo just in case, but I'm going to try and use the helicopter," Delany announced. "I guess Mr. Barkus will have a chance to show us what that noisy machine of his can do," he added wryly.

Without further conversation, the men stood and left the commanding officer's quarters. Filing into the passageway, they headed quickly for their respective stations. Sub Lieutenant Joe Brannigan made his way to the ships combat information center, stepping quietly into the darkened space. Glancing around at the group of men under his command, he noted they were all busily monitoring the various sensors that made up *Margaree's* electronic eyes and ears.

He saw that O'Hanlon was adding to the notations on the sonar scope in front of him with a grease pencil, while recording the various sounds emanating from the Soviet submarine. That information, which was priceless, would later be shared amongst the other NATO navies.

A vision of his wife, Catherine, waving up at him from the dock as they had pulled out, popped into Brannigan's head, but was quickly shoved aside by anger. Anger that Ottawa would place the value of the ship's new sonar system over that of *Margaree* and her crew, even that of the world. The ships public address system cleared the disturbing thought from his mind.

"This is the captain." There was a slight pause. "We have received orders to prevent the Soviets from acquiring the VDS system."

The crew went silent as the announcement sank in. The only sound heard throughout the ship was the whoosh of air rushing through ventilator screens as the anti-fallout system continued to pressurize the ships 'citadel'. Some of the men swore softly at the realization of what they were about to do. Others focused intently on their work, pushing the thoughts of what might happen from their minds. A few, with families at home, blinked back the odd tear and tried not to think of the possible consequences of their actions should the situation escalate. In the ward room, a sailor who had moments before been laughing aloud at the 'fishing' cartoon, fell silent; the drawing slipped from his hands, landing on the deck at his feet.

On *Margaree's* bridge, Barry propped himself up in the captain's chair. There could be no delay in carrying out the orders as he did not want the crew spending too much time contemplating the repercussions of their actions, or worse, sympathizing with the Russians in the submarine below. Reaching for the microphone hanging just above his head, he flicked a switch that would put him in direct contact with the Sea King helicopter just visible off the starboard bow. The aircraft was maintaining a steady hover at about the same distance above the water's surface as the Soviet submarine was sitting below it.

"*Buttersquare*, this is *Flapjack One*," he again gave the call sign that would identify him personally.

"This is *Buttersquare*. I read you five by five, sir."

Phillip looked over to his co-pilot and mouthed 'the skipper' in case he hadn't picked up on the call sign. The other man had though, and his face reflected the same puzzled expression that Barkus' displayed. Directly behind them, the helicopter crew sat quietly, headphones pressed to their ears, focusing only on the submarine below and the noises emanating from it. Ted, monitoring the intercom as well, said a short prayer that the message from *Margaree* was not what he expected.

"*Buttersquare*, this is *Flapjack One*," Delaney spoke clearly. He took a breath before continuing. "You are cleared for weapons release. Destroy the submerged contact. Execute immediately."

Barry stared out the bridge window across the short distance to the Sea King. He could only imagine the expression on the pilot's face.

"Ah...roger that, *Flapjack One*." Phillip paused before confirming he had heard and understood the message. "We have weapons unlock and are attacking the submerged target."

From this point on, there would be no mention of 'Ivan' or 'Ruskies'- only 'target' would be used to identify the doomed men below - standard procedure to depersonalize the enemy. Barkus glanced over towards *Margaree*, subconsciously trying to confirm that this was not just a bad dream. Next to him, his co-pilot was shaking his head.

"Damn."

"I know. Let's get on with it." Barkus said in a low voice.

"Yeah." Kevin tightened his harness before reaching ahead and flipping the weapons lock switch. "Weapons enabled."

"Weapons enabled," Ted echoed from behind them, having flipped a similar switch on his console.

"Bearing is...SIR! He's coming up!" Ted shouted so loud, the flight crew heard him clearly above the noise of the helicopter. Ted had been listening for any change in the sound from the Soviet sub and had been startled by the sudden roar of high pressure air blowing water from the submarine's ballast tanks.

"*Flapjack*! This is *Buttersquare*! The boat is surfacing!"

In the ship's CCR, Leading Seaman Brent O'Hanlon had also heard the sound of the Russian's ballast tanks being purged and hit the intercom button connecting him to the bridge.

"Target is surfacing! Target is surfacing!" It was all he had to say. Commander Delaney felt a mixture of relief and dread, for once the submarine surfaced and sent out a radio message, the Canadians would not dare attack it as the Soviets would be aware of the boat's location and threaten retaliation.

The crew on *Margaree's* upper decks and the men aboard the helicopter stared in disbelief as a sizable disturbance appeared in the water where the submarine was thought to be. Moments later, a forest of masts and antennas broke through the surface followed by the smooth, rectangular sail of the *November* class nuclear attack submarine. Seconds later, with water cascading in waves from the deck, the upper casing rose above the waves.

Reaching for his binoculars, Delaney carefully examined the Soviet submarine now wallowing on the surface. Nicely streamlined, he acknowledged. Much more so than the brand new Canadian sub he had toured upon its arrival in Halifax. Her captain had stated that the British Oberon class were state of the art, but compared to the vessel now floating alongside, it looked like a leftover from World War II.

"So that is the *November* class," he voiced in awe. Glancing over at Learner standing at the window beside him, he added, "Nice. Very nice."

He couldn't help but admire the sleek, flowing lines of the submarine. She looked like she was doing thirty knots while standing still. Or 'He' rather. Odd how the Soviets called their ships 'he'. This one certainly carried the lines of a lady, he mused, and if the reports they had heard of nuclear torpedoes were accurate, a very dangerous lady at that.

At the top of the submarine's sail three sets of binoculars appeared, their owners looking straight at *Margaree's* bridge and making Barry wonder if one of the faces behind the glasses was the boat's captain. Barely a few hundred feet above, the Sea King described slow circles around the vessel, the helicopter's crew nearly falling out the open side door in an effort to snap pictures of the sub bobbing on the surface. Delaney reached for the ships PA system and held down the coms button to the Sea King at the same time, knowing the announcement would carry across the water to the Soviets.

"All hands, this is the captain. Secure all weapons." Punching a different button on the consol in front of him, he again pressed the talk button on the microphone.

"Coms, bridge. Has he started transmitting yet?"

"Yes sir. He's really going at it and he's sending in the clear."

That surprised Barry. The Russians were bypassing their code system and using plain language. Then again, maybe that made sense. The Soviet captain would want to get the information out to his base immediately that he was derelict, with a Canadian warship sitting right on top of him.

"Coms, bridge. Ask the Soviet's if they have any casualties or require assistance from us."

"Aye, sir," replied the sailor.

Commander Delaney relaxed. He knew what the answer would be. Unless the submarine was in imminent danger of sinking, there was no way the captain was about to ask for or accept help from the Canadians.

"Bridge, coms. They are stating in rather strong language that they will not be requiring aid from us at this time."

Over the speaker the bridge crew could hear everyone around the communications consol laughing heartedly. The tension which had permeated the atmosphere aboard the destroyer for the past couple of hours had momentarily abated.

"Tell them we will stand by, just in case," Barry chuckled. That would infuriate the Soviets even more than they were now. They should be grateful, he felt, a wry smile crossing his face. A few moments ago he had been prepared to send them straight to Davey Jones's locker.

Ascending the ladder to the open bridge, Commander Delaney leaned over the rail and continued to study the submarine resting on the water's surface through his binoculars. He wondered if the Soviets gave their submarines names or simply identified them by their pennant numbers. Unlike Canadian and American submarines, this one was sailing with its number clearly painted on the side of the sail in large, white numbers.

A gaggle of men huddling on the submarine's stern were discussing the best way to dislodge the cable from their boat. One of them, obviously the ranking officer, was gesturing wildly and yelling at the men on the submarine's after casing. His voice easily carried over to the destroyer and one of *Margaree's* crew who possessed a rudimentary knowledge of Russian, was trying to take notes as he picked up snippets of the man's tirade.

A few minutes later, another sailor appeared on the submarine's deck wearing a bulky diving apparatus. Delaney watched as the diver prepared to enter the water and investigate the situation with the submarine's propellers. The Russian would quickly discover the VDS attached to the cable and once he reported the device to his CO, Barry knew the Soviet captain would try to retrieve the odd looking piece of equipment and bring it aboard.

"I bet there will be quite a reward waiting for you in Moscow when you present naval intelligence with your find, comrade captain," Barry said aloud.

The diver walked ungainly toward the stern of the submarine where the curved deck sloped down and carefully slid into the water. Unconsciously, Barry glanced down at his watch to time the dive before returning to his study of the Russian boat. What seemed like an eternity passed before the diver's head finally appeared in the water alongside and it was obvious from his animated gestures to the other crewmen that he had found the VDS and realized that whatever the strange thing was, it was important.

"Yeah," Delaney remarked quietly through his teeth. "You've found yourself a real treasure there Ivan."

"I'd say he's found it sir," Lieutenant Learner announced, also examining the boat after following Delaney up to the bridge. He too was leaning over the side of the bridge watching the action play out alongside the submarine. Henry was pondering what their options would be now. Letting the Russians haul in the VDS and leave with it was definitely out of the question. His few months of instruction in Sea Law before he had switched courses at Kingston hadn't covered anything like this, or at least not that he could recall. Perhaps he should have paid more attention in class. He smiled at the thought. Even if there was a legal precedent applicable to this situation, it wasn't likely the Russians would agree to hand the VDS back over to the Canadians under any circumstances.

"Yes. It's time to do something, and fast!"

Delaney had an idea but it wasn't a good one. Unfortunately, it was the only plan he could come up with that seemed to have any chance of success. Reaching for the intercom switch, he punched the button that would connect him with the operations room below.

"Sonar, bridge. How many feet of cable did you haul back in?"

The answer from the waterproof speaker on the bulkhead behind him was tinny but clear.

"Eighteen feet, sir."

"Thank you sonar." Good! There was a possibility his far fetched plan might just work.

"Lieutenant, see to launching the sea boat. We might need it for a rescue mission." Commander Delaney's face spread into a grin.

"Yes, sir," Henry answered, without question.

The sea boat, a twenty-seven foot motorboat attached to a launching winch on the ship's starboard side, was used primarily to ferry crewmembers to and from the ship when they were anchored. Henry had turned to supervise launching the boat when Commander Delaney stopped him.

"Not going to ask me why, lieutenant?"

"I wasn't sure I should, sir." Learner returned the commander's grin.

"You're a good officer. I like a man who follows orders without question."

Delaney turned serious. "I plan to make a fast run at the sub's stern. Hopefully he'll take us seriously and try to pull ahead which will string out the VDS cable. Then we'll chop it clear on the way by."

"That's why I didn't ask, sir," the lieutenant remarked sheepishly. "Is there a chance we might end up with it tangled in our own props, sir?"

"Perhaps." Barry's face again exploded into a huge grin. "But better ours than his!"

"It might just work sir. If nothing else, it'll give ol' Ivan over there something to think about."

"It will indeed! Carry on lieutenant."

Barry turned again to examine the Russian sub through his binoculars. This was a great opportunity to study the newest Soviet naval technology up close and he was scribbling notes as fast as he could about the submarine's visible details, especially the antennas and masts. A few of *Margaree's* crewmembers were hanging dangerously over the rail snapping pictures of the sub and Barry instructed a petty officer to go down and drag them back inboard before one of them fell into the frigid water. He understood their enthusiasm. They seldom had a chance to see any Soviet submarines, let alone a new one this close at hand.

Observing the sea boat coming into view from the destroyer's starboard side, he slipped the note pad into his shirt pocket and turned to the man standing alongside him, ordering him to sound the collision alarm. Ignoring the look of shock on the young man's face, he bellowed into the intercom, "Helm, come hard right to zero degrees, all ahead full!" Then added - "Stand by for collision!"

HMCS Margaree healed over hard as her rudders swung over to the stops and the huge bronze propellers spinning on their shafts dug into the cold water. The crew frantically grabbed onto anything close by in order to keep from losing their balance. The ship picked up speed quickly and a moment later, the men aboard the Soviet submarine stared in horror as they watched the onrushing destroyer heading right for them.

Barry noted the diver clumsily scurrying up the rope ladder hanging from the submarine's side. Through his binoculars, he could clearly see one of the officers on the bridge at the top of the boat's sail bent over, giving directions to the control room. A few moments later the water at the submarine's stern began to churn up the sea and the boat slowly inched forward - it's stern moving more to the side, than ahead, due to the damaged propeller.

"Helm, starboard three degrees!" Barry commanded as he gauged the angle and distance to the slowly moving submarine. With the VDS cable wrapped around at least one of her propellers, she wasn't going to be gaining much speed and Commander Delaney was calculating his course to miss her stern by only a few yards. He was counting on the destroyer's bow wave to act as a cushion between *Margaree* and the sub, hoping the sharp bow of his ship would cut the VDS cable cleanly. The sensor would sink to the bottom where it would be safe until *Margaree's* own divers could locate it.

Looking across to the submarine's sail he could now see two officers frantically waving with both arms at the speeding destroyer bearing down at them. Barry cheerfully returned the wave.

"Helm! Port - two degrees!" Barry again lined up the boat's stern with his trained eye and a few moments later ordered the rudder amidships. Yes, that should do it, he thought. Thirty seconds later, *HMCS Margaree* thundered past the submarine's stern, soaking the Russian crew as the speeding destroyer's bow wave crashed over the sub's after deck.

Commander Delaney felt the ship suddenly slow as it contacted with the high strength cable and he noted with satisfaction that the submarine's stern had only begun to swing around when he heard a muted 'snap' and the boat stopped moving. The cable had severed cleanly, and finally released, the VDS sank slowly to the bottom.

Margaree immediately picked up speed again and Delaney punched the intercom, already switched to 'bridge' and ordered 'engines stopped'. He felt the ship slow and thankfully noted there had been no mechanical sounds from the stern and more importantly no message from his engineering officer that anything had caught up in the props. Breathing a sigh of relief, he mentally started to compose the message he'd be sending to Halifax.

Glancing over to the helicopter still holding position directly over the submarine, he had to admit the new Sea King as a weapon just might work out. This damn variable depth sonar contraption however had so far proven to be more of a pain than it was worth.

"Bridge, Coms. Picking up more signals from the submarine."

"Jam them!" Lieutenant Commander Delaney ordered.

"Aye, sir. Attempting to jam."

Barry flicked the intercom off. He knew it was unlikely they'd be able to jam the messages for very long, but if they could even cut them off partially, it might delay the submarine's base from figuring out what had taken place. The thought of taking out the sub's antennae masts with the 3inch 50 had occurred to him momentarily, but that would be too risky and the Soviets might try to turn and launch a torpedo at the destroyer.

Barry wanted to give Halifax a piece of his mind about what happens when you hang things off the stern of a warship, but his intuition told him to wait - that this hadn't been a fair test of the new variable depth sonar system.

"Fine", he muttered to no one in particular. He'd give the new contraption another chance, on another day.

* * *

While Lieutenant Commander Delaney was pondering *Margaree's* new systems, far to the west in Canada's capital city of Ottawa, the tulips were blooming and spring tourists had already begun to fill the streets and shops of the beautiful old city. Most of them flocked daily to Parliament Hill, a majestic building constructed on a low prominence overlooking the Ottawa River.

In the Prime Minister's Office, a room as well as an institution, the man seated behind the large oak desk facing the door was trying to shake off the initial shock of the briefing he had just received. Glancing up at his Minister of National Defence who was standing uncomfortably in the center of the room, the Prime Minister began to consider the phone call he would soon have to make to the Kremlin. The Soviet submarine which *HMCS Margaree* had tangled with had clearly been well within Canadian waters. Providing proof of that would not be an issue. Not with several photos of the sleek submarine with the Labrador coastline clearly visible in the background. There would be no claims this time that their sub had been off course due to a navigational error. It would have taken great skill and diligence on the Russian crew's part to manoeuvre in the shallow waters so close to land and they would have had to know exactly where they were.

Rubbing his chin in contemplation, the Prime Minister wondered what it would take for the two super powers separated geographically by his country, to respect Canada's sovereignty. United States spy planes flew at will through Canadian airspace, totally disregarding any standard air traffic control procedures. The claims that their altitude placed them out of controlled airspace didn't cut bread with him either and the American's knew it. The Soviets on the other hand, with their ever growing fleet of submarines, seemed to share the same attitude concerning Canada's offshore limits. It was also well known in Canadian defence circles that both the USSR and the US had nuclear submarines regularly operating beneath the ice in the Arctic Ocean. Sonar sensors clandestinely installed by the Canadian navy the previous year kept a vigilant watch on the increasing traffic below the ice in the northern waters.

The Prime Minister was a staunch patriot and he had made that very clear to everyone in the first two years of his stewardship over this country he loved so much. Years before, as he had decimated his opposition during 'model parliament' in high school, he had known only one goal; to one day sit in this chair - in this office. To that end he had often forgone many of the usual activities young adults enjoyed to focus on his studies, especially history, as he was a firm believer of the old adage that those who forget history are doomed to repeat it. A short stint in the Canadian army reserves had educated him on the viewpoint of the soldier and he had sworn to never forget those long days trudging through the mud during training. He never made it to combat, a small medical problem keeping him in Canada, but that only heightened his goal of making sure the armed services were never found wanting.

His deepest regret was not having made it to this office in time to save the CF-105 Avro Arrow, and as a member of Parliament he'd had to quickly wipe away a tear on that terrible day the interceptor had been cancelled. Canadians would never realize what might have been had they only…only what? There had been problems with the aircraft and maybe that really had been the best action. But why destroy them? He tore himself back to the present.

With Canada playing an increasingly important role in both NORAD and NATO, and with the ongoing 'Cold War' continuing to escalate, more than a few Canadians had already paid the ultimate price. The Prime Minister had repeatedly pointed this out to the leaders of both super powers and had warned them that the day would come when something terrible would happen if this trespassing into Canadian airspace and offshore limits continued. These exhortations had often placed him at odds with the American President who felt Canada leaned altogether too far to the left and that the Canadians should be thankful for the protection the United States provided.

Looking up, he motioned to his Minister of Defence, who had continued to stand quietly, while awaiting his attention.

"Alright Ted, sit down. You're making me nervous standing there like that."

"Thank you Prime Minister."

"So where are we at right now? And who the hell is commanding *Margaree*? He should get a medal for keeping his cool in that mess. Man could have started World War III up there!"

"Lieutenant Commander Barry Delaney, sir," Ted replied looking down at his notes. "According to Admiral Gillis, Delany can 'be a real pain in the ass' but that is also why he keeps him around. Remember when one of our ships slipped into the US Navy base at Norfolk last year during 'Eastern Arrival'?"

"Was that him?"

"Yes, Prime Minister."

"Damn!"

Only people at the very highest levels were aware of how that exercise had culminated. The US Navy had touted the invincibility of their powerful carrier fleets for years. But one exceptionally foggy night, a Canadian destroyer had managed to slip quietly into the Norfolk naval base and carry out a successful simulated torpedo attack on two *Essex* class carriers tied up alongside.

Delaney had his radio operators use the call sign of a west coast based US Navy frigate as he sailed into the bay and in the thick fog, the ruse worked.

The Americans had been rightfully embarrassed by the incident and it had been agreed by both countries that it was in everyone's best interests that the event remain classified.

"So where is our favourite pirate right now?"

"He's been ordered here and will be on his way as soon as he finishes retrieving the VDS and debrief in Halifax, Prime Minister."

"Man should get a medal..." The Prime Minister excused him and returned to the mound of papers on his desk.

* * *

Later that evening the commanding officer of *HMCS Margaree* was aboard the ship's helicopter for the short flight west to Goose Bay, where a plane waited to whisk him back to naval headquarters in Halifax. *Margaree* would sail home under the command of her executive officer, with the mangled VDS securely lashed to her foredeck. Once the ship's divers had located the sunken sonar device and attached a line to it, the Sea King helicopter had made quick work of hauling it aboard.

Word was waiting when Commander Delaney landed at Goose that he would be flying to Ottawa to meet the Prime Minister once he was through his debrief in Halifax. The story of what transpired would soon dominate the front pages of Canada's newspapers once it broke - which it would as soon as the Soviets began their usual grand standing in the United Nations. Perhaps, Delaney thought, while speaking with the Prime Minister, he'd have a chance to clear up this foolish rumour he'd heard about sailors in green uniforms.

As Barry tried to make himself more comfortable seated at one of the weapons stations inside the Sea King, his mind went back to the confrontation with the Soviet submarine and the possible repercussions of the events which had unfolded so quickly. At the back of his mind, the nagging question of why the submarine had been so deep inside Canadian waters in the first place continued to trouble him. There certainly wasn't anything within a hundred miles of that area to interest the Soviet navy.

* * *

That evening, as Commander Delaney strapped himself into what passed for a seat in the old Dakota transport which had been waiting at Goose to pick him up; to the south in Washington, DC, his recent confrontation was being discussed in a decidedly different vein. The two men occupying the Oval Office were carrying on a heated discussion which belied the deep friendship that existed between them.

"Frankly Mister President, I don't know how the Canadians managed to stumble upon the Soviet boat. Pure, dumb luck I imagine."

The director of the CIA was livid. He had been shocked to learn that the Canadians had not only stumbled across the Russian submarine, but had damaged it as well. Unknown to the Soviets, or the Canadians for that matter, a US nuclear sub had been trailing the Russian boat for three days, having detected the submarine shortly after it had departed the Barents Sea. The Americans had been hoping to find out what the boat was doing so far inside Canadian waters, but had pulled out of the area when the Canadian warship had arrived on the scene.

Unfortunately, the destroyer's crew had detected the Soviets and after a confrontation which seemed to play out like a scene from a 'Keystone Cops' movie, the submarine had finally been towed from the area by a large Russian factory trawler. Fortunately the noisier Soviet boat had attracted the Canadian's attention and they hadn't picked up the US submarine following closely in its baffles. When he was well clear of the area, the captain of the American *Skipjack* class sub ordered his command to periscope depth and sent a message off to Groton, describing the events of the past six hours. On short notice they had been typed up and delivered to the CIA director's desk.

Before he'd had time to properly digest the information, the Director had been ordered to the Oval Office where the President had demanded to know what the hell was going on up north. The director's surprise that the White House had information he had only just received quickly turned to chagrin as the President explained to him in an uncharacteristically angry voice, how he had just gotten off the phone with the Canadian Prime Minister and had received a stern warning that Canada was not going to sit back and watch her sovereignty ignored by either American spy aircraft or Soviet submarines.

The President had guessed correctly that there had been a US naval presence in the area as well. Extremely annoyed, he had called in his CIA director who had explained to him in detail what had transpired. The US leader was an old political hack who was not used to being 'talked down to' by foreign leaders, and even less so by the Canadian Prime Minister who had always been a close friend.

"It might have been luck, but I'm sick and tired of those Canadians messing around with things they do not understand," the President lamented. His voice was calm for the first time since the director had entered the office and he stood and stared quietly out the window behind his desk before speaking again.

"I swear those damn Canadians are Communists Chuck. It's a wonder they didn't just hand over their new sonar system to the Soviets!"

The director waited quietly while the President continued. He knew there was no point in trying to reason with the man until after he had completed his tirade. Then, as always, he'd move to sit down on one of the two sofas in the middle of the room. He would sit quietly for a few moments, then invite the Director to join him on the opposite couch.

Charles Dunlop found his position as Director of the CIA to be the ultimate balancing act. Dealing with the very real danger of operating in a world which was threatening to destroy itself in a nuclear holocaust at any moment was stress enough, but at the same time, he often found himself kowtowing to politicians whose only focus seemed to be getting re-elected or looking good in the press. Fortunately, this President was in his second term meaning he was less concerned with the outcome of the next election than how his legacy would be perceived by history.

The President raised his eyes to the director. The anger had melted from his face and he now seemed completely relaxed as he moved over to one of the sofas and sat down. It was a personality trait Charles envied in the man. This uncanny ability to adapt so quickly emotionally to any situation.

"Sit down Chuck," the President invited softly. "What's done is done. So what did the last set of pictures show?"

"There's no question that Ivan put some troops ashore up there; probably a Spetsnaz detachment. The Blackbird images show they have some equipment with them, but we can't be sure what it is or what they're up to. I think it's time to send some of our people in to have a closer look."

"Our people, Chuck? On Canadian soil?"

The President sat back, clasping his fingers behind his neck, contemplating the idea. It had been done before of course, during a previous administration. But that had been comprised of visits to the Canadian Arctic by a few nuclear submarines carrying special forces. And once, by a small commando team of Green Berets he recalled, in of all places, Manitoba. The Canadians had grudgingly accepted the 'visiting' submarines as part of their agreement with the United States over the mutual defence of North America. They had never been told about Manitoba of course. This would be a different matter, and a secret operation involving combat between American and Soviet troops on Canadian soil would not play out favourably in Ottawa if they got wind of it.

"I can guarantee Mr. President, that our guys will get in and get back out without the Canadian government ever knowing. The area in question is very remote and other than their destroyer that tripped over the Ruskie sub, they have no assets in the vicinity. The closest thing to the area is a Pinetree site and that one's manned by us."

"Only toasters come with guarantees, Chuck. Who do you have in mind for the job?"

The director not only had someone in mind, but before arriving at the White House for the briefing, he had made a quick phone call to alert the group that they were on short notice for an operation.

"I was thinking a small SEAL detachment sir. We have a unit just back from Da Nang." Then with a smile, he added, "They would love a mission somewhere a little cooler for a change."

The President was not in the mood for humour. Vietnam had become an albatross around his neck and any mention of it made him wish again that his predecessor had gone in there and bombed them back to the Stone Age as he had threatened to do. At least if he had, the current administration wouldn't be spending half of its time and money dealing with the South East Asia issue instead of working on the economy. Hell, there had been more than one day he had been tempted to go out and join the protestors outside the main gate of the White House himself!

"Okay Chuck, alert them. But nobody deploys until I see plans on my desk! I don't want this leaking out to the press either or you'll be briefing my replacement next week!"

"Don't worry Mr. President. I guarantee…err…assure you that this will be kept quiet. I'll get my guys to start setting up for the operation and let you know as soon as we have some concrete plans."

The President stood without saying any more and walked towards his desk, signalling that the meeting was over.

* * *

At the same moment the Director of the CIA was exiting the Oval Office, four hundred and sixty miles east of Portsmouth, New Hampshire, an undersea game of cat and mouse was quietly playing out.

"Contact designated sierra four – bearing zero four seven degrees at two thousand yards. Identity unknown at this time."

USS Shark's sonar operator was pretty certain the contact was Russian. The other boat sounded like the old Model T his uncle owned and only brought out for a drive on sunny weekends during the summer.

"Any idea whose?"

The question had come from the submarine's captain. Dan Hetherington had been *Shark's* skipper for almost a year, yet it never ceased to amaze him how sensitive the boat's BQS 4 sonar system was. The sailor manning the sonar knew his stuff and Dan waited for the other submarine's identification which he suspected would be coming any moment now.

"Positive ID sir. Russian *Foxtrot*."

"He's a long way from home. Good work petty officer! Helm, bring us right to zero four seven. Make turns for 20 knots. Let's go wake him up!"

Dan grabbed the periscope mount firmly as the helmsman manoeuvred *Shark* to come up behind the Soviets. Underwater, the small *Skipjack* class handled like a sports car and within minutes they were coming up the *Foxtrot's* baffles. If they could catch up before the other boat's captain cleared his tail, they'd nail him with active sonar.

As *Shark's* helmsman settled onto the new course, Dan let go of the 'scope' mount and leaned over the COB seated behind the boat's 'drivers'.

"What's our speed, COB?"

"Just coming on eighteen knots, skipper."

Dan nodded in acknowledgement. They were no where near *Shark's* top speed of a little over forty knots. Making full use of the research gleaned from the experimental submarine *USS Albacore* and her unique tear-drop shaped hull, the *Skipjack* class had been designed to be the fastest, most manoeuvrable submarines in the world - and they were.

USS Shark was the fifth of the forty million dollar class of boats laid down. Commissioned in early 1961 at the sprawling Newport News Shipbuilding yards in eastern Virginia, the stubby little submarine had looked fat and ungainly sitting on the launch ways, yet it was that very shape which gave her the incredible speed and manoeuvrability she possessed. Dan was proud of his command and the many records, a few public - most secret, that *Shark* and the other *Skipjack* class boats possessed. *Scorpion* had even gone for seventy days without popping a hatch back in 1962, a feat her crew loved to brag about, and rightly so, to the chagrin of the other boat's crews.

That was fine with Dan. He'd nail this Ruskie which would bring the total for this cruise to five making him the first ace in…his thought was broken by the speaker above his head coming to life.

"Con – radio. VLF message coming in."

Dan grabbed the mike hanging on his left. "Radio – con. I'm on the way."

Taking a last, quick look at the gauges, he turned and headed aft to the radio room. Sliding the dark curtain aside he stepped into the warm, crowded compartment and looked down at the radio operator.

"What have you got, Dave?"

Ensign David Crossman turned in his swivel chair to face him. There really wasn't enough room in the cramped area for him to try and stand comfortably, so he didn't.

"VLF from ComSub Atlantic sir. They want us up right away to receive a message."

"Great!" Dan's voice was laced with sarcasm. He studied the printed note Dave had handed him. "Thank you, gentlemen. Prepare to receive as soon as we get on top. I'm going to try and make it quick so we don't lose Ivan."

"We'll be ready as soon as the antenna breaks the surface sir. I'll holler the second the message is received."

"Thanks ensign."

Dan slipped from the dimly lit radio compartment and returned to the control room. Shit! The Russians would be alerted to their presence as soon as they blew their ballast tanks to surface. All he could do was hope they could surface, get the message, and find the other submarine again before it managed to slip away. *Shark* was three times faster than any *Foxtrot* and although it would wreck his plan to scare the shit out of the Russians, that was okay.

Returning to his favourite spot, leaning against the attack periscope rails, he gave orders to break off from their chase and bring the boat up to periscope depth. Five minutes later, the long whip antenna attached to one of the masts broke the surface of the Atlantic and within a minute the speaker above him announced that Dave had copied and confirmed the message. Returning again to the radio compartment, Dan was puzzled by the wide grin on his ensign's face as he handed a scribble note to him.

"Looks like we might be getting some shore leave, sir!"

Reading the short message, Dan had to agree. They were ordered to dock in Halifax, Nova Scotia for provisioning and an overnight R+R but a feeling in the pit of his stomach told him there was more to these orders than met the eye. Especially since they noted that *Shark* was to embark for the Canadian navy base immediately.

"Looks like it lieutenant," Captain Hetherington replied with a forced smile.

Dave turned to the petty officer seated next to him and started filling him in on all he'd heard about Halifax from his buddies who'd been there before. Especially about how the girls in the Canadian port city were reputed to be friendly to foreign sailors.

* * *

While word of the impending visit to Halifax quickly spread through *Shark*, far to the north in central Labrador, a small group of men were huddled inside an old tent that had seen much better days. At first glance, they appeared to be hunters, all of them wearing a variety of heavy clothing for protection from the elements. They could very well have been planning a hunting trip into the Labrador wilderness, except that outside the torn flap which covered the entrance to the old tent, their bolt action rifles were leaning together in the classic army triangle. The weapons themselves showed heavy wear from many years of hard use but their metalwork glistened with a light coating of oil; a sign that in spite of their age, they were well taken care of.

The men were not planning a hunt. Not today at least. They were part of a group almost unheard of in the more populous areas of Canada, but revered throughout the north. The Canadian Rangers were a militia of sorts, tasked to the Canadian Army and responsible for patrolling the inhospitable wilderness areas of northern Canada. The men were trained in very rudimentary aspects of land warfare, although they were not actually expected to go into battle. They served more as the 'eyes and ears' of the regular army in the far north. While a few of the men had clearly joined the Rangers for the social aspects of the organization, most of them took the part time job seriously.

Outside the shabby tent, one of the Rangers, clearly much older than the rest, was glaring at one member of the group who was standing uncomfortably in front of him. The men called the old man Grandfather. It wasn't meant as a humorous nickname, but rather a sign of deep respect for the man who literally was old enough to be their grandfather.

The old man had appeared at the Ranger's regular meeting one evening two years earlier. Taking a folding chair from against the wall, he had sat quietly at the back of the room listening. His clothes were well worn and obviously hand made, as was the belt he wore from which hung a simple leather scabbard holding a large hunting knife. None of the men gathered for the meeting recognized him and one Ranger, thinking perhaps the old man had come into the room by mistake, asked if he could help him. The elderly man had slowly looked up at him with eyes that blazed with a fierce pride, belying their age.

"This is where we protect Canada?" He had asked in a low voice, almost a whisper.

"You could say that," replied the Ranger.

"Then I am in the right place."

That had been the end of the conversation and the stranger had sat without uttering a single word throughout the rest of the meeting. He showed up for the next two meetings as well and not sure what else to do with him, the men had inducted him into the Canadian Rangers. It wasn't much of a ceremony. There was no presentation of uniform, rank or insignia, as none existed. There was however a weapon given to every new Ranger. As had previously been issued to those before him, Grandfather was presented with a World War II surplus .303 calibre Lee Enfield, Mark 4 bolt action rifle. It had seen better days and was obviously well used but the old man took it into his hands and gently ran his rough, calloused fingers over the wood and metal.

There existed a basic training program for the Rangers concerning the use and care of the rifle. When he had arrived for his training, Grandfather had walked purposely to the range line, expertly slid back the bolt, chambering a .303 round, and without the slightest hesitation, had lifted the heavy rifle to his shoulder and fired three rounds in quick succession. The young men at the range that afternoon swore they couldn't see his hands working the bolt between shots. Afterwards, they had walked the length of the range to look at the paper target. Only one ragged hole was visible in the center of the black circle. They had stood silent for a few moments, astonished at the target hanging from the old wooden frame that acted as a holder. Finally one of them let out a low whistle.

"I guess you qualify, sir," the Ranger sergeant had remarked, breaking the uneasy silence. "I don't think we'll need to bother you with any more rifle training."

The grizzled old man had religiously attended all of the classes anyway, carefully listening to the instructor, always from the very back of the room. When overnight training exercises had taken place, Grandfather quickly demonstrated that his advanced age would not be a detriment to the group he was assigned to. There was nothing they could teach him about survival in the Canadian wilderness that he had not already mastered, and he often ended up leading the class, while the rest of the men seated around him listened intently as he shared his wisdom with them. The senior was easily able to keep up with the younger men during field training, and a new recruit had once commented how the old man seemed at one with nature.

"With nature?" one of the Rangers had responded. "Hell no, man! Grandfather IS nature!"

Late one evening, a few of the men had finally managed to pry a name out of the man who never seemed to speak unless he had something important to say. Deniigi. It was an Eskimo word meaning 'Moose'. Odd name, they had all thought. He was not a large man and certainly wasn't overly aggressive like the huge animal he'd apparently been named after. The mystery of his name simply added to the man's mystique however, and it wasn't long before he was given the only promotion a Ranger could receive. Everyone averted their gaze from the tears in his wrinkled old eyes the day it was announced that Ranger Deniigi was now Ranger Sergeant Deniigi.

Now, two years later, Grandfather was glowering intently at the young Ranger standing in front of him; a look of stern disapproval on his face as though dealing with an errant son.

"What is wrong with you!?" demanded the man in a voice much stronger than his stature belied.

The young Ranger looked sheepishly at the old man before quickly bending down to retrieve his rifle from the ground. It had slipped from his hands and before he had been able to bend over to grab it, Deniigi had appeared out of nowhere. Grandfather had stood there a few moments, silently contemplating the rifle laying on the ground as if it were a relative who had fallen there and died.

"Do you think rifles grow on trees?"

"No, I…"

"Clean it good. It may save your life someday," he commanded in a softer voice before turning away, disappointment showing in his eyes. These boys did not take their duty seriously enough, he felt. Defending Canada's northern frontier was the most honourable thing a man could do, but these young people seemed to think of the Rangers as a place to enjoy their leisure time rather than being part of Canada's defence.

The group had been on their current exercise for over a week and Grandfather understood some of the younger men were looking forward to returning home to their women. Deniigi appreciated their feelings. His own woman had died many years ago at a young age, and the vision of her flawless beauty overcame him for a moment as his mind momentarily took him back in time. Back to a day when his life had changed forever.

He had learned the importance of protecting the north from intruders that day. Back then it seemed that no one knew or cared about, what went on up here in the barren wilderness. The small towns and villages were separated by hundreds of miles and little existed between them in the way of communications.

No one in Canada realized a German U-Boat had come close to shore the previous night, allowing a group of men from the submarine to land on an isolated part of the northern Labrador coast. They had been sent there to set up a monitoring station to better predict the north Atlantic weather, an impossibly difficult task at the best of times. After a few days, the men had donned civilian clothes, hoping to appear as foreign fisherman, and had hiked the short distance to Deniigi's little village, forging for food. He had left the day before on a hunting trip into the wilderness, unaware of the lurking danger. During their search, the Germans had come upon his house and finding the door unlocked, had entered. Inside, they had discovered his wife working alone in the tiny kitchen.

Their intentions had not been to harm her, but when she had screamed at the sight of strangers walking in the door, one of the men had momentarily panicked and hit her. That had led to further brutalities and two hours later they had finally left, leaving her naked and dying on the floor. Unable to move from her injuries, she had finally succumbed to the cold - a final sleep releasing her from the pain of her battered and bruised body.

When Deniigi had returned the following day, proudly carrying the spoils of the hunt over his powerful shoulders, he had found her lying there.

After burying her body, it had taken Grandfather many hours of trudging through the wilderness to track down the men. He had followed their trail back to a small cove where they had set up camp and then waited patiently until they had settled around a small fire eating their supper, later that evening. Finding a suitable perch overlooking the encampment, he quietly brought his hunting rifle to his shoulder and chambered a round.

The Germans had never known who was shooting at them, and although they had returned fire wildly in the direction they thought the shots had come from, their bullets never came close, while they were picked off one by one. At dawn the following morning, Deniigi had buried them amongst the rocks along with their equipment. He had not understood what the strange instruments or the many maps he'd found filled with sweeping lines and numbers were for. He had exacted his revenge and after the last man had been buried, Deniigi sat upon a rock and finally succumbing to his broken heart, cried quietly, torn apart by guilt and anguish that he had not been there to protect his woman.

A few months later, when a recruiting officer had arrived in his small village, the hunter had been among the first to sign up to fight the Germans. The army had quickly discovered his natural talents with a rifle and in spite of his age, had trained him further in the art of long range killing. Deniigi excelled as a sniper and every German soldier he killed, took away some of the pain he felt for his wife's loss. When the war had finally ended, he returned home and never spoke to anyone of his experiences.

Pushing the memory aside, he re-focused on the exercise his Ranger group would be conducting the next morning. They were to hike another three miles towards the coast and then bivouac overnight before returning to their battered army truck which had been left along one of the rough roads hewn through the Labrador wilderness.

The truck, like their rifles, was a relic of a bygone era. Long disposed of by the regular army, it was patched up and kept running with spare parts and a lot of luck. The old Chevrolet four wheel drive was their only means of transportation during the summer months when the dog teams became useless. There was no fear anyone would come across the truck and take it. Everyone within hundreds of miles knew the Ranger's truck and would not have dared touch it.

Early the next morning, Deniigi was leading a trio of Rangers over a small rocky hill when a glint of light in the distance caught his eye. Dropping to the ground, he lay still, signalling the others to do the same. Carefully bringing up the pair of binoculars hanging from around his neck, he scanned the terrain ahead. The glasses were the one thing he had kept from those men so long ago. There! Again a small glint flashed from a dark area alongside a rock outcropping half a mile away.

"Stay," he whispered to the man directly behind him. Slowly the old man moved over the uneven ground. Taking advantage of every rock and bit of brush to hide his movements from whoever was out there, he crept along carefully. Now and then he would stop for a few minutes, watching for any sign that someone might have spotted him.

Deniigi had learned the importance of patience while tracking his prey, especially in a land with little if any natural cover. A land where one had to learn how to move without appearing to move at all.

Almost an hour had passed when scanning a particularly rocky area a few hundred yards ahead with the glasses, he saw the man. He had appeared from what the Ranger could see was a carefully camouflaged tent designed to simulate the terrain perfectly. Deniigi did not recognize the uniform the man wore, or the strangely shaped rifle slung over his shoulder. His instincts told him there was some danger being this close, but he needed more information before he could report back.

Another long hour passed and the Ranger had now observed four other men, all wearing the same uniform as the first. Grandfather contemplated moving close enough to the men to try and hear if they spoke English, but he knew from experience that a hunter could stalk a prey for only so long before it would finally sense him. Slowly and carefully moving back the way he had come, Deniigi returned to his men. He noted thankfully that they had followed his orders and remained where he had left them.

"Radio."

One of the Rangers, Glen Church, slung the backpack radio from his shoulders and carefully set it up on a large flat rock. Two metal bars swivelled out from the bottom of the battery compartment, holding it upright while he powered it up. The two-way device was almost ten years old but still worked well. One of the men, an amateur radio operator, treated the old backpack transceiver as though it were his child and insured that it was always in the best operating condition possible, no small feat considering its age and the difficulty obtaining spare parts and batteries. After assembling the sectional antennae, Glen checked the frequency and waited for the small vacuum tubes inside the radio to reach their operating temperature.

"Here you are sir," he announced, after making sure the handset was securely plugged into its socket.

Deniigi grabbed the handset and spoke clearly into it. The men were always amused at how the old sergeant's english always seemed to improve dramatically whenever he used the radio. They wondered if he understood how the thing worked or even cared, as they never saw him with any kind of modern electrical device and the few who had visited his small home had commented on how he had no electricity. Watching him intently for some clue to the reaction from the person on the other end of the conversation, the small group of men sat quietly. His face however, gave nothing away throughout the entire conversation. A few minutes later, passing the handset back to Church, he spoke only two words, "We wait."

* * *

"What the hell are you doing?!"

His shout almost drowned out the booming thunder and cascading rain from the spring storm – almost. The nasty weather had been making the field exercise on the sprawling army base in Gagetown, New Brunswick a nightmare. The rain had been falling continuously for two days now and showed no sign of letting up. The ground, now a quagmire of mud and water, made even the most simple troop movements nearly impossible. More mistakes than usual were being made as the cold, wet troops fought the 'enemy' and the weather, while their instructors seemed to find endless joy in their misery.

The young soldier being addressed tried to answer, but his mouth seemed to fail him as he cowered under the piercing glare of the sergeant standing before him. It didn't help that he could not stop shivering from the cold in his muddied, wet uniform.

"Have you ever seen what happens when the seven-point-six-two round is fired down a barrel full of muddy water private?! It ain't pretty! I'd hate to see your face with the ass end of that FN rifle stuck in it!"

Sergeant Ashe always slurred the 'F' and 'N' when he was angry, so that a totally new word materialized from the two letters.

"That would be a waste of a perfectly good rifle, private! Wouldn't you agree!!?"

The young man stood at attention, unable or too afraid to move; he wasn't sure which, and didn't care to find out. The cold, relentless rain ran down his face, the thunder cracked around him and every few moments, the sergeant's scowling mug was eerily lit by a flash of lightning. In the few inches between his and the sergeant's nose, the cold barrel of the soldier's FN rifle pointed skyward. In his peripheral vision - he dared not actually look down – he could see rain drops falling into the muzzle. The condom he had placed over it had come off somewhere, probably while he was crawling through the mud.

"No...err...I mean..."

"Listen here buddy," Sergeant Brian Ashe brought his face as close as he could to the young soldier's. "If it's a choice between protecting your dick and protecting your rifle, you better protect your goddamn rifle!! You can live without your dick, but by god, you will die without your rifle!"

With that, he shoved the weapon into the soldier's trembling hands and stomped away, splashing water in all directions. The private, unsure if he should move, stood trembling as much from the cold rain, as the tirade he had just endured.

"Damn kids!" Brian muttered. Heading over to the operations tent, he'd make a note to again go over the importance of taking proper care of personal weapons.

"Dumb shit!" he said louder this time so everyone around heard and hopefully learned from the soldier's mistake. "Stupid kid would have killed himself if he had tried to fire the damn rifle. Might as well just start reading Mao if that's the best I'm going to have to work with!"

Shit! This time he thought, rather than spoke the word. When we get to Germany next month... His muttering was broken by a jeep splashing to a stop behind him.

"Sergeant! They want you down at headquarters. Colonel's looking for you."

Maybe some other idiot had shot his foot off, Brian pondered. "I'll be right there. Any idea what's going on?"

"Didn't say Sarge. Just asked me to get you there right away."

"Okay, Thompson. Give me a second to grab my maps."

Ashe slipped into the tent and picked up his tactical maps which were safely secured inside a plastic sleeve to protect them from the weather and grime. Folding the sleeve carefully into one of the cavernous pockets of his combat pants, he rejoined the soldier waiting in the jeep outside. The colonel probably wanted to go over the plans for tomorrow night's exercise, he presumed. He could not know how wrong he was.

"Okay corporal, let's move!"

"Oh, sorry Sarge. Colonel said to bring your kit with you."

"Did the colonel say where I'm going?" Brian asked. He was more annoyed than curious.

"I'm 'fraid not Sarge."

"Damn army," Ashe muttered out loud, laying his FN on the passenger seat before returning to the tent.

A few minutes later the sergeant was dropped off at the base commander's headquarters building. Walking inside, Brian stopped for a moment to shake the water from his beret before stepping up to the sergeant seated at the desk outside the colonel's office. The other man gave his soaked uniform a disapproving look before beckoning to the door behind him.

"Colonel's expecting you, Ashe"

"Thanks," Brian replied, reaching for the doorknob.

The office was sparsely furnished and decorated with the flags, banners and crests of the various regiments which were or had been based at Gagetown. Also adorning one wall was a collage of souvenir plaques from the many foreign military units which had trained or passed through the sprawling base. A large, old desk sat in one corner of the room facing the door and a few well worn chairs were spread out in a semi-circle in front of it. Seated behind the desk was a man who looked fearsome in the combat kit which he wore at all times – some believed even to bed. Gagetown's CO was a vet of WW-II and Korea and bore scars from more than a few battles, not all of them in combat. He was a bear of a man and had the voice to match.

"Ashe!"

Brian swore the plaques vibrated on the wall.

"Sorry to drag you from the exercise." The colonel looked up from the piece of paper in front of him. "How is it progressing so far?"

The memory of the kid with the water filled rifle barrel flashed through his mind, but Brian thrust it aside. "Very well, sir. They're young, but eager to learn" God, he thought. That sounded like something out of an old John Wayne movie.

"Good!" The colonel's voiced boomed again. "Have a look at this."

Brian reached for the single piece of paper the colonel had been reading when he'd walked in. Glancing quickly through the two short paragraphs, he noted there had been a sighting of strange troops by one of the Ranger units in Labrador but no other information was available. Sergeant Ashe was familiar with the Rangers, having spent a few weeks with them during an Arctic exercise the previous winter.

He had been surprised by their resilience and in spite of their limited training, the odd group of men had performed fairly well. He had wondered at the time however, what would happen if they ever came up against professional soldiers.

"Anyone have any guesses as to who they are, sir?" Ashe queried, handing the page back.

"No, but they want someone to go up there and investigate. You came to mind right away." The colonel smiled before continuing. "You were just up there working with those guys and have an idea of what they can and can't do."

"When do I leave?"

"The jeep's outside and a Dakota is waiting for you on the runway. Ottawa wants this looked into quickly and quietly." He paused. "And Ashe?"

"Sir?"

"Watch your ass up there. It sounds like Russians and if it is, they're probably Spetsnaz. Confirm who they are and get your butt out of there. I don't want you getting into a clash with no one to back you up but a bunch of untrained seal hunters."

"Yes, sir."

"Get going and this is secret. Keep it to yourself."

In a rare event - the army reacting to any event with lightning speed - Sergeant Brian Ashe soon found himself strapped into a hard metal seat aboard a Royal Canadian Air Force Dakota and three hours after leaving the small air strip at Gagetown, his stomach lurched as the aircraft descended in a turbulence filled landing at Goose Bay, Labrador.

"Shit!" was all he could mutter as the aircraft bounced violently during the final approach before slamming down hard on the runway.

* * *

As Sergeant Ashe's unplanned flight lifted off from the strip at Gagetown, a few hundred miles to the south west, the stubby form of an American nuclear submarine was slowly making its way to a pier down the hill from the Shearwater air base. People in buildings overlooking the harbour paused for a moment, giving the boat a cursory glance before dismissing it, accustomed as they were to the coming and going of naval warships in the harbour.

Aboard *Shark*, half a dozen sailors lined the deck in customary fashion as the submarine slide towards the pier. They anxiously stole peeks over their shoulder at the vibrant city, while those of the crew not standing watch waited impatiently below to escape the confines of the boat.

Nova Scotia's capital city did not disappoint them. Many of the crew found it very similar to Boston, with its narrow downtown streets and historic buildings. More than a few of the sailors returned to the sub with the addresses and phone numbers of girls they'd met in the city's clubs and bars. A few of the older, married crew had rented a car and driven to Peggy's Cove to explore a different kind of scenery.

The visit passed all too quickly and the next evening, having replenished the submarine's stores, Dan gingerly manoeuvred *USS Shark* from its berth alongside the navy pier at Shearwater. The radio operator had announced their departure to the harbour traffic control centre and was standing by for a reply.

"November Oscar Kilo Mike, this is Halifax Traffic. Confirm you are north of McNabs."

"Halifax traffic, November Oscar Kilo Mike is north of McNabs; entering the traffic lane."

Granted clearance into the busy entrance of Halifax harbour, the communications officer replaced the microphone in its holder and reported to the skipper that they were cleared to leave the harbour and that all radio transmitters were now locked down. From this point on, nothing short of an emergency action message would allow their use until they had resurfaced just off their base at Groton, Connecticut.

Dan turned to the task of making sure *Shark* would arrive on time at a navigation point he had received in a coded message earlier in the day. They were to rendezvous with and pick up a detachment of SEALs who would be jumping from a navy Herc' at the location and it was crucial that *Shark* be there when the commandos arrived.

The commander had earlier confirmed their speed and heading with his navigation officer, insuring they would reach the rendezvous on time since SEALs were known to get upset when their 'taxi' did not show up as scheduled. Dan was aware that many of *Shark's* crew saw the navy commandos as pompous glory seekers, but he also knew a lot of that attitude stemmed from simple jealousy. He had no doubt however, that few of his men would trade places with the SEALs and the dangerous missions they undertook.

They would easily make the rendezvous, and only then would he be informed of their actual mission. Dan suspected another trip to Russian waters although he tried not to spend much time wondering about their destination. He was zero and seven so far trying to guess ahead of time where his orders would be taking them and he didn't relish being proven wrong yet again.

The sonar crew, he knew, would be happy to head up there and harass Ivan. During the time it took for *Shark* to reach deep water southeast of Nova Scotia, they hadn't heard anything that might have been another boat; a disappointment to the crew who were intent on capturing the award 'unofficially' given to the US submarine crew who successfully stalked the most '*Ivan's*' that year.

"We're clear the shelf, sir."

"Thanks Jed," Dan replied. Turning to the COB, he gave the order to dive the boat.

"Dive the boat, aye sir!" The Chief of the Boat echoed.

"Make your depth three two zero feet COB."

"Make my depth three two zero feet, aye!"

Ahead and behind the sail, vents opened atop the hull, allowing air to escape from the submarine's ballast tanks with a loud whoosh as seawater entered through open valves in the bottom of them. The tanks were much smaller than one would imagine – carrying just enough water to break the boat's neutral buoyancy and causing it to sink when full or surface when high pressure air blew the water from them. Now, as seawater rapidly displaced the air in the tanks, *USS Shark* sank beneath the waves to the chagrin of two dolphins who had been playfully riding the bow wave created by the stubby nose of the submarine as it pushed its way through the water.

Once *Shark's* sail disappeared below the surface, control planes mounted on either side of the fin-like structure bit into the water, allowing the 'drivers' to better control the submarine. With the endless energy from the S5W nuclear reactor turning the huge propeller at her stern. *Shark* soon settled at the ordered depth and silently cruised toward her destination.

PART II

THE DISCOVERY

As the crew of *USS Shark* were falling into their quiet, monotonous routines, Sergeant Brian Ashe was kneeling against the cold ground of eastern Labrador. He gazed intently through binoculars at a site he never would have imagined he'd see this side of the Atlantic ocean.

"Holy shit…" Brian whispered, although the subject of his comment was nearly half a mile away.

Not allowed even a quick call to his wife before leaving Base Gagetown, he had landed at Goose bay the previous evening. The base commander had assured him that he would personally inform her of Brian's mission, in very generic terms of course. Ashe was not so sure that would be a good idea. His wife might just drag the colonel out back and make him cut the spring grass which was sprouting at an alarming rate with all the rain they'd been having.

Climbing down the few steps from the Dakota, temporarily blinded by the bright lights of the air base, Brian had been met by a man in civilian clothes which had obviously seen better days.

"Sergeant Ashe?"

"Yes, I'm…"

"Jeep this way."

He had turned and walked away without waiting for Brian to respond. The man certainly didn't waste words, the sergeant had thought as he walked towards what at one time had been a military issue jeep. It was little more than a wreck now, camouflaged with badly faded green paint and rust.

"Shit", Brian had muttered out loud. "Park this thing in a scrap yard and no one would ever find it."

Climbing in, he had barely grabbed the side of the windshield before the driver took off with a clashing of gears. Heavy blue smoke seeping in from wherever the rusted exhaust system ended below the porous floor, competed with the stench of burnt oil coming from beneath the scratched and dented hood covering the engine.

Sergeant Ashe looked over his shoulder to confirm that his weapon was secure and did a double take when he noticed the cargo behind his seat. Securely mounted in the back of the battered jeep was one of the army's new PRC-515 radio sets. Ashe had been told about the new equipment back in Gagetown a month ago, but he had also been informed that it would not be issued to active units until later this fall. Somebody had pulled hard on some strings to get their hands on one and have it sent up here.

In spite of the jeep's decrepit condition, the driver continued to push the small vehicle along at break neck speed on what would have barely passed for a logging road back in New Brunswick. Almost two bone jarring hours later, they arrived at a small Ranger camp made up of a small shack and a battered old tent. Driving over a small bush which caused the jeep to momentarily teeter on two wheels, the man who Brian was now convinced planned to die before the jeep did, expertly swerved to a stop just feet away from a group of men.

Before stepping from the jeep, Sergeant Ashe surveyed the men, unable to avoid staring at their ragtag clothing. Their garments were a combination of multi-colour, handmade and store bought attire which all shared the same quality – dire need of replacement. The men on the other hand, had given his well-kept combats a brief once over, while showing no outward sign of embarrassment over their lack of uniform attire. The tent they stood beside reflected their appearance. It had obviously been patched and repaired many times and Brian was not sure that it had ever been complete or wasn't simply assembled from bits and pieces of other discarded tents.

Climbing painfully out of the vehicle, he had been introduced to the men, who had all warmly shaken his outstretched hand. One of them held back during the introduction, shyly standing aside. The man was obviously the eldest member of the group and remained quiet while eyeing the new stranger suspiciously. Afterwards, he had hesitantly came over and shaken hands. Grandfather hardly paid any attention to Brian, but had eyed the FN assault rifle slung over Ashe's shoulder with obvious longing before turning away from him.

You have got to be kidding me, Brian had thought at the sight of the frail-looking senior. The man looked like he belonged in an old folk's home. When later on, he had to choose a couple of Rangers to come with him to reconnoitre the intruder's encampment, the old man had insisted on leading them there. Sergeant Ashe soon came to realize that the man possessed more than a passing knowledge of soldiering and a seemingly endless amount of energy for his age. Brian also noticed again how Deniigi, as he learned the man's name was, kept eyeing his FN, while carefully clutching his old Lee Enfield.

Now, laying in the limited shelter afforded by a few wild bushes growing through the rocky ground, Brian realized the old man had stumbled across something much more serious than army headquarters in Ottawa had expected.

The sighting of the Russian assault rifles hadn't meant much to Ashe when he had first read the Ranger's report concerning them. The AK-47 was now a common site around the world with more than one communist country turning them out by the thousands every year. He had assumed that it was probably an exercise by Icelandic troops ignoring international boundaries or perhaps the old Ranger had mistakenly identified the weapon. More than likely he had thought, whoever they were would probably be gone by the time he had caught up with the Rangers.

One look through the worn old binoculars that Deniigi handed him had sent a chill down his spine. The clothing worn by these men bore no insignia, but the three years Brian had spent in Germany patrolling the 'line' had given him plenty of opportunity to see Russian army uniforms up close and he recognized these ones instantly. The lack of insignia on them meant only one thing – Spetsnaz.

"Shit," he whispered again. Deniigi nodded slightly before pointing behind them, indicating that he thought they should go back. Brian nodded in agreement and together the men carefully retraced their steps through the rough countryside.

"Did you see any more than five of them Deniigi?" Brian asked when he felt it was safe to speak.

"Only five," the old man replied.

"Okay, good." Brian was quickly learning that the guy didn't waste words.

They made their way back to the Ranger camp and Brian immediately reported what he had seen using the new long range radio. The process was a long one as he had to use a one time cipher code to send the information. As modern as it was, the new radio did not posses any encryption capability.

Keeping his message as short as possible, he described the uniforms and noted there seemed to be only five soldiers present in the group but the possibility existed there might have been more inside the carefully camouflaged tent. He had been unable to see anything indicating what the commandos were doing and had not noted any activity other than the men looking bored. He noted that it appeared as though they were waiting for something.

When the report was received at the main Ranger base, it was relayed via secure phone lines to Goose Bay and from there, to Gagetown, New

Brunswick, where the communications officer seeing the 'Blue' tag attached to it, immediately forwarded the message off to Canadian army headquarters in Ottawa.

Powering the radio off as he knew there would be no replay anytime soon, Sergeant Ashe looked over at the Rangers and spoke his thoughts aloud.

"And now, gentleman. We do what the army does best. We wait."

* * *

"All clear sir."

"Thank-you, Mr. Johnson." Dan turned to his right.

"Helm, come left to heading zero four zero degrees."

"Zero four zero degrees, aye sir."

USS Shark's crew had been lucky so far. They had not come across anything during their travels to the pickup point other than an occasional biological contact. Dan allowed himself to relax a little. He knew if they could pick up the SEALs without any outside interference, that would greatly increase the odds for their mission's success. Once the SEALs were safely aboard the submarine, they would go deep and maintain silence until they reached their objective. This close to Canadian shores in the relatively shallow waters just off the Grand Banks, they were in constant danger of being discovered, or worse yet, getting caught up in fishing gear as *USS Skipjack* had managed to do not far from where they currently cruised.

"All ahead slow."

"All ahead slow, aye."

The huge propeller at *Shark's* stern slowed until it was barely turning. The blades quietly displaced water behind the boat, giving the submarine only a slight forward motion. With little headway, the sailor 'chasing the bubble' had his hands full. The planes at the stern and on either side of the sail, had little effect on the boat's movement through the water at this speed.

"COB, periscope depth! Sonar, one more check!"

"Periscope depth, aye sir," responded the COB.

"Still all clear, sir," Petty Officer Johnson announced from the sonar console.

They had reached the rendezvous point without incident and would now sit quietly just below the surface waiting for the SEAL paradrop. Once the navy commandos hit the water, they would deploy a small noisemaker which would sink while emitting a faint high frequency buzzing sound that the submarine's passive sonar would pick up, signalling the boat's crew that their 'passengers' had arrived. The noisemaker used a short range frequency that ensured it would not be detected by any other warship which might happen to be in the area.

Dan hated the waiting. Patience was not one of his attributes and as a fast attack boat captain, sitting around doing nothing was not something he relished. He'd much rather be stalking some unsuspecting submarine. That was fun albeit so one-sided. The poor Ruskies never did seem to hear the Americans hiding in their baffles. Most times Dan found it all too easy to simply pull behind the noisy Russian boats and follow along after them until he became bored. At that point he would amuse the crew by nailing the hapless adversary with a good sonar lashing. His thoughts were interrupted by a shout from behind.

"Contact sir! Noisemaker. Five hundred yards astern."

"Thank you sonar. COB, surface the boat! Slowly, COB."

"Surface the boat, aye. Helm, all stop. Bring her up nice and steady."

The commander did not hesitate to order *Shark* to the surface. The SEALs would have had an excellent view for miles around during their descent and would have never given the 'pick up' signal had they spotted any other ship in the area. If they had, they would have floated in the water, their black painted faces barely clearing the waves, and waited patiently until it was apparent there would be no danger to the submarine. Doctrine was very clear on that subject. The submarine was a MUCH more valuable asset than the squad of SEALs.

USS Shark rose silently through the frigid waters. The petty officer at the helm performed an excellent job of keeping the submarine on an even keel during the ascent; a difficult job at the best of times but made even more so as the boat had almost no headway and the controls were now almost useless.

Above, buoyed by small inflatable vests, the SEALs saw the disruption on the water's surface and recognized the turbulence caused by a submarine slowly blowing its ballast tanks clear. They watched carefully to make sure the surfacing sub did not appear to be coming up right beneath them, possibly causing injuries.

There was no cause for concern however as *Shark's* stubby hull broke the surface a few hundred feet away. Starting to swim towards the rounded black hull, the SEALs quickly covered the distance and were soon being helped up the curved sides of the submarine. At the top of the sail, a pair of crewman searched the horizon for any ship or aircraft which might chance upon them. The early morning skies and the water's surface remained clear of any contacts however, and they soon relaxed, leaning into the sides of the sub's sail and periscope masts. Both sailors were certain they wouldn't see anything. They seldom did this far out to sea and besides, the boat's radar would pick up a target long before they could spot it.

Shark's radar would indeed pick up a target at long range, but the operator had neglected to set the system to 'fast search'. The small radar antennae atop its tall, retractable mast, was rotating slowly, allowing for a more intense search, but also taking precious seconds longer before it covered the same area twice.

* * *

According to Greek mythology, the god Argus Panoptes possessed many eyes, making him the perfect sentinel. It had therefore seemed fitting to name the new Canadair CP-107 maritime patrol aircraft after the ancient god who had been capable of seeing everything around him at once. The new Argus also possessed many 'eyes'. Not only to see over the surface of the oceans but beneath it as well. With a wingspan of one hundred and forty-two feet, it was a huge aircraft, crammed with numerous electronic sensors and manned by a crew of well trained operators.

The machine's most distinguishing features were a powerful radar dish mounted in a large bulge beneath its 'chin' and a long tapering point or 'stinger' at the aircraft's tail which housed a magnetic anomaly detector. At low altitude, the sophisticated MAD device could distinguish a distortion in the earth's natural magnetic field caused by the large metal hull of a submarine lurking below the surface.

The aircraft's ability to detect submarines was paired with a capacity to deploy a variety of torpedoes, bombs, depth charges and mines as well as 'special weapons' (unofficially of course) with which to kill them. The Argus crews laid claim to the title of World's Best Sub Hunters, with any doubt being eliminated during the annual Fincastle sub hunting competition in which the Canadians had demolished their foreign rivals the previous year.

The deadly submarine hunter's roots lay in a civilian airliner, the Bristol Britannia. Years earlier, another long range patrol bomber, the WW-II German Luftwaffe's FW-200 Condor had also been born of a civilian passenger aircraft. Unlike the Condor however, the Argus used an entirely different fuselage and power plants than the original aircraft. The engines were also the source of another of the aircraft's obvious traits - it's sound. Running at full throttle, the earth literally shook when the huge machine thundered overhead and when it approached at its maximum speed of over three hundred miles per hour, the effect on anyone standing below it on the ground was stunning, as the aircraft's sheer size and noise simultaneously enveloped them.

The feature that secured its place as the premier anti-submarine patrol bomber in the world was the aircraft's incredible range. The crew members were supplied with bunks where they could take short naps during the long patrol missions which could, and usually did, stretch for hours on end.

Five hours into this morning's mission, Argus 709's pilot was preparing to make the gradual course change which would lead them back to their base at RCAF Station Greenwood. He stole a quick glance out the side window at the ocean streaking by in the bright morning light as he held the aircraft steady, just over one hundred and fifty feet above the water's surface. The sea was relatively calm today and flying in 'ground effect' as they were, added another ten knots to their top speed.

Seated deep inside the dimly lit fuselage, surrounded by equipment that not only permeated the air with an 'electronic' odour, but also kept him warm, the radar operator was quietly pondering his future in the airforce. Although the Argus employed one of the more advanced versions of airborne radar in the world, the adversary he was tasked with hunting had made a recent technological leap of its own, that he felt would send his trade the way of the Dodo bird.

The new submarines sliding down the ways in the Soviet Union were being powered by nuclear reactors which allowed them to submerge and stay submerged for days and weeks at a time. Great for the MAD guys, the radar operator considered, with their strange device and even stranger displays, but surface radar was…a slight flash on the screen in front of him caught his attention.

"Guess I won't be joining the Dodo birds today," 'Pudgy' Cormier muttered aloud before pressing the intercom button.

"Sir," he called over to the officer who's duty was to co-ordinate between the operators and the flight crew. "I have a surface contact bearing three two three degrees, two thousand yards. It's either a very small ship all by itself, or a surfaced submarine."

"Show me what you have," replied the officer, moving down the aisle towards the radar operator. Leaning over, he smiled, "Oh yeah, that's a sub and out here, it has to be Russian!"

They hadn't received any information regarding NATO submarines in this area during the pre-flight briefing before their take off from Greenwood earlier this morning.

"Kind of cheeky for Ivan to be messing around this close to Canadian waters," Cormier remarked.

"Watch it close Pudgy. I'll be right back."

With that he navigated his way forward to the cockpit where he informed the flight crew of the discovery. The pilot nodded and immediately lowered the aircraft a few feet closer to the water, causing the aircraft commander's stomach to churn a little as he looked out the cockpit window on his right and realized he was looking across at the wave tops now and not down at them.

The commander of Argus 709 had been flying ops in the patrol aircraft for years now and had no problem with low altitude flying, but he still found it hard to think of what would happen should they hit a downdraft and the aircraft belly flopped into the Atlantic. The pilots always joked that the Argus was so tough, it would simply bounce off the surface of the water and continue flying. He found THAT idea even more distressing.

* * *

Aboard *USS Shark*, the petty officer watching over the ECM console was enjoying the rhythmic rolling of the submarine as it sat on the surface. The motion was hypnotic and threatened to lull the man to sleep until he was suddenly jolted by the ECM gear beeping madly. Turning in his seat, he read the screen and quickly confirmed what the device was trying to tell him.

"Oh hell! COB! Airborne radar contact right on top of us! He must be on the deck!"

The warning came too late. Above him, the last SEAL had just made it up the rope ladder to the pitching deck of the submarine. The captain, standing on the bridge to observe the pickup, turned in unison with the men on the deck below as a steadily increasing sound caught their attention just as the bridge intercom buzzed.

The SEAL commander stared in disbelief at the sight of a huge four engined aircraft coming straight towards him. His initial reaction was to duck, but as the bomber grew closer, he could see it was flying about a hundred feet above the water. His expletive was drowned out as the blast of noise hit him. The sound waves felt as much as heard, followed by an explosion of air and heat from the plane's engines as the Argus roared low over the submarine, missing the extended periscope mast by less than a dozen feet. The submarine's captain, looking directly into the transparent nose of the aircraft, clearly saw a crew member leaning into the perspex nose with a camera in his hands aimed directly at him.

"COB!" he yelled down the open hatch at his feet. "What the hell…?" He stopped when he realized that a voice was coming from the bridge speaker. His ears were still ringing from the wave of noise that had just washed over him.

"…contact overhead," the speaker finished. Way too late! Dan noted. The picture of *Shark* sitting on the surface was a prize catch for that patrol crew. He hoped they had not managed a good shot of the men on the after deck – especially the guys wearing wetsuits.

* * *

"Sir," called the navigator from his position looking out the clear nose of the Argus. "I have in my hands a photo worth more free drinks than you can imagine!"

"I don't know about that," replied the pilot. "I can imagine a lot of drinks!"

He looked over at the aircraft commander and gave him a smiling thumbs up. Pushing the intercom button on the control wheel, he then ordered the radio operator to inform Greenwood that an American nuclear sub was dead in the water south east of Newfoundland and to give them the coordinates. Banking the Argus in a tight starboard turn, he brought the aircraft back on the reciprocal bearing but as he levelled off, he could see the submarine was already beginning to submerge. Too bad, he thought. An amateur photographer, he would have liked to have another shot of the sub from the opposite side, silhouetted in the morning sun.

* * *

"Damn it COB! Why the hell didn't anyone pick up that aircraft!?"

Dan knew the answer probably lay in the altitude the Canadian patrol bomber had bore in on them at. Everyone knew that flight level 10 down to the surface off Canada's coasts was 'Argus Country' and those pilots could work magic keeping the huge aircraft so low over the water that nothing would pick them up until it was too late. US Navy pilots had tried similar tactics with their Neptunes but had written off the manoeuvre as being far too dangerous.

"Sorry, captain! They were so low that by the time they hit the screens, it was too late."

"Okay. We'll spot them next time. I'm sure they already radioed our position but hopefully they didn't notice the SEALs on deck."

Dan had his doubts about that. The Canadians didn't miss much.

He was right.

* * *

Four hours later, a navy lieutenant was spreading out the photos taken by the Argus crew across a large mahogany table inside the main headquarters building of the Canadian Navy in Halifax. The film had been rushed with a military police escort from the airbase at Shearwater to the photographic lab next door to the headquarters building where the technicians had been ordered to be both fast and careful processing the celluloid. The Argus had been diverted to the airbase just across the harbour from Halifax when her crew had reported the submarine sighting and the news that they had managed to get photos of the boat. The aircrew had been disappointed at first, not being able to continue their hunt of the American boat, but had accepted the unexpected trip to Halifax as a worthwhile alternative

Rushed through processing, the prints were still damp from the developing fluids used to bring the images out on the photographic paper. The officer held them carefully by their edges as he laid them out in chronological order. He was also trying hard not to attract the attention of Admiral Hunnicut, who was shuffling through papers at his desk across the room.

Tossing one of the papers aside, the admiral grunted and walked over to the table, ignored the startled look from the lieutenant, and glanced down at the images, slowly examining every detail in them.

"I'll bet money she's *Shark*," he commented. "Pretty little thing. Just left here earlier this week."

The lieutenant tried to make himself as inconspicuous as possible and hoped the admiral was just talking to himself and didn't actually expect a comment from him.

"So, what do you make of this, lieutenant?"

The young officer looked up nervously. He'd just been posted to the admiral's staff and was still unsure how to deal with the man.

"Yes," he replied hesitantly. "She certainly is a pretty submarine, sir."

"Not the sub, son! What do you make of this!?"

The admiral's pen was jabbing at one of the photos which showed the submarine sitting on the water. Looking closer, he could see a group of men standing on the deck behind the sail.

"Looks like some men just climbed aboard, sir." The lieutenant wished now that he had simply dropped the photos off and waited outside.

"Ever see submariners dressed like that, lieutenant?" It sounded more like an accusation than a question.

"Err...no sir. I can't say that I have." He paused. He hadn't seen many submariners period and didn't care how they dressed on their smelly vessels. He could never understand what would motivate a sailor to volunteer for that duty.

"They look more like scuba divers, don't they, sir?"

"Good for you lieutenant! Don't ever be afraid to give an opinion! Now go find that Argus crew and send them in," he ordered. "I want to know where that boat was headed."

The lieutenant straightened up, and realizing the admiral was no longer paying any attention to him, turned on his heel and left the office. In the main reception area of the headquarters building, the Argus crew was standing together. Still in their flight suits, they were enjoying a cup of coffee and discussing the mission.

"The admiral will see you men now," the lieutenant announced before thankfully dropping into his chair behind his desk.

"Okay fellows, now remember, let me do the talking," the aircraft commander warned them quietly as they headed into the room.

Stopping inside the doorway, the men allowed their eyes to sweep the expanse of the room. The size of the space, dominated by a huge table in the middle, surprised them and they stood quietly at attention, waiting for the admiral to acknowledge them. He was bent over the table, examining what they presumed to be the photos from their flight and seemed oblivious of their presence. Without looking up he grunted more than asked, "Which one of you picked the Yank up first?"

"I did, sir," the radar operator spoke up without thinking, immediately regretting that he had brought attention to himself.

The admiral stood and turned towards them, an unreadable expression on his face. Walking over to the radar operator, he looked down at him. The man towered over Pudgy by a good five inches.

"At ease, gentleman. Damn good work son!" His voice boomed around the room.

"You showed the Americans they can't just sail into Canadian territory and not be found out! Good work...all of you!" He turned and walked back towards the table.

"Come over here and look at these pictures of yours. Tell me what you make of them."

Crowding around the table, they saw the images of the American submarine, sharp and clear, sitting on the surface. Unlike the lieutenant earlier, the aircraft crew noted immediately that the submarine appeared to have picked up a group of men from the water. The admiral asked them to speculate on what the mission of the submarine or the men might have been, admonishing them to speak openly. He was also inquisitive about the direction the submarine had taken after it submerged.

"Well, I wondered about that, sir," Pudgy offered. "He definitely headed west, but only after running north-east for almost half an hour." The radar operator paused before continuing. "Our MAD operator had him dead to rights."

"Do you think he was heading for Labrador with a team of SEALs, flight sergeant?"

The young man was visibly shaken by the unrelenting gaze from the old man's bright gray eyes, but he did not cower.

"Possibly."

"And what the hell would they be heading there for?" Admiral Hunnicut's voice boomed out again and the question echoed around the large room.

"I don't know admiral, but they were definitely headed that way."

The admiral liked this man. He didn't fall apart under pressure from high ranks – a rare trait in the military these days.

"What's your name son?"

"Cormier, sir. Flight Sergeant Pud...Robert Cormier." He'd almost given the admiral the nickname which had followed him ever since an incident in the 'dunker', when he had become wedged tight in the escape device while under water.

"Well Flight Sergeant Cormier, you've got balls! Don't ever lose 'em! And you're right about where *Shark* is headed." He continued thoughtfully, "We're just not sure why yet."

For another hour, the admiral spoke with the crew, pulling out every detail of their mission and discussing at great length the MAD equipment and its reliability. As the sun was starting to set over the navy base in Halifax, the men finally left the building and headed back across the harbour to Shearwater to clean up after which they would spend the evening on the town – a reward for their diligence.

* * *

As the crew of Argus 709 left the Shearwater air base headed for Halifax, far to the north, a grim faced Spetsnaz Senior Lieutenant Kristoff Nikolev was looking up at the gathering darkness over the Labrador landscape. Pushing up the sleeve of his olive green jacket, he checked his watch. It was time again for them to start up the generator. Using what light remained in the evening dusk, his men carefully removed the specially designed camouflage covering to reveal an odd looking antenna anchored into the rocky ground just outside their equally well camouflaged tent.

His team, all members of Spetsnaz Group Four, had been encamped on the Canadian coast for a week now, awaiting the proper time to begin their operation. After carefully checking each part of the antennae for damage which might have occurred during their transit to this place, they had assembled it the previous night using low output flashlights. With the camouflage netting in place, the antennae beneath was nearly invisible and prying eyes from any direction would only see what appeared to be a few large rocks on a landscape littered with them.

Inside the tent, Spetsnaz Starshina Abashev primed the portable gas generator which burst to life with a low rumble. Used to power the electronic equipment which had been carefully set up, the SY-32 power unit was designed to supply electricity using an amazingly small amount of specially developed fuel. The tent itself was originally a standard issue mess unit but this one had been modified and dyed to the point that it looked more like a rock outcropping than the rocks themselves did. There had been a brief moment of concern for Kristoff, when coming back from a short patrol of the area the day of their arrival, he had found the tent had been erected incorrectly and was far too square in shape. He had quickly ordered the men to take it down and reassemble it properly.

From where he stood outside, Nikolev heard the generator start up with a muted rumble. Stepping inside, he found Gefreiters Danshev and Narinsky seated at their consoles, carefully watching the displays for signals they would diligently record for future use. The senior lieutenant hated the inactivity this kind of mission forced upon himself and his men. An elite Spetsnaz infiltration and operations team, they would need a lot of hard physical training to get back into proper shape when they returned to their base at Jaroslavl, north east of Moscow.

During their briefing before leaving the Soviet Union, it had been explained that the mission they were embarking on was very important to the Motherland. It had been made clear that if they were successful, the information collected could save the lives of many of their comrades in case of war.

When the briefing had concluded, Kristoff had sat down alone with General Ustinof, the head of Spetsnaz, and suggested that perhaps this mission was too dangerous - that the Canadians and Americans would react very strongly if they discovered the commandos on Canadian soil. The General had brushed aside his fears and assured him the Western powers were too frightened of war to respond forcefully. He had gone on to explain that this show of Soviet technology was vital and would further warn the West against ever attacking the Motherland. Kristoff realized there was no point in arguing further. The general's mind was made up and if the commando pursued this line, they would simply replace him and he dared not risk one of the other leaders taking over his team. Especially for a mission so fraught with danger as this one.

After more briefings, had come hours of training with the unfamiliar electronic equipment they would carry with them on the mission. Not only did they have to be skilled at operating the devices, but also in repairing and maintaining them in the event of a failure. The team would also have to carry everything else they would need with them as there would be no possibility of resupply once they came ashore. Special, high energy, low bulk food items had been selected for the men which were also unfortunately, very low in taste. A location had been chosen for them to carry out the mission based on

71

availability of the one thing they would not be able to carry enough of - fresh water. The site selected had a small brook running close by which would have thawed this late in the spring, providing them with drinking water.

The submarine voyage to a point just off the Canadian coast had proven uneventful and before disembarking, the commandos had exchanged friendly jabs with the submarine's crew who had teased them relentlessly in return about how they would appreciate real food and real women on their return home after completing the mission.

He was jarred back to the present by a flashing light on the front console of the receiver. The unit had already detected a signal, captured from the air by the odd looking antenna outside the tent. Although at this latitude it was very weak, the sensitive circuits inside the mysterious box were able to amplify the signal sufficiently to record the information being transmitted. The data was encoded of course, but when the information was retrieved upon their return to the Soviet Union, scientists would manage to decipher it, perhaps with a little help from the KGB – and a greedy Westerner.

Somewhere in the night sky, he mused, a Canadian or American interceptor must be in the air. Its datalink system would be picking up the signal transmitted from one of the NORAD radar sites. Pinetree, they called them. The radar operators manning the station must have detected something in the skies worthy of a closer look. They would have no idea that their signals to the interceptors where themselves, being intercepted.

Kristoff had been impressed with the ingeniousness of the Pinetree radar line during the team's indoctrination in the North American Air Defence Command system. The men had found the unique partnership between Canada and the United States curious, unable to imagine the Soviet Union having such an open relationship with another country, let alone trusting them to help defend the Motherland.

The string of radar stations making up the Pinetree Line, they had learned, stretched across Canada and parts of the northern United States. One of the stations, upon spotting an intruding aircraft, would then relay the information directly to the intercepting fighters through a secure datalink. The information would show up on a display in the aircraft's cockpit, giving the fighter's crew all the information they needed to make a successful intercept.

The major advantage of the system, they had been briefed, was the ability it gave the pilot to close in on the adversary without using his own radar or radio until the very last minute. Thus no warning was given to the intruder of his presence until it was too late to take evasive action. Fortunately, the Committee for State Security had managed to acquire information about the Pinetree system from an American technician whose love of money and weakness for women were more powerful than his patriotism.

And this, Kristoff mused, was why he and his team were sitting on this uninhabited, rocky part of Canada. They would be monitoring the signals from three of the Pinetree sites located on the east coast of Labrador and would hopefully compile a history of data transmissions to the interceptors, both Canadian and American. The signals traveled only one way – the aircraft not being able or needing to reply to the radar station along the datalink.

One piece of equipment sitting in the tent had been unused so far, and would remain so for a couple more days. The high powered transmitter was capable of completely jamming the datalink communications, leaving the intercepting aircraft blind and relegated to using its own search radar which was incapable of long range detection. More importantly, it would easily be picked up by the radar warning equipment on Soviet aircraft, allowing them to successfully evade the fighters.

Nikolev was happy the mission would soon be over. This boring vacation in the Canadian wilderness could not end soon enough. Kristoff sat down on one of the packing boxes now being used for a seat and relaxed. Closing his eyes, he began going over the plans for their departure, which involved a rendezvous with the submarine tasked with bringing them back home. It would be nice to have a hot shower again - even the limited ones available on the sub. Those sailors had such an easy life, he thought, before nodding off.

* * *

The tourists taking advantage of Ottawa's warm spring weather for an evening stroll over the grassy mounds of Parliament Hill, were oblivious to the increase in vehicular traffic at a time when most of the employees in the building had gone home for the day. The setting sun over Canada's capital city painted the majestic buildings with a beautiful crimson glow. They were closed now; the last public tour having left an hour earlier. In the Prime Minister's office, a grim faced Minister of Defence was sitting uncomfortably across the desk from the Canadian leader.

"And that's what we know so far, Prime Minister," he concluded as he sat back in an overstuffed chair. "I've also spoken with the US ambassador, but he either doesn't know anything about what is going on, or he's not talking."

Ted hated to be the bearer of bad news for his boss, especially when he didn't have much information to go on. The details of how the Soviets had been discovered were still somewhat sketchy and he had been expecting a briefing from the army but that had been delayed due to the sensitivity of the information. Because communications regarding this matter were under the highest security level, any information pertaining to this situation was taking far longer than normal to arrive.

"Okay Ted," the Prime Minister reflected. "A group of Soviet soldiers is sunbathing on the rocks in Labrador, an American nuclear submarine with a group of commandos is probably heading their way, and we have a small group of civilians…Rangers, with a regular army sergeant, caught in the middle. This isn't good, Ted."

"I think…," the Minister of Defence began.

"No, the time for contemplation is over," the Prime Minister interrupted, reaching for his intercom.

"Sarah? Get me the President on the phone. Yes, I know what time it is and if he's napping, tell them to wake him the hell up!"

Winking at Ted, the Canadian leader felt empowered for the first time since their meeting began an hour and a half ago.

"If the President finds what we do to his spy planes upsetting, he's going to be furious about this! Call your guys in Greenwood and Summerside, Ted. I want everything they have in the air NOW! And I want that American submarine found."

The Prime Minister paused, contemplating his next order. "Tell them when they do, tail the bastard and await further instructions. Oh, and Ted, have the navy get a ship or two up there as well. I want a serious show of force to make it clear that Canada is a sovereign nation and we are NOT going to be walked all over!"

"Yes, Prime Minister."

"And not a word about the Soviets is to leak out to the press. It looks bad for us that they were able to land at all, let alone set up a base camp. I want to kick their asses out, but on our terms."

"Yes, sir."

Ted stood and walked over to the adjoining office where he grabbed the phone and contacted the RCAF Station Greenwood operations center. Getting through to the squadron leader, he passed along the Prime Minister's instructions and laughed at the question from the patrol squadron's commander before replying.

"No, Keith. Just find him for now. But we'll be sure to let you know right away if it's okay to sink the bastard."

Hanging up, the Minister of Defence made a call to the squadron commander at the base in Summerside, PEI and repeated the orders. Satisfied the men would do everything possible, he dialled the army base in Gagetown to find out what was known about the sergeant working with the Canadian Ranger group in Labrador. After coming on the line, the commanding officer assured Ted that Sergeant Ashe was one of his best, and more importantly, he was very level headed. Good thing, Ted thought. The man could start World War III up there if he screwed up badly enough. He paused for a moment at the thought. That was exactly what the Prime Minister had said earlier in the week about *HMCS Margaree's* captain. He had been impressed by how level headed the ship's commanding officer had been in a situation that was at best, exceedingly dangerous. Hopefully, the minister thought, Ashe would be as well.

The Prime Minister meanwhile, quietly contemplated the situation. He had more than a passing knowledge of the Rangers and fully understood that they were not trained to go up against any professional force, let alone a Spetsnaz team. There was something unique about this Ranger group though, or rather someone. He smiled at the memory of his short stint up north with the army and picked up the phone. Hopefully he'd be able to get a message up to them without it arousing too much suspicion.

* * *

The next day in Halifax, the admiral responsible for the sprawling naval base was on the phone with the 'level headed' commanding officer of *HMCS Margaree*. Barry had just returned that morning from a very quick trip to Ottawa and had spent the day making sure his ship was ready and that the VDS had been replaced and tested. His visit with the Prime Minister had been cordial and he felt the man was genuinely interested in what had transpired. He had also felt the tension around the room as they spoke. Obviously, things had not quieted down any after the incident.

"Are you sure it's working properly?"

"Yes admiral," Barry replied. "I was there for the final test myself and the new VDS is working like a charm. The XO ran some extra tests on the range in the basin and everything calibrated perfectly."

There had in fact been one minor flaw with the huge pulley that reeled the VDS in and out, but that had been easily rectified and the ship was again ready for operations. Lieutenant Commander Barry Delaney was anxious to get his destroyer back to sea. Since returning from Ottawa, he had heard rumblings all over the base that something big was afoot and he wanted *Margaree* and her crew in on it.

"Okay Delaney, warm her up and call me when you're prepared to drop lines - and listen, Barry," he paused measuring his words. "This could get sticky. Make sure you're carrying a full load. *Terra Nova* will be sailing with you. She's ready to depart now and you will have operational control of the two ships." There was another moment of silence on the line. "And Delaney? I want both my ships back in one piece."

"Aye, sir. I'll bring them both home." Barry stood silent, the phone receiver against his ear for a few moments before he continued. "Thank you for the opportunity, admiral. I'll give you a call as soon as we're ready. I expect that will be in less than six hours."

"Some opportunity! I'll be expecting your call." The admiral hung up the phone and looked over his desk. His 'in' box was filling up rapidly as the current crisis was monopolizing all of his time. No matter, he thought. One way or another, this was going to be all over soon and if things went wrong, there would be no more paperwork to worry about…ever.

Standing up and gazing out the window behind his desk at the fading daylight over the harbour, Admiral Hunnicut reflected on the changes in the Royal Canadian Navy which had occurred over the past twenty years. At the end of the last world war, when the battered and broken old Corvette he had been a boatswain on, had sailed back into Halifax, the Canadian navy had been a huge and powerful force. Within months however, the government had set plans in motion to cut it back drastically. Then had come the frantic rebuilding as the cold war took hold, but now, half a dozen years later, the navy was working hard just to keep its only aircraft carrier in service. She would be heading to Quebec in a couple of weeks for a needed refit, leaving the navy without a flight deck for six to eight months, although if past refits were any indication, they'd be lucky to see *Bonnie* back in a year.

The other problem sitting on his plate right now was the ongoing protest over unification and the coming new uniforms. Recently an incident had gotten out of hand in the dockyard, but calmer heads had prevailed and in spite of Canada's rich naval traditions being brushed aside by the powers that be, the admiral knew his sailors would do their job. Hell yes! His men would grumble and complain, but they'd get the job done regardless of what the pencil pushers in Ottawa made them wear.

Back aboard *Margaree*, Delaney was also pondering the future as he took in the space delegated to him as his office and cabin. The mementos of his career were spread around like trophies, some indicating achievements from his past, while others were simply humorous reminders of good times. One in particular caught his eye. It was a simple plaque from *USS Joseph P Kennedy*, given to him by her captain when they had sailed together escorting an American carrier during the Cuban missile blockade. That had been the last time, before the incident off Labrador, that he had felt as though events around him were spiralling out of control.

Barry recalled how the newspapers and general public had thought themselves closer to World War III at that time than ever before, but as most soldiers knew, while the leaders involved were busily trying to shout each other down and posturing at the United Nations, there was little real danger. That came when small events rapidly escalated before the politicians were given the chance to step in and slow things down.

Over the next few hours, Barry was all over the ship giving orders, confirming that earlier orders were being carried out properly and making sure that *Margaree* was ready for battle. He made a mental note to run a test on the anti-fallout spray, just as a precaution in case the unthinkable did happen and they had to sail through a contaminated area. The system was designed to drench the entire outside of the ship with water, washing off any radioactive particles that might land aboard.

During a brief inspection of the 'bear trap', Barry noted *HMCS Terra Nova* slowly making her way south through the harbour. She had been berthed at the Bedford magazine earlier and her weapons lockers would now be fully stocked.. Along her deck, the special duty crew stood smartly at attention and Barry wondered how many of them were aware of the seriousness of their mission. Probably best they didn't know, he surmised. Some of them might have jumped overboard and swam for home.

*   *   *

At RCAF Station Chatham, Ben gazed at the Voodoo parked silently inside one of the alert hangers. Even sitting on the ground, it looked to be going supersonic. He ran his fingers through his hair thoughtfully as he examined the weapons door which was currently in its typical half open position, when the aircraft was powered down. On one side, the familiar pair of Falcon missiles were mounted and armed - the standard load out for an alert aircraft. It was the other side of the door that held his gaze and kept him frozen in place. Mounted opposite the Falcons was a pair of Genie rockets. Not the ones like he had seen the ground crews occasionally practice with - painted blue to denote their inert status. No, these were all white with a pair of coloured bands circling the nose. He had only seen live Genies outside of the storage bunkers located south west of the field twice before. Something had gone wrong in the world tonight he thought…terribly wrong.

"Looks like the shit hit the fan somewhere, sir"

Ben turned towards the voice. A young airman holding an FN rifle that seemed about as large as he was, stood beside the aircraft. He was trying to look tough - and failing. His eyes showed fear. Not fear of his current job, Squadron Leader Jones knew the man would defend the station to the death if necessary, but fear of the unknown and unthinkable that hung like a distasteful odour over the base.

"Seems like it airman. I'm sure someone just woke up on the wrong side of the bed this morning and we'll be playing baseball again this weekend." The officer versus ranks ball games were a huge hit on the base and he received the expected response from the young man.

"You think, sir? Sure would be nice to win another game." The airman smiled and visibly relaxed. The officers had won a game once. Everyone swore it had happened - once. It was just that no one could remember how many years ago it had been.

"I'm sure it would," Ben answered with a forced grimace, and then added with a stern tone, "but in the meantime, don't let anyone mess with my airplane!"

With that, he turned and headed back to the alert room to join the growing group of air crew sitting around waiting for something to happen.

"You can count on it sir!" the young airman called after him, his voice sounding more confident.

As Ben walked into the room, Cam came up to him and reported that their assigned aircraft was fully operational and pointed to the red page attached to the flight document.

"I'd never seen one of these forms before today," he commented, making a few marks on the page. "Looks like if we misplace one of the Genies, we might as well not come back."

He had carefully read through the special instructions regarding the use of the nuclear rockets and decided it would be much better if they didn't have to fire one. The resulting documentation would take longer than the ensuing war would last.

"Probably wouldn't be anything to come back to anyway, Cam. If we have to fire them, I'm thinking we head due south to the Bahamas afterwards…if the fuel lasts."

* * *

Sunrise the next morning cast long shadows over the parking lot behind the nondescript structure next door to the Parliament Buildings in Ottawa. Obscured by the darkness, a blue four door car pulled up to an unmarked entrance behind the ordinary brick building which neighboured the Hill. A lone figure emerged from the vehicle into a ray of bright sunshine. He stopped for a moment, allowing his eyes to adjust to the bright light, and squinted up at the sunlight streaming through the towers of the capital building.

The Prime Minister closed his eyes for a moment allowing the image to slowly fade from his retina. Blinking it away, he walked briskly towards the door, stopped and turned, gazing back once again at Parliament Hill. Earlier that morning during a heated debate with his advisors, he had refused outright to evacuate from the capital. After being briefed on the current situation, they had strongly suggested he head to Carp where the new shelter was located, but the PM had argued against the move, preferring instead to remain where he felt certain his presence would do the most good.

The Prime Minister had also pointed out to them that the press would immediately notice his unscheduled departure from the city and with enough digging, they would soon uncover that something was amiss. That, in spite of the threats he'd made to everyone aware of the situation that the entire affair remain top secret. If news of the past day's events were broadcast, it would cause panic to break out. No, he had stated with a firmness which had finally ended the debate, he was staying put.

Throwing one final glance towards the capital building, as though to an old friend he was seeing for the last time, the Prime Minister spun around and walked through the small unmarked door. An army officer standing just inside the entrance jumped to attention.

"Good morning sir," he almost hollered, snapping a salute so forcefully the Canadian leader thought it might break his arm. "I'll be escorting you downstairs."

'Downstairs' was a euphemism for the cavernous space, one of Canada's best kept secrets, two stories below where they stood. The men strolled quickly to an elevator at the end of a short hallway, and as it opened, stepped inside. The shiny grey doors had barely brushed together when the floor seemed to drop from under their feet, leaving a feeling of nausea in the Prime Minister's stomach. Before he had time to react, the elevator shuddered to a stop, leaving him clutching the handrail for a moment to regain his balance, and breakfast, as the doors swished open in front of him.

"Sorry, sir. The elevator is designed to drop quickly...in case of an emergency..."

"That's okay," he replied, secure now that the bacon and eggs he had for breakfast would remain in his stomach. "I understand."

He had toured the facility shortly after being elected but had never seriously contemplated its use. The Prime Minister had always assumed that in case of a national emergency, he would be taken to the huge underground complex in Carp, just west of the city. The new facility had been built to withstand any kind of attack, as opposed to this room which was smack dab in the middle of Canada's capital city and only protected by a few feet of concrete and the building standing above. Designed during WW-II, it would never survive even a near miss from a nuclear weapon.

When he had previously visited the command centre, he could not help but gaze down upon the large open space in awe. Huge wall displays and consoles filled every inch of floor space, and while standing there, he had also seen the irony of its existence. There really was no point in a portion of Canada's government surviving a nuclear war. The northern hemisphere, and especially Canada due to the prevailing winds, would be uninhabitable far longer than any human would be able to survive.

The Prime Minister could not fathom existing for weeks or even months waiting for the food and water to finally run out, while above, his beloved country lay devastated and dying. He was not an overly religious man, but he remembered enough from his Sunday School classes to equate surviving in the bunker to a macabre sort of purgatory, where he would wait before finally being sent, not to Salvation, but to hell – his punishment for deserting the people he had sworn to protect. He had vowed that day to never seek refuge in this room or the even larger, new purgatory over at Carp, if the bombs ever started to fall. If that happened, he would take the elevator back up to the surface and go home to his wife.

And yet, a few short years later, here he was. Not seeking refuge. He meant to keep that vow, but he did need to make use of the command, communications and control systems the 'Baby Bunker' possessed. As he entered the command center for the second time during his leadership, a pathway opened in a wall of people standing in the centre of the room, creating a human hallway to a lone desk which held a commanding view of the wall displays in front of him. Spread out before the displays were three rows of consoles, each manned by at least two uniformed men or women.

His own desk held only a few note pads, a glass of pencils and pens, and two telephones. One of them, a large multiline affair, connected him to all of the stations in the bunker, as well as to most of the offices in the Parliament Buildings above. The other phone was a plain white version similar to what one would expect to find in any home, except that a round disk containing an amber light occupied the spot where the dial would have been. The smaller one hadn't been there the previous time he had visited, but the Prime Minister remembered reading about its installation shortly after the Cuban affair. When he had commented on the new 'red phone' while reading the notification, an embarrassed look had crossed his aide's face who then explained that the phone was in fact white. He had started to assure his boss that a red one could be installed but that was as far as he got. The Prime Minister had cut him off with a hearty laugh. The white phone would do fine.

The largest wall, the one containing the displays, was actually three separate panels forming a semi-circle. On the centre one, the huge video display currently showed an outline of eastern Canada. On the floor area directly before it, a few of the consoles were occupied by various military personnel who were busily checking over the control consoles in front of them. The various 'systems' they controlled, kept in a constant state of readiness, operated all military communications, and more importantly, the highly classified, secure networks used amongst Canada's nuclear armed forces. He had been taken aback when asking about a particular part of the control console, an embarrassed captain had referred him to a general standing nearby who quickly corralled the conversation in a different direction. It had been the general's polite way of noting that even the Prime Minister was not privy to everything.

Behind the front row of consoles, another row of desks broken into three sections stretched across the room. The uniforms of the men and women hovering over them indicated that each section was assigned to one of the armed services. A large group of high ranking officers stood or sat around the area talking, most of them, he surmised, discussing how they should be in the 'Big Bunker' at Carp, rather then under the bull's eye Ottawa would represent in their minds.

The nation's capital held no strategic military value of course. It was probably targeted by only a single Soviet warhead of low yield. As had most of the world's major powers, Canada had long since decentralized control of its armed forces, spreading its command centers out over the country lest one of the new thermonuclear weapons wipe them all out in one horrendous fireball. Ottawa would be what the military referred to as a 'symbolic target'. That wouldn't matter much to him, Canada's political leader thought. Being 'symbolically' dead was still dead.

The Prime Minister walked over to his desk, well separated from the rest at the back of the room. From here he had a bird's eye view of the entire space. He noted how the floor sloped down slightly to the huge video displays mounted on the wall in front of him. The centre one was still showing the east coast but the image had zoomed in and was now only showing the area from Nova Scotia's eastern tip to the southern coast of Baffin Island.

He sat down and quickly scanned a few reports which had been placed on the desk prior to his arrival. The one from Goose Bay, where the land forces commander had relocated a couple of days ago, reported the Ranger team had observed no changes in the Soviet activities.

The next report confirmed that *HMCS Margaree* and *Terra Nova* had left Halifax and were making for the Labrador Sea at high speed. It was obvious they would only arrive in time to pick up the pieces, which would be fine with him, as long as none of the pieces to be picked up were Canadian.

His mood lightened as he read the last report. One of the Argus patrol aircraft from Greenwood thought they had found the cagey American submarine and were waiting for a second aircraft to join them in a convoluted 'reverse wolf pack'. The Prime Minister had been well briefed on the submarine hunter's capabilities and he was confident the aircrews would make quick work of finding the little bastard.

"Okay Ted," he looked over to the Minister of Defence who had stood quietly as the Prime Minister finished reading. "Lets get this show going. Have your guys move in, but stand by for orders."

"Yes, Prime Minister. I'll send the signal to the army unit observing the Russians."

Ted strode over to a brigadier general who had just hung up the phone at his console. After listening to the minister for a few moments, the officer frowned and sat down heavily. Reaching again for the telephone, he prepared himself for the order he was about to give. This action, the general thought as he pressed one of the buttons across the front of the device, could very well be the start of the final world war. It would never be given a number – there would be no one left to do so.

"Doug?" The general's voice was gruff, belying his true feelings. "It's Hector. Yeah, we're down in the 'hole.' No, the Man wanted to come here instead. I think I understand."

There was a long pause as the officer on the other end of the line made small talk, as if by stalling he could somehow prevent the order he was anticipating.

"Doug. Send them in and tell them to await further orders." He listened for a moment longer. "Yes, I did tell him again that you had a force ready to go in with a paradrop. The Man still wants this handled quietly and he still feels the Rangers can pull it off." A brief pause. "Yeah, you too and thanks!"

General Hector LeBlanc slowly replaced the receiver on the phone. Now it was up to a small group of men he had never met or even spoken to. He sincerely wished he could have spoken personally to that young army sergeant up there in Labrador, and explained to him that although it might seem like he was being sent in alone, there was a huge force ready to back him up if things went badly. Of course, by then it would be too late for the sergeant and his little band of men. Hector remembered years earlier when he had been on a northern exercise with the Rangers. He hoped that the ones in this group were half as dedicated as those men had been. Even so, he realized that this was a hell of a lot to ask of a bunch of civilians.

He has briefed the Prime Minister at length regarding the Ranger's training and had stated outright that sending them in against the Soviets was a mistake. The PM had countered that highly trained commandos would be expecting tactics they themselves would use and this might catch them off guard. He had given in, and after thinking it over, had agreed that the man might have a point. The Spetsnaz wouldn't be expecting this.

The Prime Minister's orders stated that the Soviet soldiers had to be removed at any cost. They also stipulated that prisoners were neither necessary nor expected. General LeBlanc knew that Sergeant Ashe and the Rangers might have something to say about the 'any cost' part, but he was certain they would be the first to agree that this situation had to be resolved quickly – and quietly.

Many good men and women had already paid the supreme price for this nation's sovereignty and others probably would in the future, but a free Canada was a prize worth fighting for. Hector pictured the landscape where the sergeant would be operating with his ragtag band of citizen soldiers. Although the harshest part of the northern winter was past, the land was still cold, barren and rocky. Not a good place to try and ambush seasoned commandos.

Pushing up from his chair, the general walked over to the Prime Minister who was speaking in hushed tones with Hector's navy counterpart. It was too bad one of the navy's destroyers wasn't in the area already, he thought. A few rounds from its three inch guns would have put an end to the Soviet picnic in a hurry.

Looking over the situation map to kill time while the Prime Minister finished his conversation with the admiral, Hector noted that the view was now showing only Labrador, enlarged to detail every little town and village. He saw the three Pinetree radar sites which lined the coast of Labrador clearly indicated with a forth one situated closer to Goose Bay. The Soviets had landed just south of the site at Hopedale, the central of the three coastal stations.

The American troops stationed there had been alerted to the Rangers being in the area on the premise that they were conducting a security sweep exercise, but nothing had been said of the Soviets. Earlier, the Prime Minister had asked his military advisors if they thought the Americans were aware of the intruders, and if they were, did they know that the Canadians knew? He and the other men in the room had broken out into laughter at the question. It had been a light moment in an otherwise gloomy meeting.

Hector was pretty certain the Soviets would never be foolish enough to attack one of the radar sites directly, especially on foot. Each base was well guarded by a good sized security detachment and more help was only a parachute drop away. An attack on any of the Pinetree locations would be suicide. So just what were the Soviets up to, the general pondered. A simple exercise to see if they could land a small team on Canadian soil perhaps? That made no sense. There was no strategic value to that and besides, as this group was about to discover, they would be severely dealt with.

"I guess we'll know soon enough," he said out loud to no one in particular.

* * *

"Damn! Are you sure about this lieutenant?"

"I'm afraid so, Sergeant Ashe."

The officer understood his concern. Lieutenant Sanderson had arrived at the makeshift camp an hour earlier after enduring the same heart stopping ride Brian had previously suffered through. Recovering from the initial shock of seeing the Rangers in their rag tag clothing, he'd taken the sergeant aside and given him his orders.

"Colonel Anderson in Ottawa asked about reinforcements for you and the word is they will send them in only if it becomes necessary. There's a couple of squads of paratroopers standing by in Gander," he noted, trying to sound positive. "Their gear is sitting in a few Dakotas that are ready to roll, but the Minister would rather this be handled quietly. None of the troops on standby know what's going on and Ottawa is too afraid of a leak to brief them."

Sanderson looked down, averting the sergeant's blank stare. After seeing the Rangers, he felt the paratroopers should be called in now, rather than wait for what was surely to be a disaster in the morning. Hopefully Ottawa knew something he didn't. The sergeant certainly seemed capable but he could see the deep concern in the man's eyes. No wonder – these men were not trained combat troops.

"It will be an interesting day tomorrow," Ashe sighed. "We'll see what we can do with Ivan. Better stand close by that radio, sir."

Brian thought someone at headquarters must had lost their mind. They might enjoy an initial element of surprise over the Russians, but failing that, he and the Rangers were dead. For that matter, even if they did catch the Ruskies napping, the results would probably be the same – it would just take a little longer. And Grandfather, he thought, would most likely die of a heart attack when the first shot rang out.

"I'll be right here waiting for word, sergeant." The lieutenant looked at him and held out his hand. "Good luck."

Brian shook it and saluted before walking over to the tent where the Rangers awaited his return.

"A leak," Brian muttered, as he reached the ragged tent. There will be something leaking all right, he thought but did not say. Throwing the flap aside, he walked in, dropped his map holder on the floor and laid out the orders to the men. He didn't want any of them to doubt they were heading into dangerous territory.

"Okay fellows, here's the story…"

He went over the plans carefully, making sure they understood how critical the mission was and how so much would depend on their not being detected by the commandos until it was too late – for who, he wasn't sure.

When Brian had covered everything, he made it clear that if any of them, even for a moment, thought they might not be up to the mission, now was the time to back out. As he expected, no one spoke.

Grandfather summed up their feelings.

"We done talking?"

"Yes…we're done talking, sergeant," Brian sighed. None of his years of training had prepared him for this.

"We leave now," Deniigi announced. "Safer in the dark."

"You're right," Ashe agreed. "Pack up men. We'll move out in thirty minutes. Full ammo, but don't worry about your kits. We won't be camping out anywhere on this trip. Jimmy, grab the radio and don't drop it. If we need help, that radio is our only hope."

The men carefully checked their rifles over and packed ammunition for the Lee Enfield's into the old canvas ammo pouches they carried. The lieutenant had brought along a case of new .303 rifle rounds for the Rangers, as well as a few extra bandoleers of 7.62mm clips for Brian's FN. The Rangers sat around the small fire they had cooked supper on earlier and carefully cleaned their weapons one last time before heading out into the night.

Brian looked down at them and pictured the same scene playing out as a different group of young men prepared to storm the beaches of Normandy, or some numbered hill in Korea, or around the world in the growing mess that was Vietnam. In the past, the enemy had been different, but the anticipation and fear, a fear so real you could taste it, was always the same. He had always imagined that if he ever found himself in this situation, it would be in Europe along 'the wall', not here. Anywhere BUT Canada.

There was no false bravado in this group. They could have been preparing for a hunting party instead of what was akin to a suicide mission. Brian watched as Deniigi cleaned his rifle for the fourth time. He wished he could teach the troops back in Gagetown that kind of respect for their weapons. Pushing the thought from his mind, he sat down on the ground with the men. Grabbing a few empty magazines from his ammo bag, he started sliding five round clips into one of them. Half a dozen mags should do fine, he mused. If one hundred and twenty rounds didn't do the trick…well, it wouldn't matter.

* * *

As Sergeant Ashe filled his twenty round magazines, a similar scene was playing out forty-eight miles to the east of the Ranger's camp. Nikolai and Vladimir were sitting in the dark chatting. A fire was unthinkable, although they certainly would have cherished the warmth on this cold, crisp night. They were practising field stripping and cleaning their rifles by touch. Nikolai had just fastened the folding bayonet in place and as usual, had managed to cut himself in the process, causing him to swear.

"One of these days," he hissed. "They will make removable bayonets for this rifle." Vladimir roared in laughter.

"Sure they will comrade. And then you will never again have this problem with your bayonet, for surely you will drop it in the dark and never be able to find it."

"Perhaps, but do you think we will ever use this thing?"

Nikolai saw the bayonet as a throw back to the Great Patriotic War and his country's inability to embrace anything which might be construed as modern. The design he considered to be a flaw had actually come about as the result of so many soldiers dying in that conflict when after their ammo had run out, and having lost their bayonets earlier, were unable to defend themselves. Part of the design specifications for the new rifle which had become the AK-47 was that the bayonet not be detachable.

"Someday you might need it, comrade. Remember, you can only carry so many bullets."

"Vladimir Narinsky, you are a hopeless romantic. Those days are long over. When I run out of bullets, I will simply throw a bomb, and when I run out of bombs I will call in an air strike."

"With what? You would have dropped the radio in the dark hours ago and…"

They were interrupted by Senior Lieutenant Kristoff 's shadow looming in the darkness.

"It is time. Word has come that we go operational in one hour."

"Finally!" Vladimir exclaimed. "We will soon be out of this dreary land."

Forty-five minutes later, additional elements of the large antennae which until now had been safely stowed inside the camouflaged tent, were fully assembled and connected to the powerful transmitter. When they had completed testing the array, the commandos carefully camouflaged the new sections while Kristoff slowly walked around the antennae in the moonlight, looking for any obvious sign of its existence. He was satisfied that unless you knew exactly where it was and what shape it held, there was no possibility that anyone would think it was anything but a large rock.

"Good job," he remarked, turning to enter the tent. Inside, the air was warm, heated by the powerful transmitter which had been slowly brought up to operating temperature, lest something inside be damaged from the sudden change from the cool ambient air.

"Are we ready to turn it on, Anton?"

"Yes, sir," he replied. "It has reached operational temperature and all readings are stable. We must be sure that none of the men come within three metres of the antennae when the transmitter is operating."

"Very well. The men are clear. Leave it on standby and await my order to activate."

The transmitter unit sitting on the floor of the tent hummed slightly but other than that, there was no outward sign of anything different taking place on this night. Stepping outside, Kristoff sat against a large rock and looked up at the starlit sky. It was very peaceful here in the middle of nowhere. He enjoyed the solitude for another few minutes before beginning to remove the material draped over the antennae. The night was still, with the only sound being a gentle wind whistling around the rocks. Halfway across the country in Ottawa, the same could not be said.

* * *

A horn sounded from within the ceiling of the underground command center, and the centre wall display immediately changed to show eastern Canada, including a good part of the Atlantic Ocean. Off the coast, a line appeared on the map, with the western end of it showing an arrow shape aimed at southern Labrador.

"Unidentified aircraft – heading two five three degrees…," a hidden speaker blared. The information was being given in the order that one of the Pinetree sites was sending it out… "Range – two hundred and twenty miles – speed three hundred and forty knots." The station's FPS-93 radar had zeroed in on the intruder. "Altitude unknown. Reporting station Cartwright."

The unknown altitude was an indication the aircraft was coming in low - lower than the FPS-90 height finding radar at the Cartwright site was capable of reaching. The Prime Minister, sat quietly for a few moments as the Royal Canadian Air Force officers in the room digested the information. When he could wait no longer, he stood and walked over to the airforce control console, trying hard not to appear concerned.

"What's going on air marshal?"

"We have an unidentified aircraft coming in low towards Labrador, sir. Based on its speed, probably a Bear. That's a Soviet bomber sir. It is…"

The Prime Minister cut him off. "I'm familiar with the aircraft."

"Sorry, sir. Chatham will have interceptors after it in a few minutes."

* * *

In the ready room at RCAF Station Chatham, Ben was absentmindedly thumbing through an old car magazine while at the same time keeping an eye on the television set tuned to the CBC. Stanley Burke was reading through the day's news and had just begun a story on Russia's continued support of North Vietnam when the alert horns went off.

Before the magazine had settled to the floor, Ben had burst through the door and out into the cool night air. He had only a few dozen feet to cover before reaching the four-door alert truck whose driver had the engine started and the transmission in gear. The seating was prearranged and Ben slid into the 'shotgun' spot while Cam raced around the vehicle and dropped into the seat directly behind the driver. Flight Lieutenant Jeffrey Talbot crammed in against Cam from the rear passenger door while his radar operator Jack Morrison slammed the door shut as he practically landed on Jeffrey's lap.

Before the aircrews had settled into their places, the driver simultaneously mashed the gas pedal and released the clutch, causing the truck's tires to squeal in protest before sending them racing across the floodlit apron to the alert hangers.

Braking to a hard stop just outside the opening doors in front of one hanger, the driver yelled a quick 'good luck!' at his passengers who were already scurrying from the vehicle.

Sprinting inside the hanger, the crews of the two alert aircraft scrambled up the boarding ladders clamped to the Voodoo's sides and quickly slid into their cockpits. As they adjusted themselves in the ejection seats, the waiting ground crew rushed up the ladders to help strap them in. The two pilots, oblivious of the men adjusting their belts, flew through the pre-flight checklists with their radar operators as they powered up the various systems which would turn the CF-101 from a quiet, stationary aircraft, to a roaring beast.

Outside, the sergeant put the alert truck into gear and slowly drove across the apron to his favourite vantage spot from where he could survey the Voodoo's as they roared into the sky. Night takeoffs were spectacular and he never tired of watching the aircraft roar off with long tongues of flame shooting from their afterburners as they clawed their way into the air.

"You belted in, Cam?" Ben called.

"All safe and secure, sir."

Cam gave his vertical belts one last tug to make sure he'd stay securely in place in case they had to perform any extreme manoeuvres or worse, eject from the aircraft.

"Ground crew clear!" came a shout from the left side of the aircraft as the men tasked with making sure both crewmembers were securely fastened and their helmets plugged into the aircraft radios, stood well back from the engine intakes.

"Dropping canopy, starting left engine." Ben continued quickly through the 'scramble' check list, only pausing for confirmation from Cam when one of the items required his participation or acknowledgement. The canopy lowered above their heads and a small light flashed on both instrument panels indicating that it was locked securely in place just as the whine of the left engine's starter motor filled the hanger.

At this point only one ground crew remained close by the interceptor. Just before leaving the hanger, he tugged the yellow wooden chocks clear of the Voodoo's main landing gear. A piece of rope connecting them allowed him to remove both wheel restraints with one swift movement before he held one of them up over his head, indicating to the pilot that they were clear and not in danger of being sucked into the engines.

"Starting right engine."

In the cockpit, Ben confirmed with a thumbs up that he'd seen the man holding up the chocks and gave him a wave to indicate his help was no longer needed. Tapping down on the brakes to keep the aircraft in place while both engines reached operating temperature, he made one final confirmation sweep with his eyes over the instrument panel that the rest of the aircraft's systems appeared to be functioning within proper parameters.

Cam was busily running through the weapons system, which had its own pre-flight checklist. He paused for a moment before closing the armament door after completing the Genie connect test procedures. It was the first time since the alert horn sounded that he had contemplated the 1.5 kilotons of nuclear energy stored within each of the rockets now sitting just below his seat inside the weapons bay.

"Weapons check complete - all okay, sir." Cam turned to the radar system and set it to standby where it would warm up, but not transmit.

"Roger weapons check – beginning to taxi."

Ben lifted his feet up gently from the brakes and the aircraft immediately lurched forward. Even with the engines only turning at idle, the Voodoo seemed eager to leave the ground. Looking to his left, he saw the second alert aircraft's nose appear from the adjacent hanger, preparing to follow him along the short taxiway to the runway.

"India two, India one, how do you read?"

"Five by five, one. All systems okay," Jeffrey replied from the second aircraft. He carefully maintained his distance from Ben's aircraft, making sure not to follow directly behind the lead interceptor's exhaust.

"Chatham tower, India flight is ready for takeoff." Ben pulled off the taxiway and positioned his aircraft on the left side of the runway centerline, giving Jeffrey enough room to line up on his right.

"India flight, you are cleared for takeoff," announced the controller in the tower. "Winds are one eight four at two knots and altimeter is two niner niner three. Contact Sunflower on three four six decimal nine on departure."

"Sunflower on three four six decimal nine on departure."

Cam had already dialled in the frequency for St Margaret's on the UHF radio as he would be contacting the Pinetree site as soon as they reached five thousand feet.

"I've got them tuned in sir," Cam reported as Ben braked the aircraft to a stop on the runway threshold. "Setting MG-11 to semi-active."

"India one, this is two. Lined up and ready."

"Roger two. Rolling in three – two – one..."

Sitting in the alert truck, the sergeant watched as four long streams of flame shot back from the two aircraft which were barely visible on the dark runway. The sound was deafening as the engines spooled up and through the distortion caused by the tremendous heat of the jet exhaust, he could see the aircraft beginning to move ahead slowly before suddenly appearing to leap forward; marked only by twinkling navigation lights and the roar of flame from their afterburners.

The crews were shoved into their ejection seats as the aircraft rapidly gained speed - the Pratt & Whitney J-57 engines quickly thrusting the aircraft forward. In moments they accelerated past one hundred and fifty five knots and both pilots eased back on their control sticks, lifting the nose wheels free of the ground. Seconds later the aircraft pulled up into a sharp climb as their wings bit into the cool night air.

"Chatham tower, India flight is airborne." Ben called, pausing briefly - all the time it took to pass through five thousand feet before announcing, "switching to Sunflower control."

"Roger that India flight, good luck."

Ben smiled. They might need that luck tonight. For a brief moment he let his mind wander to thoughts of his wife. She'd still be sleeping unless the departing aircraft had waken her. That wasn't likely. The sound of jet engines carried on at all hours on the base and everyone soon grew accustomed to their roar - so much so that it often lulled them to sleep rather then kept them awake.

"Okay Cam, where are we off to tonight?"

"Nothing up yet, sir," Cam replied from the rear cockpit. "Okay - data coming through now." He watched as a section of the radar scope suddenly filled with numbers and symbols.

"We have a single bogie - low and slow in sector seven. Turn to course zero seven six and maintain two five zero feet. Sunflower reports probable Bear."

"Roger the Bear," Ben acknowledged before switching to the radio. "India two, do you have the data?"

"Roger one. Looks like we're Bear hunting tonight."

Jeffrey chuckled. A Russian TU-95 Bear low over the water was probably just out testing the NORAD defence coverage. Someone in Ottawa was over reacting, sending them out with the Genies. Damn politicians! They would finish this intercept, try to get some pictures in the gathering dawn, and head back home.

* * *

Two hundred miles east of Labrador, the object of the interceptor's attention was sweeping towards the Labrador coast at low altitude. The pilot of the TU-95 – Codenamed 'Bear' by the West - had his eyes glued to the altimeter on the instrument panel in front of him. His co-pilot was equally engrossed in the compass readings, making sure they were following the exact course as ordered by their base commander. The general had taken the two men aside before takeoff and had repeated his earlier warning during the crew briefing on how absolutely crucial it was they not stray from their course. The consequences of such action would be severe, he had warned them. The two men were made to understand that the repercussion of failing in this would be onerous not only to them but to the Soviet Union as well.

Six hours later, they were rapidly approaching the Canadian coast and the imaginary line that signified the NORAD defence zone. Outside the aircraft, the rising sun had just begun to glint off the bottom of the engine nacelles, sending haphazard beams of sunlight into the cockpit while the huge counter-rotating propellers of the sleek turboprop aircraft pulled it through the air.

Behind the pilot and aircraft commander, the TU-95's crew were monitoring the various pieces of electronic equipment that filled the tight, narrow fuselage. This version of the bomber carried no weapons but was instead crammed with monitoring equipment with which to record NORAD radar and radio transmissions. Even the casual observer would immediately spot the difference between this aircraft and its bomber counterpart. A veritable forest of antennas lined the top and bottom of the fuselage giving it the appearance of a flying porcupine.

The crew knew flying directly into Canadian airspace was likely to draw a lot of attention from the RCAF, but they were not overly concerned. More than once, a TU-95 had inadvertently strayed over the invisible line delineating international airspace from Canadian territory, sometimes accidentally, and other times…well no one admitted to those. The radar defences would have picked up the Soviet aircraft by now and there would already be fighters on the way to intercept them. The radio intercept crew concentrated on the frequencies known to be used by the NORAD defence system's data links and the chat frequencies used by the fighters themselves.

The navigator, sitting in the clear nose of the aircraft had two cameras ready in case a chance opportunity came to take a photo of the colourful Canadian interceptors they called 'Voodoo', in the early morning light. In the cockpit, the first streaks of sunlight were beginning to make things uncomfortably warm and the pilot was adjusting the temperature controls when he heard a warning over his headset.

"Sir, EECM operator reports activity in the datalink band."

"That will mean Canadian fighters are already in the air and will be arriving soon," announced the flight engineer, who was also acting as a go between for the flight crew and the operators behind them. The airmen made as little use of the intercom as possible, leaving it clear in case of an emergency.

"Thank you," the pilot replied, not taking his eyes away from the altimeter for a second. They would soon reach the point in their flight plan where it would be time to gain altitude and make a hard right bank to head north along the Canadian coast, before turning once again out to sea.

* * *

One hundred and twenty-three miles north of where the TU-95 was boring in on the Labrador coast, another aircraft was cruising low over the surface of the Atlantic. The pilot had been flying a modified race track pattern while behind him, the crew was working diligently trying to find an elusive American submarine. The Canadians aboard Argus 709 were blissfully unaware of the drama unfolding just south of them.

The Argus' crew had been flying through their search area most of the night since departing from RCAF Station Greenwood late the previous evening. As the first rays of dawn appeared over the horizon, the aircraft commander was beginning to think they had guessed wrong as to the location of the American submarine, after the MAD had picked up a slight disturbance early into the flight.

At the radar console, Flight Sergeant Robert 'Pudgy' Cormier was busily tracking a few fishing boats sailing out from one of the small Labrador ports that dotted the coast. Probably heading out early for a day of cod fishing, he presumed. Robert almost envied the men on the boats, their lives filled with hard work but a lot less stress. Trying to get more comfortable in the small chair he was wedged into, Pudgy changed the range setting on the Argus' radar for a long distance view. He was surprised when far to the south of them, he thought he noted a brief flicker on the screen. He watched carefully for a few minutes but it failed to reappear. Noting it on his contact chart, he went back to following the fishing boats which had now split up and were headed off in different directions.

Five minutes later the pilot brought the Argus into a slow, graceful one hundred and eighty degree turn to starboard, bringing the aircraft back onto a southerly heading down the opposite side of the huge racetrack shaped holding pattern they flew. He winced as the first rays of direct sunlight came streaming through the cockpit windows on his left, momentarily blinding him as he settled the aircraft on its new course. Twenty feet behind him, at the radar console, Pudgy again noticed a small flash on the scope.

"Commander, I've got something, but it's only there for a second and then it's gone again. It might be a small boat but it could be a periscope, although I can't imagine the radar picking up a 'scope at that distance. Might have been a snorkel though."

He was so focused on searching for any sign of the American submarine that it did not occur to him that his surface search radar might be picking up another low flying aircraft.

* * *

Stretching his arms out to relive the stiffness in his muscles after leaving the tent, Senior Lieutenant Nikolev looked out at the rising sun and was once again amazed by the rugged beauty of the landscape surrounding him. The early morning sunlight caused the land to literally shimmer as the rays of sun reflected off the condensation covering the terrain and made it appear as though the ground was alive with tiny lights. He was amazed that no one lived here. Of course, he thought, in January, it would be a very different scene than it was on this early spring day.

Kristoff looked down at his watch and his mind wandered. The rugged time piece had once belonged to the father he had hardly known. It had been given to him when he was seven years old by a naval officer who had come to the small house where he and his mother lived. He could still clearly remember that day.

As a young boy, he had been excited to see a sailor coming up the tidy walk outside his home and had run outside to welcome the man with a proper navy salute as taught to him by his father. Standing at attention, looking up into the man's eyes, Kristoff had recognized a sadness in them and his hand had dropped limply back to his side. His father had been away at sea with the Soviet navy for over a year fighting the Germans and a foreboding in his young heart told Kristoff that something was terribly wrong. The man had reached down and touched his shoulder gently and asked where his mother was. The officer didn't have to say anything else.

Sitting down on the stoop, Kristoff had bent over and cried. He didn't remember for how long, but he could still see his mother's face as she had opened the door to investigate the commotion outside. Seeing her son sitting there in tears and the expression on the naval officer's face, her own had immediately registered the knowledge that the man she loved would not be coming home. The woman had dropped to her knees embracing her son for what seemed to him a very long time. When she finally did let go, his mother had looked down at him and with tears streaming down her cheeks had made him promise that he would never marry and leave his wife to go off to war.

Years later, an officer had come to visit them who had been with his father the day he had died. The man, wearing medals which glinted in the light from their fireplace, told them how a German submarine had stalked his destroyer. Although the Russian sailors had fought valiantly to save the ship after a torpedo had ripped into its hull, setting fuel oil ablaze, their battle had been in vain. The Soviet navy officer went on to tell how almost the entire crew had perished, freezing to death in the frigid Arctic waters after escaping the roaring inferno aboard the ship. The lucky ones died quickly when the dying warship's depth charges exploded as the destroyer sank into the deep. Those who escaped the explosions, floated hopelessly, hanging on to life vests and wreckage, waiting for the frigid water to claim them.

The visitor told them of the heroics performed by Kristoff's father that day. How mortally injured, he had helped as many of his men as possible to safely abandon the sinking ship, getting them into the remaining life boats and trying to calm the ones who were panicking. Then laying on the deck, weak from blood loss, he had given his watch, the only personal possession he had, to this officer, beseeching him to bring it to his son when he returned to the Soviet Union. Only a few of the crew were rescued by a Soviet patrol boat the following morning, but they had all told the same story of how their commander had fallen, after making sure his men were safe.

In the ensuing years, Kristoff had wondered if the officer had embellished the story to lessen the pain of their loss, but his doubts had been laid to rest when the selfless sacrifices his father had made that day had finally became public, and his mother had been presented the Order of Lenin in his father's name. The red star and ribbon now hung in a simple wooden frame above the fireplace in their small home.

After graduating from high school Kristoff joined the Russian army – the image of dying men on a sinking ship still haunting him. His mother's admonishment remained with him so in spite of frequent dates and even a few serious relationships, he had yet to marry. As the son of a hero of the Great Patriotic War, he rose quickly through the ranks and when the opportunity had come to apply for Spetsnaz, the elite branch of the Soviet Army, he had jumped at the chance.

Again he looked at the old watch. It was showing its age now, but scratched and well worn, the old timepiece still functioned perfectly. The hands on the dial read oh six hundred. He was grateful that he had this cherished memento of his father. Fond memories of the short time they had spent together brought a quick smile to his face as Kristoff threw open the tent flap and stepped inside.

"It is time to find out if this magic box of yours works, Anton. Switch the device to jam."

* * *

Descending to hook around the Bear, the pilots of the Four Sixteen Squadron Voodoos closed up their formation and prepared to switch their interceptor's MG-11 radar to active for the final intercept. The CF-101's onboard radar had been set to standby since takeoff to avoid it being picked up by the Bear's sensitive warning receivers.

"Shit! Sir, we've lost the datalink," Cam exclaimed. "I've tried recalibrating the receiver and still no joy."

"India two," Ben called over to his wingman. "Do you still have datalink?"

"India one, negative data link. I was just about to report that."

"Roger, India one. Go on active radar. I'll alert Sunflower."

Switching to the intercom, he instructed Cam to start searching with their radar as well but with the limited range of the Voodoo's system, Ben realized it would be pure dumb luck if they found the Soviet aircraft which would be flying just above the waves somewhere below them.

"Sunflower, this is India flight." They would know something was wrong the moment they heard him calling.

"India flight, Sunflower reads you five by five."

"Sunflower, India flight has lost datalink."

"Roger that India flight, stand by."

Ben scanned the air around them as he waited for a response. It was only moments in coming.

"India flight, this is Sunflower. All systems are checking fine here. Confirm frequency calibration."

"Confirmed calibration. Both aircraft have lost link," he added.

At RCAF Station St. Margarets, the maintenance team double checked their equipment while the technicians at the datalink transmitter site in eastern Newfoundland went over their transmitters but found nothing out of order.

"Sunflower, this is India flight. We will try to continue the intercept on our own. We have the unknown's last coordinates and will conduct a search in that area," Ben announced before adding, "Suggest a backup be scrambled in case our equipment is faulty."

He really didn't believe there was any possibility both Voodoo's were suffering identical equipment failures, but with no other explanation, a second flight would have to be sent up.

"Roger that India flight. A back up flight is being scrambled now."

"Thank you Sunflower. We will monitor this frequency and continue our search. India flight out."

"Sunflower out."

Moments later, just across the New Brunswick border at Loring Air Force base in north-eastern Maine, a pair of F-106 Delta Darts roared into the morning sky and rapidly turned east towards the Atlantic ocean. Within minutes, the combination radar scope and map readout mounted low on the instrument panel of the sleek delta winged interceptors was directing the American pilots to their target which was now rapidly approaching the Canadian coast.

Going to full afterburner, the two single seat fighters quickly accelerated their climb while controllers at the air traffic control center in Moncton, New Brunswick frantically diverted civilian air traffic away from the interceptor's route.

Five minutes later, the pilot of the lead F-106 was in contact with Sunflower control.

"Sunflower, this heah is Canyon flight. We have lost datalink," his Texas drawl belying the seriousness of the report. "Could yo'all confirm that India flight is still unable to receive yo' signal as well?"

"Confirm that Canyon flight. India flight is still reporting no joy. Technicians here report all okay and we are transmitting at full power."

"Okay Sunflower, we'll try ta join up with India flight and switch ta a manual intercept. Break. India flight this is Canyon flight lead, how do yo'all read?"

The pilot of the F-106 was certain that Sunflower's technicians were obviously wrong about the transmitters working properly, but hopefully the combination of four interceptors would easily be able to track down the elusive Bear.

"Canyon flight, this is India flight. Have you five by five. We are just entering sector five, awaiting manual directions from Sunflower." Ben glanced over, confirming that India two was still holding position to his right and slightly behind.

"Roger that India flight. We are about ninety miles behind yo'all now."

Making judicious use of their afterburners, the Delta Dart pilots had caught up to the Voodoo's and were flying a loose formation a thousand yards astern and above the Canadians. With the operator at St. Margarets directing the crews manually, the flight of four interceptors turned slightly to the north and spread out, while beginning to descend closer to the altitude being flown by the intruder.

Far ahead, the TU-95's pilot was making a turn of his own to the north, having brushed by the Labrador coast, fulfilling the mission he and his crew had been sent on. The Soviet officers were discussing the unusual lack of interception and wondered why the familiar Voodoo's had not appeared to harass them, especially where they had flagrantly crossed into Canadian airspace.

The pilot of the Russian aircraft was not about to press his luck however, and had pushed his throttles forward until the four NK 12 MV turboprops were pulling the sleek aircraft quickly through the air at close to its maximum speed of four hundred and fifty knots. A fog bank suddenly enveloped the aircraft which gave him a moment's concern and he pulled back ever so slightly on the control column, bringing the aircraft's altitude a little higher.

* * *

Thirty miles ahead of the fast moving TU-95, the radar operator aboard Argus 709 was still trying to locate the elusive contact which had once again appeared briefly on his scope. Pudgy Cormier was beginning to think it had to be the American submarine - probably riding low in the water and picked up by his radar when it rode the crest of a large wave. He reached up to reset the range on his scope when the mysterious blip appeared once again, much closer, and this time it stayed on the screen. Damn! he thought. That sub couldn't have moved that fast...

"Sir! Radar contact!"

Realization of the contact's identity suddenly hit him.

"Shit! It's a..." His call to the cockpit was too late.

The Argus pilot had just glanced down for a moment to check his altimeter and had looked up again just in time to see a flash of silver appear out of nowhere through the light fog.

"Damn!"

On the TU-95's flight deck, the Soviet pilot, still engrossed in his own altimeter never did see the Argus but instinctively reacted by pulling back and kicking the left rudder pedal as he felt, rather than heard, something collide with his starboard wing.

The two aircraft barely brushed their wingtips, but at the rapid closing speed it had been enough to cause both of them serious damage. The TU-95 nosed up and immediately stalled, causing it to flip over onto its back and splash inverted into the ocean.

The Argus pilot had also reacted instinctively, kicking his rudder pedal in a desperate bid to straighten the aircraft back on course, while at the same time attempting to maintain level flight. The aircraft commander quickly ordered a mayday sent out but the radio operator, having felt the impact, had already begun to transmit their status and location. He was unable to confirm a reply before the mortally wounded Argus settled slowly into the thankfully calm waves of the Atlantic.

The crew, strapped securely into their seats were jostled about but suffered no serious injuries. The countless drills had prepared them well for this eventuality and they quickly but calmly unfastened their seat belts and moved to the emergency exits. The pilot had attempted to follow the emergency ditching procedures as best he could, considering the damage to the control surfaces. Pulling back hard on the control column just before the plane struck, he had protected the nose of the aircraft from taking the brunt of the water's impact. As it was, the crew had to escape with due haste from the aircraft as it immediately began to settle into the water.

Pudgy, kicking out the observation window directly across from his station, fought to squeeze through the small rectangular opening and finally slipping through, landed hard on what remained of the port wing. Moving speedily, he pulled the emergency release on the life raft storage in the wing root and was rewarded with a whoosh as the inflatable boat popped free of the small opening and instantly filled with gas from its internal CO_2 cylinders.

On the starboard wing, the MAD operator was accomplishing the same thing and in moments, the crew had scrambled from the sinking aircraft onto the two life rafts. In a matter of minutes, the vertical stabilizer of Argus 709 was all that remained above the surface. It pointed to the sky like some macabre, metal shark's fin with the Canadian ensign showing clearly against the white painted tail in the morning sunlight.

Until this point, no one had spoken a word as the men had reacted instinctively, fortunate that the smooth landing had allowed them to carry out a textbook evacuation of the sinking aircraft.

"Damn small escape hatches…" Pudgy muttered, finally breaking the silence. The men in the two rafts, their adrenalin starting to abate, stared at him silently for a moment and then burst into hearty laughter, as much from relief, as amusement at Cormier's constrained expression.

Just over a thousand yards away from the rafts, the TU-95 had landed hard on the water, its fuselage splintering apart before immediately disappearing below the waves. Only a stream of bubbles and small pieces of debris marked where the aircraft had come to rest. A moment later, two heads popped to the surface. The Soviet co-pilot and navigator had been miraculously thrown clear of the wreckage when the fuselage had disintegrated upon impact with the water.

The men bobbed on the water in their life vests, riding the gentle swells in a see-saw motion. Both men realized there was little likelihood that the radio operator had been able to get word out of the collision, and without an inflatable boat to protect them from the ice cold Atlantic waters, they had resigned themselves to their fate. The Soviet airmen immediately began to feel the first numbing signs of hypothermia. As the cold water enveloped their bodies they found it harder and harder to focus their thoughts and the co-pilot, the smaller of the two men, began to drift in and out of consciousness. The navigator, on the verge of passing out, looked up and through a hazy film, saw a hand reaching down for him from the heavens.

"God?" He asked in Russian, barely able to get the word out through his violently chattering teeth. "You...you are real?"

"Grab hold, Ruskie!" God was shouting down at him in English. That was odd he thought, as a feeling of serenity seemed to envelope him. If God were real, wouldn't He speak to him in Russian?

"Shit, he's almost passed out. I'll go in and get him," Pudgy shouted, dropping into the cold water and struggling to push the half conscious Soviet aviator into the raft. Hauling Pudgy back aboard with a grunt, the pilot smiled at the now soaked flight sergeant.

"Hell Pudgy," he asked, "How the hell did you ever make it through that observation window?"

"No problem, sir. I'd of torn the fuselage open with my bare hands, before going down with the ship," he answered, the cold causing his body to shiver uncontrollably. Flopping down into the raft alongside the Russian airman, he grabbed the blanket offered to him by one of the other men and quickly wiped the water from his face. He then used it to cover up the man he had just saved. Beginning to recover from the mind numbing cold, the TU-95 survivor looked up, managing a weak smile. Fighting the chills wracking his body, Robert smiled back and held out his hand.

"Welcome aboard Ruskie!"

In the second raft, the Canadians were roughly hauling in the co-pilot who had not responded in any way to their shouts, forcing them to paddle the raft over to him. They carefully laid the unmoving man in the bottom of the raft, covering him with a couple of blankets. The Argus pilot instructed two of the men to lay next to the Russian, hoping their combined body heat would help bring his temperature back up. The airmen were all trained in cold survival techniques and they were well aware that life in these northern waters was measured in minutes.

Satisfied that they had done all they could for the half frozen man, the aircraft commander hollered over to the other raft, asking the radio operator if he had gotten out a Mayday call. The answer came not from him but in the roar of jet engines as a pair of CF-101 Voodoo's followed by two F-106 interceptors roared low over the rafts. The lead Voodoo pilot vigorously rocked the jet's wings, signalling to the men below that they had been spotted.

"Would you look at that!" Cam remarked, gazing down at the rafts bobbing in the waves below. "Those are our guys but I wonder where the Bear got to?"

"I think I have an idea," Ben replied. "Check out the bottom of the raft on the left when we come around. That's not airforce blue that guy is wearing. I'd better let Sunflower know."

Ben flicked the microphone switch on the control stick while banking around to keep the men in the water in site.

"India two, switch to guard in case they have a working radio in one of the rafts. I'll alert Sunflower. Canyon flight, India leader, you might as well head home – looks like the Bear went for a swim." He didn't mean it to be funny.

"Roger that India leader. Yo'all take care. Canyon flight is returning to the roost." The two F-106 pilots banked their fighters into a step climb and headed southwest, back to Loring AFB.

"Sunflower, this is India flight. Our boogie seems to have gone in as well," Ben reported, knowing the excitement that information would create. "We have the Argus crew in site. Two rafts in the water."

"Break! This is India two, Sunflower. We have contact with the survivors. All crew from Argus 709 report they are safe as well as two survivors from the Bear."

"This is Sunflower. Received that India flight. Alerting Halifax SAR."

* * *

"They're ALL okay?" The Minister of Defence was incredulous after hearing that the entire crew had survived the crash. "Are you sure?"

Having ditched two Spitfires in the English Channel during WW-II, the minister was astounded the entire crew could have survived a water crash in such a huge aircraft.

"Yes sir," replied the officer from the Halifax Search And Rescue center. "They are in contact with a Chatham Voodoo right now and everyone is accounted for with no injuries. The two Russian survivors suffered some moderate hypothermia, but they'll be fine."

"An airforce transport has dropped another raft to them, as well as food and water and with the calm seas, *HMCS Margaree* will reach the area to pick them up in about eleven hours. Unfortunately," he added, "there aren't any other ships in the area. They're well off the beaten path."

"Thank you lieutenant. Pass the word – damn good job everybody!" The minister hung up the phone and repeated the good news to the Prime Minister, who was visibly relieved.

"Damn it Ted. This will really rattle things in the Kremlin."

"It will that, Prime Minister. Are you planning on calling the Premier to let him know?"

"Not a chance in hell!" the Prime Minister replied sternly. "I'll talk to him when I can hand over his troops on a silver platter."

The Minister of National Defence detected anger in the man's voice and remained silent while the Prime Minister continued. "He thought he had a rough time with Kennedy over Cuba a few years back! Wait until I get through with him!"

"Very well sir," the minister responded. "I'll let you know when *Margaree* picks up the air crew."

* * *

"An Argus crew and what?!"

"You heard it right, sir. The Argus and Bear collided at low level in some fog." Lieutenant Learner continued to explain the situation to Lieutenant Commander Delaney on *HMCS Margaree's* bridge. "The Argus crew made it out okay," he continued, "and two of the Russians survived and are with them in the rafts."

"Damn." Barry was silent for a moment, contemplating the situation. "Call down and see if we can get a couple more knots out of *Marge*, Henry. I don't want those men floating around out there one minute longer than necessary. Oh, and contact *Terra Nova* and let them know we'll be pulling ahead but for them to maintain their present speed. No need both of us burning up all our fuel." Pausing again for a moment, he added, "and Henry? Better find out who's got an oiler out here. We'll be needing it before this run is over."

Barry gazed out the window, picturing in his mind what the men in the life rafts were going through. The weather for now was mild and the seas fairly calm but that could change in a heartbeat in these waters. It would be more than ten hours before they reached the location where the two aircraft went in - a little less if the guys below could coax a few extra pounds of steam from the boilers. If the situation dictated it, he could send the Sea King ahead once they were closer, to pick up the men and fly them back to the ship, but he'd rather not risk the helicopter on a rescue mission unless it was absolutely necessary. Not with Ivan probably slinking around in the depths up there.

As he continued to gaze ahead, he felt the vibration through the deck plates increase slightly as the stokers below persuaded *Margaree* to give all she had in the rush to reach the downed airmen.

* * *

Six hundred and forty miles northeast of were *Margaree* raced through the water, the ocean was anything but calm. The crew of a small cargo ship wallowing in heavy seas, was desperately trying to make sure that the wooden crates lashed to the freighter's heaving deck were secure. The sea state was growing worse from a small but intense approaching storm and waves were beginning to crash over the bow, threatening to rip the cargo completely from the ship. The captain stood on the starboard bridge wing, directing his crew through a megaphone as they scurried about on the deck below trying to tighten the ropes that held the cargo in place and at the same time avoid being washed overboard.

The ship's master looked up as a strange sound reached his ears over the roar of the wind through the ship's rigging. To his left, barely skimming over the wave tops, a group of aircraft roared past, the power of their huge turboprop engines causing the bridge windows to rattle in their frames. "Russians", the captain, a veteran of the last world war, muttered aloud as he recognized the red star markings on the wings and fuselage of the aircraft closest to him. He shrugged off the momentary distraction as the formation disappeared over the horizon and returned his attention to his men working feverishly below.

* * *

"How's the fuel, Cam?"

Flying Officer Camille LeBlanc had been watching the CF-101's fuel gauges carefully for the past ten minutes. They would soon reach the limit of their range and have to head back to Chatham.

"We've got another fifteen minutes sir," he replied. "That relief cover had better get here soon."

"They're on the way," Ben acknowledged. "Still nothing on the datalink?"

"Nothing. Sunflower still claims there's nothing wrong at their end."

Well something is definitely wrong somewhere, Ben thought. They had tried a few different frequencies and it had almost kicked back in for a second before dropping off again. The other Voodoo crew was experiencing the same problem and the '106 guys had claimed to be receiving okay until halfway to this sector when their mapping screens had simply gone blank.

"India flight, this is Rescue 681, how do you read?"

"Loud and clear 681!" The relief aircraft had finally arrived. Looking down, Ben could see the Dakota flying low over the water and noticed something drop from the open door in the side of the venerable transport aircraft.

"Roger India. You guys can head back to the barn. We'll take over."

"Thank you, sir," Ben replied and brought the CF-101 into a sharp bank towards the west with his wingman following closely behind.

"Okay Cam. Point me in the right direction and let's go home. Mother will be worried that her little boy has been out playing this long."

Cam laughed at Ben's reference to his wife. He always called her 'mother' because of the way she scolded him when he returned late after a scramble. His own wife, he knew, would be waiting for the sound of jet engines which would signal the return of the alert flight. All of the wives handled the possibility of their husbands never returning home in different ways but they shared one common trait; they knew how important the job was. That knowledge, as well as the support of the other airforce wives kept their morale up.

An hour later, Ben and Cam were sitting in debrief, explaining to the intelligence officer about the odd problem with the datalink, which had mysteriously started working again on the return flight to Chatham.

"Gremlins," the base radio techs had claimed, but Ben felt it was more than that. He'd had a strong feeling that something was amiss after the Blackbird intercept days earlier and the feeling was only getting stronger.

"Gremlins," he muttered aloud while leaving the room a couple of hours later. "Right."

∗   ∗   ∗

In the operations room at the Cartwright Air Station, a United States Air Force manned Pinetree site, an airman on watch had just reached for the cup of black coffee on the stand next to him when a group of white dots caught his eye on the lower right portion of his radar scope. He blinked instinctively, his mind telling him that he couldn't possibly be seeing what was on the screen. In the second it took his eyes to refocus, the small white dots, fuzzy circles really, had moved a tiny bit further from the edge of the scope.

"What…?"

The operator seated next to him was staring at the same spot on her screen and she had instinctively punched the alert button, notifying the senior officer on duty that they had detected an unknown.

"What is it?" The airforce sergeant queried as he moved behind the two operators who were now leaning close into their scopes. He too stared blankly at the white shapes as the passing scanner ray highlighted them. He counted quickly, and noted their heading.

"I count fourteen, sir," the woman said, without looking up at him.

"Confirmed, fourteen," echoed the airman sitting next to her without looking up. The duty sergeant didn't hear him as he was already halfway across the room reaching for the telephone that would connect him with the new air defence facility in North Bay. He punched a single large button on the console in front of him and seconds later, a voice on the other end of the line acknowledged his presence and waited.

"Alert - bogies fourteen - sector forty-three."

"Alert – bogies fourteen - sector forty-three," was repeated through the earpiece.

"Affirmative."

The duty officer replaced the receiver and rushed back to the operators who had now been joined by their relief crew – a spare team was constantly available for any of the positions in the 'scope room'. He noted that the aircraft were now entering the adjoining sector and the radar was reporting their speed at three hundred plus miles per hour. Probably a squadron of Bears, but he knew better than to assume.

"All other areas clear, sir," one of the relief crew informed him.

"Thanks, Bob. North Bay is alerted. Now we wait for the interceptors."

* * *

Ben turned his car into the driveway of the modest little house he shared with his family and turned the engine off. Sitting for a few moments, he enjoyed the quiet peace of the late hour. The neighbour's cat, whose name he learned was Molly, sauntered over to the front steps and sat there looking at him expectantly. He smiled and contemplated discussing with Joanne about acquiring a cat for the kids when the stillness was shattered by the alert horn. Molly looked up in disgust before scurrying around the house. Exhausted from the long flight, Squadron Leader Jones climbed stiffly from the car and walked up the small, concrete path to the steps. Joanne had just opened the door to great him, having heard the car pull in, when the phone rang in the living room behind her.

"Oh, Ben!" she exclaimed, as he brushed past her to answer the phone.

"Don't worry hon," he called back over his shoulder. "I can't go back up this soon anyway. Besides," he quipped, "it's probably just Cam checking to make sure I filed the summary report."

He walked quickly into the living room and picked up the phone.

"Jones."

"Squadron Leader Jones? This is Flight Sergeant Cudmore in base ops. We need you here immediately!"

"Maybe you are not aware. I just…"

"I'm sorry squadron leader," interrupted the flight sergeant. "The wing commander is aware you just landed and said to tell you there's a bit of a dust up going on."

"Were those his exact words?"

"Yes, and he made certain I put it to you that way."

"I'm on the way!"

Ben dropped the receiver, not noticing that it bounced from the phone and fell to the floor. He rushed to the door where Joanne was about to protest when she saw the look on his face. Ben was about to say something when the sky was suddenly filled with the screams of the base air raid sirens drowning out the alert horn. Joanne had never heard them go off before other than during pre-publicized alert exercises.

"Go hon! I love you!" She touched his shoulder as he ran past her.

"I love you too!" Ben yelled back as he tore open the car door. Throwing the transmission into gear, he smashed the gas pedal and than had to slam the brakes as another car went roaring by the end of the driveway. Hitting the gas again, the car roared on, leaving Joanne standing to stare at the taillights as they disappeared around a bend in the road.

Ben recognized Cam's Ford and followed it down the street and onto the main road which ran parallel to the base's runway. Reaching the gate, Cam slowed quickly, bringing his car to a stop only long enough for the guards at the entrance to quickly scan his ID and then himself before waving him through. Ben followed suit and they drove to the base ops center where an assortment of civilian vehicles were parked randomly along the lane. A few had been abandoned haphazardly on the carefully manicured grass in front of the building.

Rushing from their cars, Ben and Cam ran up the concrete steps to the entrance and ploughed through the door. The wing commander was standing inside, talking into a phone and held up his hand, signalling them to wait.

"Yes sir. I have two more going up in ten minutes," he spoke into the telephone. He pointed to the flight brief room and at their clothing, indicating that they were to suit up immediately. "Their aircraft are being refuelled from the crash run this morning. Yes sir. We have three more in…"

Without waiting to hear any more, the two men rushed through the briefing room they had left only twenty minutes earlier, to the pilot ready area, where they quickly grabbed their flight suits and started to change.

"Any guesses?" Cam asked breathlessly. He tore off his civilian clothes, simply adding them to the pile on the floor left behind by an earlier crew.

"Nothing I can think of," Ben responded. "Unless it has to do with that Bear collision this morning. Maybe the Kremlin wasn't impressed with what happened."

"That's probably it," Cam agreed. The men stopped talking. The few seconds wasted speaking might be crucial later. In the air defence business, all time was measured in seconds, and seconds could mean the difference between life and something too horrific to imagine.

* * *

Far to the north of where Ben and Cam were quickly changing back into their flight suits, time seemed to have come to a stop for Kristoff as he looked forward to his mission coming to an end. The submarine that would take them back home to the Soviet Union could not arrive soon enough.

Kristoff fidgeted as he stood alone outside the tent. The commando was becoming increasingly bored with little to do but watch the strange birds that inhabited this area flying over him. He was anxious to get back to real missions. This one was a complete waste of his and his men's talents. Once again, he looked down at his father's watch. It was almost time to activate the jamming system and this time the orders indicated that it was to stay operating for a much longer period than previously. He wondered if the jammer had created the desired effect when it had been turned on earlier that morning. Hopefully, it had annoyed the interceptors and interfered with their communications enough to cause them some grief.

Perhaps the general's plan might work, Kristoff thought. This would certainly give notice to the West that the Soviet Union was capable of their own great advancements in technology. Before departing, the commando had suggested to the general that Sputnik might have been a clever enough show of Soviet prowess, but the man had laughed and brushed the comment aside. He called Sputnik 'old news', insisting they must go through with this mission to prove the USSR was capable of even greater things.

"Who am I to stand here and question my orders?" Kristoff asked himself out loud and pushing the doubts from his mind. Besides, he thought, Moscow must have carefully weighed the risks before endorsing this plan, and after examining all the dangers involved, the KGB would have given it their blessing as well – or so he hoped.

* * *

One man who harboured no doubts about HIS leader's blessings was Captain Dan Hetherington. Unfortunately for him and his crew, their mission had not progressed very smoothly so far. Five hundred and fifty feet below the surface near a point where the Atlantic Ocean became the Labrador Basin, the nuclear powered attack submarine *USS Shark* hovered motionless. The boat and its crew had been sitting silently for the past five hours, everyone aboard being careful to make no unnecessary noise. Having earlier ducked a Canadian patrol aircraft by slipping below a double thermal layer and going 'quiet', Dan had ordered the 'drivers' to proceed slowly northwest to this point. He had then settled the crew down for a long wait, just to make sure 'the coast was clear'. Now, the waiting was finally over.

"Cob, make your depth three hundred feet," he ordered, before adding; "Quietly Cob."

"Aye sir. Helm, make my depth three hundred feet. Bring her up nice and slow, Mr. Cale."

"Make my depth three hundred feet, nice and slow. Aye."

USS Shark gently began to move through the water. Four valves opened quietly, allowing high pressure air into the ballast tanks which expelled the sea water out vents in the bottom of the hull, thus increasing the buoyancy of the submarine. The addition of a specially designed venting system, similar to that installed in *Scorpion* the previous year, allowed a slow, steady stream of air into the tanks, almost eliminating the noisy, tell-tale turbulence of water being blown from them. For both spy submarines, the modification had prevented their being detected on more than one occasion when they had been operating where they didn't belong.

Crammed into the confines of the torpedo room, the SEALs were becoming increasingly unhappy with their current lot in life. Being caught on the surface had been disastrous; the worse case scenario for the commando group. They knew there would be hell to pay when they got back to Virginia. At least the sub's crew had finally managed to evade the Canadians after hours of silent running and remaining motionless. It had been discussed at great length among the men as to whether or not the Canucks were in fact a communist ally posing as a friend. They had all come to agreement on one point - life for a submariner in Canadian waters was not boring!

"Maybe they invited the Russians to land there," a petty officer had suggested.

"No way man! The Canuks are different alright, but man, I tell you, they're just like us," one of the SEALs had vehemently declared. "They just don't get all uptight like we do 'bout stuff."

"I don't know man. I think they're just a bunch of commies! I bet if the chips were…"

"Hey!!!"

The two men fell silent as their heads turned in unison in the direction the shout had come from. Ducking through the hatch, *Shark's* weapons officer angrily made his way to where the two SEALs were sitting against one of the torpedo racks. He was at least three inches taller than either of them and his huge forearms threatened to tear the sleeves out of his uniform. He glared down at them with a cold, piercing stare.

"My wife is Canadian. You two pin heads wouldn't be calling her names now, would you?"

Realizing this man could probably carry one of their boats singlehanded, and maybe even the crew with it, the two men remained silent. Finally, the one who had made the comment spoke.

"Sorry L-T. We're just lettin' off steam. We don't mean nothing by it, man."

"Alright. You two look like you've been sitting on your asses long enough. Your lieutenant asked me to come and drag your sorry butts back to the mess. Maybe we're finally going to be rid of you guys before you stink the boat up any worse than it is now." The lieutenant's expression softened somewhat as he added, "Come on, Caps' even ordered some special chow for you guys."

"Hey, man. Now you're talkin'," the SEAL replied.

The two men stood up carefully in the confined space and squeezed past the lieutenant. Ducking through the hatch, they made their way through 'officer country' and then down the ladder to the crew area and mess. The rest of the SEALs were already seated at one of the tables and with the final two members present, the lieutenant began.

"Okay guys. The captain says we're going to be turning back for the coast tonight so make sure your gear is checked. I don't want anybody dropping their ammo into the drink this time," he finished with a stern look at one of the men.

"Jeeze, LT! I tol' you a hundred times - it was an accident!" In response, the men broke into hearty laughter, taking turns punching the disgruntled man's shoulder.

"Hey Johnson, maybe you'd better carry the clips in your underwear," one of them joked. "I'm sure there's plenty of extra space in there!"

"Yeah, sure there is you little honky," Johnson snarled. "Man, you could carry an RPG with room to spare in yours!"

"Alright!" barked the lieutenant. "You can play 'mine's bigger than yours' when we get back home!"

"RPG up…"

The rest of the sentence was lost as the group filed through the passageway to the ladder and back up to the torpedo room. Lieutenant Gary Land watched as they disappeared, then grinned himself, before looking back down at the map spread over the table. It showed a rugged coastline which he knew was strewn with rocks and rugged precipices. They would have to use ropes to scale the low cliff from the beach where the team was expected to land, if you could call that small sandy patch a beach, the lieutenant noted as he studied a reconnaissance photo of the area. He and the team had landed on worse though. One 'trip' to Siberia had been very similar and at least here, they weren't likely to face the whole Russian army - just a few of its best men, he reminded himself.

Land sat down and continued his study of the photo. Clearly marked was the location of the Russian encampment, as well as the few areas of higher ground nearby. It was assumed the men were Spetsnaz, the Soviet equivalent of the SEALs. Both groups were highly trained and motivated – expected to go anywhere and do anything without hesitation. He hoped the commandos were more out of shape from their long campout, then his men were from being cooped up in the boat's torpedo room for so long.

The lieutenant glanced at his watch and folded the image back into its waterproof pouch. This mission was certainly the strangest one he'd ever been called out for. Nobody up his chain of command seemed very sure of what the Russians were up to. The Canadians, on the other hand, had no idea about their uninvited guests. If the Canuks had been aware of the commandos, all hell would have broken loose and they'd have sent a regiment up there to clean them out. Ah, the Canadians, he thought to himself. All about peacekeeping these days, or so they claimed. He knew better. Reaching for a cup of coffee one of the sailors had brought them before the meeting, he drank it down quickly and headed to the control room.

"Well Canuks," Lieutenant Land muttered beneath his breath while ducking through the hatch. "We'll take care of this one for you."

* * *

Slowly scanning the terrain ahead through his binoculars, Sergeant Brian Ashe was not happy about the situation he and the Rangers had found themselves in. The sun was just above the horizon and blinding him as he tried to locate the Russian camp through the morning haze. A warm front had moved into the area overnight and brought unseasonably high temperatures with it, along with a persistent light ground fog.

"Got it," he whispered to the Ranger laying on the ground to his left. From what he could see, nothing had changed within the camp since they had last visited this spot. He did however note an odd rock outcropping that had escaped his attention the first time he and Grandfather had examined the site. Focusing the binoculars on the rock, he examined it carefully.

"Shit," he hissed quietly. "It's a damn antenna!"

"Why would they have anything that big up here," Ranger Karnes asked, examining the camp and the oddly shaped antennae next to the tent through his own binoculars. Now that he knew where to look, it was obviously not a rock formation, although it had been exceptionally well camouflaged.

"I don't know," Ashe replied. "I really don't know. Look - I'm going to stay here. You return and have Church radio back that they have a large antenna of some sort set up." Looking back at the departing Ranger, he whispered loudly, "Make sure he tells them that it's camouflaged to look like a big rock!"

He returned to his position, laying prone on one of the rare spots of ground not covered in sharp stones. The sergeant was careful to practice proper observation techniques, making sure nothing reflected sunlight back to the Russians, especially the binocular lens which could act as a mirror and signal his presence to the enemy.

His rifle lay propped against a nearby rock, turned so he could quickly grab the FN with one hand and bring it to bear. There was little natural cover here and he envisioned that a fire fight between himself and the Russians at this point, would be a very short affair.

Looking across the open ground, he saw the man he had speculated earlier must be the Spetsnaz leader, emerge from the tent and lean against a large rock with his back towards him. He knew to look for a soldier who appeared by himself more often than the rest. This was generally the sign of a leader and as officers in commando groups, like their men, seldom wore any rank insignia, it was the only way to discern who was in charge.

Across the broken terrain, Senior Lieutenant Kristoff Nikolev was looking out over the frigid water. The transmitter appeared to be operating properly and again he could only assume that an unknown Soviet unit somewhere was monitoring the Canadian Air Force communication frequencies for a sign that the system was having the desired effect.

He thought again of home and how his mother had looked at him when he had last seen her. Her eyes had been filled with a strange sadness. The Spetsnaz officer could tell she was more worried about him than usual, although she had no idea what it was her son did in the army. He surmised it was some kind of maternal instinct mothers possessed. She was a good woman and had brought him up to the best of her ability after his father had been killed. Yes, he remembered, feeling a wave of sadness wash over him, it had been a hard life for all of them in the post war Soviet Union.

Kristoff often wondered what life might have been like had the hated German U-boat captain not sunk his father's ship. Perhaps he would have gone to university and become a doctor. The psychological testing he had gone through, as all Soviet children did, had indicated a much higher than average mental ability. Later in life, he had admitted to himself that he had found little difficulty with school work, and was bored with most of it. Only his mother's constant attention kept him focused on his studies and he received consistently high marks as a result.

Dragging his thoughts back to the present, he took a brief stroll around the secure perimeter his men had set up. Nearly invisible in the rough terrain, they had constructed a simple detection system, ringed with grenades which would incapacitate any intruder and alert his unit to their presence. At first he had worried that some wild animal might come along and set off the crude arrangement, but he soon realized that not even wildlife seemed intent on inhabiting this barren corner of Canada. Only the strange looking birds which constantly hovered over the nearby cliff seemed interested in calling this piece of land home.

Kristoff again checked the time. The mission seemed to be mostly a test of their ability to complete a task at a given time. This occasion, they were to operate the jammer for three hours. That should be long enough for whoever was out there to measure its effect he thought, not wishing to ponder any further who that might be.

Sergeant Brian Ashe meanwhile, continued to gaze through his binoculars at the mysterious looking antennae. Its purpose was a mystery to him and he had never seen one quite like it. He was working on possible assault options when a noise directly behind him sent a shiver down his spine causing him to turn quickly. Crawling slowly along the ground towards him was the Ranger's oldest member. One look at the expression on Moose's usually inexpressive face told him the news wasn't good.

"Headquarters says we go in," Deniigi whispered hoarsely. "Now."

* * *

"Six hours to the crash site, commander," the lieutenant announced, steadying himself with the compass mount against the speeding destroyer's motion.

"Thank you lieutenant."

Commander Barry Delaney leaned against the forward bulkhead of the open bridge, enjoying the view as *Margaree* crashed through the waves. Occasionally a large swell would send spray flying over the bow, covering the 3"50cal. turret and causing a few forward deck fittings to be ripped away.

They had steamed at full speed throughout the night and for a couple of hours, had hit speeds not seen since *HMCS Margaree's* shakedown cruise. The crew had been running rescue stations drill but had been unable to implement a full man overboard practice due to the ship's high speed and the waves crashing over the bow. Barry was not willing to risk one of his own men being washed overboard in the rush to rescue the downed airmen.

"Coms, let Halifax know we're six hours out," he ordered. They had picked up a transmission from one of the aircraft watching over the downed aviators, and learned that the men in the rafts were fine. Extra rations had been air dropped to them as well as a new radio to replace the original one which had exhausted its battery.

Just under two hundred nautical miles directly ahead of the speeding destroyer, the Argus crew were trying to make themselves as comfortable as possible. The rafts now seemed half the size they had been when the men had first climbed into them. It was the same phenomenon experienced by prisoners, who would sometimes hide tape measures away to reassure themselves that their cells were not magically creeping in on them inch by inch as they slept.

Sleep for the airmen was another matter. Although not immersed in the cold Atlantic waters, they fought to remain awake, allowing their bodies to better fight off any effects from the cold environment. They also kept a close watch amongst each other for any sign one of them might be dozing off. The Russian airmen had obviously been trained in a similar manner, as they too reached out and shook awake any of the Canadians who appeared to be falling asleep.

Back aboard *Margaree*, the medical team had set up a make shift hospital ward in the PO's mess, ready in case any of the aviators required immediate medical attention. Everything aboard the speeding destroyer which would be needed had been prepared for when they snatched the half frozen men from the sea.

"Bridge, sonar. Contact bearing three five one degrees," announced Leading seaman Brent O'Hanlon, knowing it was not what the commanding officer wanted to hear right now.

You've got to be kidding me! Barry thought to himself, reaching for the intercom, "Sonar, what have you got down there?"

"Submarine, sir. Sounds like he's just starting to move. No positive ID yet, but I'd bet it's a *Skipjack* – just not 100%."

Brent was pretty certain of its identity, but not certain enough to confirm the contact as anything but an unknown at this time. Of course that didn't really matter. There was no such thing as a 'friendly' submarine and all submerged contacts were treated as hostile unless identification was one hundred percent positive.

"How did you hear it at this speed?" Barry had to ask. He recognized O'Hanlon's voice and wanted to test the young man's mettle further. O'Hanlon was destined to go places – if the navy could convince him to stay in.

"Passive sonar picked him up sir," came the answer over the speaker. "He's either making a lot of noise or he's in a sound tube. Otherwise, I wouldn't have heard him."

"Good work O'Hanlon. Keep a close watch, but we have to pass him up this time."

Barry knew the fleeting contact was a fluke and would soon be lost.

"Will do sir. If he comes near us I'll shout...err...let you know sir."

"You shout your ass off if he does, Leading Seaman O'Hanlon!"

"Yes sir," the voice over the speaker answered. The other men on the bridge exchanged knowing glances. One thing you could say for their commander - he never minced words.

* * *

Aboard the two rafts, now securely fastened together, the men were gratefully enjoying a meal of rations dropped an hour earlier by a rescue aircraft flying out from Goose Bay. Although only consisting of a few cold items, they tasted wonderful to the men who had been without a meal for a long time. The unseasonably mild spring temperature made the waiting bearable – just.

"Hey," joked Pudgy Cormier. "This tastes just like steak! You have to hand it to the airforce! No one can make food from - looks like 1959 - taste like it was just cooked last year."

"Be grateful we have that," the MAD operator quipped. "The Russians are sure enjoying it."

"Yeah, their rations were probably world war two surplus," Pudgy noted.

"Nyet," spoke up one of the Russians. "From great patriotic war." He broke into laughter at the look on the Canadian's faces.

"Damn! Ivan speaks english!" exclaimed the MAD operator.

"Da," the man continued in hesitant but clear english. "We learn it for air traffic control." He smiled, showing teeth with a few stainless steel fillings. "I am comra...Dimetry. Man in other raft is co-pilot, Asimov. We are thankful for your help."

"Well I'll be damned," Cormier remarked, reaching out to shake the hand extended towards him. "Nice to meet you guys." His expression turned serious. "How many were aboard your aircraft?"

Dimetry's face changed to a look of sadness. "Nine, beside us."

"I'm sorry Dimetry," the aircraft commander said solemnly. He meant it. As with seafarers, aviators belonged to a universal fraternity and their common enemy was foremost the science that allowed them to fly.

"Da. Thank you."

The men fell silent. Each living through his own thoughts of relief at their survival and sadness for those who did not make it. Most of the airmen had been touched by tragedy at some point in their aviation careers and they never became accustomed to the feeling of loss when one of their own was gone.

* * *

In Moscow the day had dawned cloudy with a few spring showers falling over Red Square. Sitting at the large oak desk in his opulently adorned office, General Ustinov enjoyed a glass of hot cider to ward off the chill from his brisk morning walk. The plan he had devised and put in motion was unfolding perfectly and he would soon be the toast of the Kremlin when he stood before the Politburo and announced its success. The fools in the planning office had panned his idea as being far too dangerous and even capable of bringing the Soviet Union to war with the cowardly West, but he knew better.

"West." – he spat the word commonly used to describe his enemies – "All puppets of the Americans!" Especially the Canadians, who claimed to be peacekeepers while they sat on a cache of nuclear weapons. Why couldn't the Politburo see as he had, that NOW was the time to strike fear into the hearts of these capitalists?

America was embroiled in a useless conflict in Vietnam where they were fighting a hopeless struggle to save the corrupt government of the south. The general knew from television reports that the American people were losing patience with their leaders and wanted this costly war ended. Watching the protests taking place all over the United States and regularly broadcast on the American television stations had shown him that even their once mighty military was becoming tired of the conflict. It was weakened now by dissent from within, especially in the lower ranks.

"Yes," he muttered, slowly moving over to a map of North America adorning one wall. Now was indeed the time to take advantage of the low moral which permeated the American heartland.

His experiment would show the impotent capitalist military leaders how weak their forces really were and further demoralize them. How foolish the Politburo had been to refuse implementation of his plan. Of course those who had protested it would be quietly sent away, while he would be given a place of even greater power and prestige in the leadership of the Soviet armed services.

A knock on the ornate door disturbed his thoughts and he growled for whoever it was to enter. An aide walked in and saluting briskly, handed him a note. Reading it over quickly, Ustinov brushed the aide away with a wave of his hand. The note contained excellent news. He smiled broadly as he examined the piece of paper in his fingers. Everything was in place and the bombers would be commencing their runs at any moment. He thought for a moment of the traitor who had sold the information on the SAGE datalink to a KGB operative, sharing with her how a tiny flaw in the NORAD communications system could be exploited to jam it. The others had said the information was too valuable to make use of except in time of war. He had tried to argue with them that this was indeed a war, but they had brushed his ideas aside.

Out of nowhere, a wave of doubt washed over him and a worried expression crossed his eyes and just as quickly vanished. Yes, tomorrow at this time, his name would be spoken with respect and pride throughout the Motherland.

* * *

In the wilderness of north eastern Maine, the quiet peace was broken by alert horns going off at Loring Air Force Base, the sprawling home of the Strategic Air Command's 42nd Bomb Wing. Thick plumes of black smoke rose from the alert stands as the eight jet engines on each of the huge bombers poised there were started in quick succession. Within minutes six Boeing B-52 Stratofortresses had began a slow, lumbering crawl to the end of the runway. In each of the swept wing aircraft's bomb bays, four B28 hydrogen bombs swayed indiscernibly in their racks.

Before the bombers could reach the runway where they would roll straight into their takeoff runs, a detachment of Convair F-106 Delta Darts, also stationed at the base, had taxied from their alert hangers on the opposite side of the runway and roared into the air. They would head east, while the B-52's would turn to the north for a rendezvous with KC-135 tankers from the Maine Air National Guard. The 'flying gas stations' would be departing from their base at Bangor International Airport and heading north as well, along the Stratofort's flight path. After topping up from the tankers, the B-52 pilots would begin a long, steady decent over northern Canada, preparing for their runs over the pole and into the Soviet Union.

In Ottawa, over which more than a few B-52 bombers would fly this day, the Prime Minister was reading over a report which had just been handed to him by a sombre looking airforce group captain.

"Is this verified?"

"Yes sir. All Area Three bases are on alert or have scrambled their aircraft."

"What the hell is the Soviet Premier thinking?" It was a rhetorical question and the Prime Minister did not expect nor want an answer.

"Thank you. Please carry on."

"Yes, sir." The group captain came to attention and returned briskly to the airforce console. It was connected directly to the sprawling underground complex in North Bay, where the smell of fresh paint lingered faintly in the air within the newly constructed facility.

The Canadian NORAD headquarters was in turn linked through secure communications channels to what was playfully called its 'big brother' buried deep in the Cheyenne Mountains of Colorado. Protected by the massive mountain range above it, the home of the North American Air Defence Command housed an army of men and women whose responsibility was the aerial protection of North America. As in North Bay, everyone from lowly private to general was busily trying to determine what was going on. Was this the beginning of an all out attack, a squadron of Soviet bombers which had fallen off course, or the unvoiced possibility of a deranged squadron leader who was trying to start World War III on his own.

That scenario had been played out in the movies over the past few years and although the governments of all nuclear armed nations had denied even the most remote possibility of such an event ever occurring, it had come very close - once.

That scenario was going through the Prime Minister's mind when a buzz from the phone on the desk in front of him interrupted his thoughts. Reaching over to answer it, he smiled, already knowing who was on the other end.

"Hello Mr. President."

"Hello Prime Minister. How's the weather up there today?"

"A little more threatening than I like," the Prime Minister responded sharply.

"Same here. NORAD's still stewing but there hasn't been any other activity to suggest a further threat and I think we just have a bunch of flyboys who're lost and trying to find their way home. What are your boys saying?"

The President had some misgivings about the Canadian leader but in times such as these he had no choice but to trust the man and seek out his help. After all, Canada was a huge buffer between the United States and the Soviet Union and on more than one occasion the Prime Minister had quietly stepped in to quell a dangerous dispute between the two super powers.

"We're seeing the same thing here," the Prime Minister replied, making it clear that he was not simply agreeing with the President. His country's sovereignty had been ignored enough this week.

"The first interceptors should reach them shortly and then we'll know for sure," the President noted.

"Yes. I say we wait for that report. I'll call you the minute it's in and we'll go from there."

"That sounds good. I'm already in the bunker. I presume you're at Carp?"

"No," the Prime Minister responded. "I'm 'next door' for now. I didn't want to stir a panic up here."

"Right," the President answered. Damn! He'd just been 'one upped' by the Canadian. "I'll talk to you soon."

The line went dead. It had not been the Prime Minister's intention to embarrass the US leader, but he certainly didn't regret it.

* * *

Roaring off the end of runway twenty nine at Chatham, Ben rolled his CF-101 into a tight right turn until the Voodoo was heading north east. Climbing rapidly past ten thousand feet, he heard Cam call Sunflower control for their initial bearings.

"Sunflower, this is India flight; we are angels ten and climbing." He knew they would already be tracking the pair of Voodoo's and were waiting for the initial contact from them before starting to transmit information to the interceptors through the datalink.

"Roger India flight, we have you – data sending."

Cam looked down at the scope and sure enough, there was the information on their target's bearing, heading, altitude and speed.

"Looks low and slow, sir," he announced to Ben over the intercom.

Ben had just gotten a thumbs up from Jeffrey who was flying his Voodoo low and behind his leader's starboard side.

"Sounds like another 'lost Bear' problem Cam," he chuckled into the mouthpiece.

"I'd say so sir. Datalink is working fine now. Turn right ten degrees and maintain this altitude," he ordered.

"Coming right ten and maintaining this altitude, roger," Ben replied. He didn't mind taking directions from the guy in back. It was part of the team work that made them the professionals they were.

"Sunflower, we have secure datalink," Cam radioed to St Margarets. This would be their last voice communication during the intercept stage. The two Voodoo's tore through the air beyond the sound barrier, disregarding peacetime noise abatement procedures out of necessity, leaving broken windows and upset civilians in their wake below.

Ahead of the interceptors, the Soviets had split the TU-95 formation into two groups with one heading directly for the Labrador coast and the other further north. The Russian crews were impressed with the arrogance of this exercise and had their cameras ready knowing they'd be getting some great photos of Canadian and American interceptors on this day. They presumed incorrectly that by now, the Russian government would have notified the West of the upcoming exercise so that in spite of their intention to 'accidentally' stray into Canadian airspace, NORAD would have been alerted and would just assume the Russians had 'miscalculated' their position.

There would be the usual wagging of wings and veiled threats over the emergency frequencies, as well as the universally understood hand gestures, but everyone would just end up taking pictures and waving before heading for home. The crews flying in two TU-95RT's along with the bomber versions knew this was going to be a great day for radio and radar intercepts, allowing them to record a little more Western technology.

Aboard India one however, the situation had just taken a turn for the worse.

"We've lost datalink, sir."

"Oh shit, Cam! Don't tell me that!"

"Sorry, sir. I rechecked the other frequencies. No joy," Cam announced with a finality that told Ben the source of the problem, like the last time, was not with them.

"Okay. Call Sunflower up and tell them we'll need vectors - again," he grumbled. "This is going to be a mess with all the interceptors up here right now."

Ben was right. Four F-106's from Loring AFB had just lost their datalink information as well and one controller was busily trying to unite the two pairs of fighters so she could control them as one unit. The other controllers at St Margarets were also busily trying to shepherd interceptors towards the incoming aircraft and the control room was flooded with strained voices. One of them looked up in frustration and spoke what was on all their minds.

"This was not how SAGE was supposed to work!"

The situation was made worse by the Bears sweeping in low, just above the surface of the water. This caused them to intermittently fall off the radar scopes. The job of directing the interceptors to the intruders was becoming more frustrating by the second.

A controller would give coordinates to a pair of fighters only to lose radar lock on the target. An armada of KC-135 tanker aircraft were flying out from numerous east coast air bases to refuel the F-106's which didn't have the long range the CF-101 Voodoo interceptors possessed.

Technicians meanwhile, were frantically going through the entire SAGE system and rumours that sabotage may have played a part in its failure were rampant. These were based on the notion that the datalink itself was impossible to jam. A few people in NORAD were aware of the one weakness the communications system's design did posses. The possibility that someone had discovered the flaw and was exploiting it however, had been quickly brushed aside.

Ben looked down for a moment to check their fuel state as the Voodoo's orbited aimlessly while his controller waited for the bogies to pop up on her radar again. Adding to the tension was their wait for nuclear weapons release from Sunflower which would signal use of the Genie rockets nestled inside the aircraft's armament bay.

A few hundred miles south east of where India flight orbited impatiently, another radar operator had just picked up the incoming Soviet aircraft.

"Bogies! Bearing three five five degrees," the petty officer manning *HMCS Margaree's* air search radar announced. "Very low. Speed, approximately three hundred knots. Multiple targets!"

"Lieutenant! Sound action stations!" Barry jumped from his chair and through the blackout curtain leading to CCR. Reaching the radar console, he didn't have to ask what was being tracked. A group of targets appeared to be heading just across the top of the screen. How many there were was hard to tell as they kept showing up on the radar scope and disappearing - a sign they were low over the water.

"Coms! Alert Halifax! Now!"

Barry could feel the hairs come up on the back of his neck. He knew they would have been informed if there had been this many Soviet aircraft expected along his route.

"Contact *Terra Nova* and let them know what's going on! Have them go to action stations as well."

"Yes sir," replied a voice across the room. He didn't see who it was, and didn't care. "There is trouble aloft," he murmured. "Big trouble!"

"Sir, I have Halifax coms and *Terra Nova* has acknowledged the signal," the anonymous voice announced. "They report picking up speed and following our track."

Barry made his way to the communications room, actually a small alcove in the newly designed CCR.

"Tell Halifax we have multiple bogies, low and slow – approximate heading, two seven five degrees."

"Yes sir," the leading seaman acknowledged. "Informing them now – Hotel X-Ray, this is Charlie Golf November Juliette, we have…" He continued the message and within seconds, an acknowledgement had come back from the naval communications centre in Halifax, Nova Scotia. The voice was slightly distorted by the single sideband radio, and the urgency in the operator's voice was apparent.

Barry thought for a moment and then turned back to the radio operator. "Someone must be up there after those guys. Give a call on the air guard channel and see if anyone is around."

"Yes, sir." The operator turned slightly in his chair and reached for the UHF radio used to communicate with the Sea King on military aviation frequencies.

"This is Charlie Golf November Juliette on guard. Tracking multiple bogies approximately fifty-five degrees north, fifty degrees west." He waited for a response, doubting there would be any with the rather cryptic message he has sent. Less than five seconds later, he was surprised to hear a voice filled with static come over the radio speaker.

"CGNJ, this is India flight out of Chatham," Cam knew from the call sign that it must be a Canadian warship but had no idea which one. "We are no joy with data from Sunflower control; can you vector us to the bogies?" Cam thought it was unlikely but they were getting nowhere at the moment with Sunflower.

"India flight this is CGNJ. That is affirmative." The destroyer's radio operator had no idea who or what 'Sunflower Control' was. That didn't matter. The ship's IFF indentified the aircraft as 'friendlies'. "Waiting for radar ID on you." He turned as he spoke to the radar operator who was trying to pick out the interceptors from the many targets he had on the ship's SPS 12 long range search radar.

"Got him," the radar operator reported. "Have them come right to zero three seven and maintain their present altitude."

"India flight, come right now to zero three seven degrees and maintain present altitude. Stand by for further."

Barry unconsciously gave the man a thumbs up. Hell, he thought. It's starting to get mighty crowded around here. They had been tracking a submerged contact but as expected, it had soon disappeared and now they were tracking multiple airborne targets on the search radar.

To the north, India flight was following the directions from *Margaree's* radio operator and had informed Sunflower of their alternative tracking source.

"Sir, we should have them in three more minutes," Cam called into the intercom.

"Roger that, Cam. That was a bit of luck running into that ship." They still had no idea which warship it was but Ben had noted the call sign on his knee board. He'd look into it when they had a chance later on.

Cam was about to comment when a call came over the command frequency. It was not an order he'd ever expected to hear.

"Ben?"

There was a perceptible tremor in Cam's voice. In the moment, he had used the pilot's first name – something not lost on Ben.

*   *   *

Five minutes earlier, the Canadian Prime Minister and his Minister of Defence were speaking in an office adjacent to the control room. Crowded around them were high ranking officers of all three branches of Canada's military and the atmosphere was tense.

"I don't see what choice we have," an airforce general was explaining. "The Falcons might do the job but there are so many targets I wouldn't be able to guarantee that our guys will be able to bring down all the bombers."

"We need to get all of them," the Prime Minister spoke with authority. "Something is fucking up Pinetree and those interceptors are flying around blind out there."

Normally these men would have been shocked to hear the Prime Minister use such strong language, but with the current situation, no one in the room seemed to take notice.

"General, any idea at all what's going on with the radar?"

The Prime Minister was becoming increasingly frustrated over the failure of the Pinetree sites. They had been touted as the perfect, secure defence line and now they appeared utterly useless.

"It's not the radar, sir. It's the datalink from the ground up to the aircraft. Something seems to be jamming it but the techs are saying that's impossible. They're pulling their hair out up there trying to find out what the hell is going on – sorry sir."

Daniel L. Little

"Okay, this is getting us no where. Send the order to the interceptors. Code word 'Flyswatter'!"

"Right away, sir!" The general turned and rushed from the room. Oh my god, he thought. This was it.

* * *

"What have you got, Cam?" Ben had noted the distinct change in his weapons operator's voice.

"Just came in over the command net. We're clear for 'Flyswatter'."

There was a moment of silence over the intercom while Ben turned towards his wingman's aircraft, flying a few hundred feet to his right. He saw Jeffrey's head nod, almost imperceptibly, letting him know that he too, had received the order. Ben knew that behind his sunshield, the other pilot's face was reflecting the same combination of anger and fear his own must be showing. As the momentary shock wore off, his first thoughts were for Joanne and the kids back in their tidy little home back in Chatham. Ben wondered if he would ever see them again. There were no shelters for the families and it was grudgingly accepted that they would be among the first to die in an all out war as nuclear warheads landed on the base.

"Okay Cam. Confirmed unlock on the Genies."

"Roger sir. Genie one and two unlocked," Cam responded uncovering the pair of switches he had always looked at with an almost childlike curiosity, knowing he would never have to flip them on. He was rewarded by a pair of green lights on the left side of his instrument panel. Oddly, it suddenly struck him that he hadn't mowed the lawn this week. Christina would be on his case about that when they got back.

Behind his instrument panel, a seldom used circuit switched on and the armament door below the two men quickly rotated, exposing the two Genie rockets which were now fully armed. They contained no guidance system of their own; nor was there a need for one. Their detonation, initiated by a proximity fuse, would take out any aircraft within a large radius, including the one which had fired the rocket, if the pilot was lax in following the proper procedure for evading the explosion.

* * *

Unlike the sleek interceptors, the old RCAF Dakota rumbled slowly through the sky with its twin radial engines reverberating through the fuselage. Their vibration, accompanied by a steady drone, threatened to lull the men aboard the aircraft to sleep. The CC-129 Dakota did share one attribute with the speedy jet fighters however. Crudely mounted below its bulbous fuselage, was the same stubby datalink antenna found on the NORAD interceptors, and inside the empty cargo aircraft's fuselage, Corporal Graeme Johnson was busily adjusting the radio receiver he had jury-rigged aboard the old World War II aircraft back at his base in Chatham.

"You really think this is going to work corporal?" asked the flight sergeant seated across from him.

"Sure do, sarge! I'm picking up the signal from the Pinetree transmitters just fine right now. We'll see where it breaks off."

After the last datalink failure, Graeme had developed a theory about the problem and grabbing a UHF directional antenna, had mounted it below the old Dakota transport along with the regular datalink antennae carried by the interceptors. The airmen helping him had joked about mounting a few Falcons on the old transport's wings and one of them had even drawn up a caricature of the Dakota with missiles and rockets mounted under the fuselage while a fearsome looking pilot glared out from the cockpit. They all had a hearty laugh over the drawing and then returned to the task of connecting both antennas to a receiver capable of picking up the datalink signal. Although he wouldn't be able to decipher them, Johnson would be able to see a video rendition of them on the small display tube built into the receiver.

"See this wave on my scope?" Graeme spoke loudly to be heard over the din of the engines. "That is the signal from the datalink. We should be able to see if it drops off. The techs at St. Margarets are saying their systems are working fine but something is definitely amiss."

"I'll say," laughed the sergeant, pointing to his temples and twirling his finger before pointing it at Graeme. "The CO said not to come back if your plan doesn't work."

"Hey man, that won't be a problem. Between my brains and your…err, what was it you claim to have again, sarge?" Graeme ducked the oily rag that came flying at him.

Corporal Johnson kept an eye on the scope and noted no changes in the signal as the aircraft continued slowly in a north easterly direction. Sitting on the floor of the C-47, he fought to stay alert in spite of the hypnotic drone of the radial engines. He forced himself to focus on the sine wave which flowed and flickered across the receiver's display like a heart monitor. Stretching out, he rubbed his eyes and began to question whether this get up of his was going to work after all when the sine wave suddenly wavered, disappeared completely and was replaced by a perfectly straight line.

Graeme looked at the scope suspiciously, catching the sergeant's attention and bringing him over to where the corporal was sitting on the floor.

"Something?" he asked.

"I think so," Johnson answered. Turning the crudely designed system he had installed for adjusting the directional antennae below him on the fuselage, his face broke into a huge grin. "Well I'll be damned!"

* * *

With each passing moment the Prime Minister was becoming more concerned with the situation. Could he be witnessing the start of the war which would truly end all wars? And would it be his actions that precipitated it? The unidentified aircraft had still not been positively identified although it was almost certainly a squadron of Soviet bombers.

So far, there had been no indications of any other unusual Soviet activity anywhere in the world, which was both reassuring and alarming. The 'rogue nuclear commander' scenario kept playing out in his mind and that possibility was much more of a threat than an all out attack, which could possibly be called off through diplomacy.

A mad man however, could not be negotiated with and he would be hell bent on reaching his target. The Prime Minister was pondering which possible target, when an airforce squadron leader rushed over.

"Sir! We know what's happening with the Pinetree sites," he gushed out, making no attempt at decorum.

"What is it?"

"They're being jammed!" He smiled broadly, as if that knowledge alone would solve all the world's problems.

"Jammed?" The Prime Minister stood and walked swiftly over to the airforce console where a group of officers were talking excitedly with the squadron leader trailing behind him.

"By whom?"

"The damn Ruskies I imagine...sir," the officer stammered and immediately blushed at his choice of words.

"That's okay, son," the Prime Minister smiled. "Damn is the right damn word today."

They reached the group of officers who immediately fell silent, studying him.

"Well?" he asked. "What have you got?"

"Sir, an aircraft out of Chatham was flying a test run and they were just over..."

"Spare the details! Tell me what you've got!" The Prime Minister's face twisted into an angry scowl.

"It's a jamming station. Somewhere in Labrador," the Air Vice Marshall went on. "We assume it's our visitors and they've set up some sort of radio equipment strong enough to break into the datalink. The techs are still saying it can't be done but they're not quite so sure now." He smiled before continuing. "I already informed army command and they're moving on it now."

"Good work, Stan. I'll get the details later."

Turning to look for his army liaison, the Prime Minister was startled to find him standing right behind him.

"Sorry sir. I wanted to let you know that the Rangers have gone in and are no longer in radio contact. We tried to send a message," he continued, "to let them know what is going on, but we don't know whether it was received or not."

"When will we hear something from them?"

"I'd say as soon as they either mop up the Russians or… sorry, as soon as they mop up the Russians, sir."

The general had caught himself. He personally didn't give the Rangers much of a chance and had already rushed a second contingent of men from camp Gagetown onto a Flying Boxcar to Goose Bay.

"Let me know the minute you hear anything…anything at all!"

"Yes, sir," the general responded. He hoped the Prime Minister hadn't detected the doubt in his voice.

He had.

Returning to his desk, the Prime Minister wished he could just slump into the chair and close his eyes for an hour but he knew that was not an option. Somewhere in the bleak landscape of Labrador, a group of men with no real military training – with one exception – was Canada's first line of defence. No, he thought, remembering. There were two exception. His eyes suddenly felt very heavy and he quickly rubbed them while reaching for the cup of steaming coffee an army warrant officer had just brought him. Looking up at the young man sporting an impeccably pressed uniform, the Prime Minister smiled in gratitude.

"Man should get a medal for timing," Canada's leader said under his breath.

* * *

Sergeant Ashe had completed reconnoitring the area as best he could without being spotted by the Russians. The order to take out the intruders had been delivered earlier by a breathless Ranger who must have run all the way from their camp before crawling as quickly as he could to where Deniigi was waiting for Sergeant Ashe to return from observing the Soviets.

This wasn't going to be a cakewalk, Ashe acknowledged, studying the terrain. Ideally he would have preferred a two pronged assault, taking both flanks and splitting the defenders, but the landscape would never allow much movement before one of the flanking groups would be spotted. He decided to send one man out on the right flank as weak enfilade, or at worst, to draw fire while he and the rest of the Rangers went straight in.

It was not a great plan, he surmised – not even a good one. Looking again at the men crouching and lying behind the sparse cover around him, he realized the element of surprise was the only thing in their favour. In this fight, that would have to be enough.

The Sergeant had spent nearly an hour studying the lay of the land, and then going over his plan one last time with the men. Upon learning he would be the one going off on the right flank by himself, Ranger Church seemed a little shaken but said nothing.

Brian didn't blame him. If anything went wrong, Church was also expected to make it back to their base camp alive and send help.

"Okay, any questions?" Sergeant Ashe said a silent prayer that there were none as he had laid out the operation as simply as possible for his rag tag bunch of men. Thankfully, he was rewarded with silence.

A few hundred yards away from the relieved Canadian sergeant, Senior Lieutenant Kristoff Nikolev was staring off into the west. He hadn't seen anything move, nor had he heard any sound, but his soldier instincts were warning him that he and his men were no longer alone out here on this barren patch of land.

Looking again over the landscape he saw nothing move. You've been here too long Kristoff, he told himself. You're starting to imagine things. He knew in his heart that they had indeed been on this spot far longer than should have ever been allowed. The mission was almost over however and in two more days, the submarine would return to pick them up, returning him and his men to their base. He could taste that first hot meal his girlfriend would prepare after... A smile played on his face at the 'after'.

He wondered if their mission had been a success. There was no way of knowing, and in all likelihood, if past excursions were any indication, they would never be told. Perhaps that was for the best, Kristoff considered. Tonight they would commence taking apart the strange looking antenna and begin the task of packing up the equipment they had carried up and over the steep cliff to this spot. The commandos would be sure to leave no sign that they had ever been here.

Looking around again at the scenic terrain, he shrugged off the earlier feeling that someone was watching him and this time enjoyed the view. This Labrador is a ruggedly beautiful land, and yet strangely, a hostile land as well. Again that feeling of...what was it? He would be more careful. Perhaps, the man pondered, he had been part of the commando unit for too long and he was growing paranoid.

Kristoff did know from experience that the most dangerous time was always the end of a mission. This was when he had to watch the men closely for signs that they were letting their guard down – thinking more of home than their safety.

A short distance away, other concerns plagued Sergeant Brian Ashe's thoughts.

"Look," Brian whispered to the Ranger next to him. "That's him. Their leader. We have to make sure to take him out first." Then looking over to his right, he signalled Church to start moving along the right flank.

Ranger Glen Church crawled carefully through the short brush and slowly made his way to the higher ground on his right. Fear drove him to hug the ground closely, expecting any moment that a Russian bullet would tear into his flesh. He wasn't a coward, but he was a realist and he was fully aware of his limitations in the world of soldiering. His study of history had shown him that. The training given the Rangers was not what he would have considered thorough, but for today he knew, it would have to be enough.

What Ranger Church did have in his favour was the knowledge he possessed of hunting and trapping in this land, taught to him by his father and grandfather. This give him a remarkable edge over the men he was stalking. Unlike the Soviets, who trained mostly in the dense forests of East Germany, he, as his ancestors before him, had learned to make use of the most minute cover in the mostly barren northlands.

Their clothing, which had surprised the Canadian Army sergeant with its worn and tattered appearance was in fact perfect camouflage for this terrain. Ashe noted how effective it was as Church seemed to disappear into the landscape.

Brian marvelled at how he managed to blend into the earth. Shit, he thought, watching the man move carefully over the area he himself would have avoided as 'open ground'. He made a mental note to bring some of these guys back to Gagetown in the future, to share their craft with the regular army troops.

Studying the Russian camp, he noted that none of the commandos were visible at the moment. Perfect! It was the moment he was waiting for. Brian signalled the Rangers to start moving forward. Agonizingly slow, they moved over the ground, using whatever rock, brush or small plant was in front of them for cover. Even the smallest rock outcropping, used properly, would break up the silhouette of a man sufficiently enough that someone glancing casually in his direction might fail to notice him.

The Rangers moved carefully, stopping occasionally to make sure they had not been seen. As taught in their basic training course, half of them would move towards the objective, while the remainder watched for any sign they might have been spotted. Sergeant Ashe began to move for the tenth time and glancing back, was dismayed by the small distance he and his men had covered. This was going to take some time, he surmised. Perhaps it was just as well. He didn't want the sun in their eyes should – no, he corrected his thought - when a firefight broke out. None of them thought for a moment that the Soviet commandos would just lower their weapons and surrender.

Pausing again, his mind drifted momentarily to his wife and young daughter back home in Oromocto. A look of sadness briefly flashed across his face as he imagined the base commander coming to inform them that he would not be coming home. Pushing the thought to the back of his mind, he again inched forward.

Damn! In the war movies, this was where John Wayne would come over a nearby hill with the reinforcements. This was no movie however, and there would be no reinforcements.

* * *

"Charlie Golf November Juliet, this is India flight." Cam was calling for another update on the unidentified aircraft. The radio operator on the Canadian warship had warned that he would soon lose the aircraft on the ship's radar and he wanted to make sure the interceptors were headed in the right direction before that happened.

"Roger India flight, we are showing the contacts at your one o'clock - no more than twenty-five miles. They are just about to fall off our scopes so you're on your own sir."

"Okay Charlie Golf November Juliet, thank you and we will take it from here. Be warned that we are cleared for 'Flyswatter'." Cam did not want the warship sailing into the radioactive fallout of their Genie rockets if it came down to that.

"Roger, cleared for 'Flyswatter'. Good luck India flight!"

The sailor had no idea what 'Flyswatter' meant, but jotted down the word to check in his code book later. Looking over, he saw the small indications that represented the Russian aircraft disappear off the upper left of the radar scope. The airborne intercept was no longer his problem.

Casually grabbing the well worn, dog-eared code book from the shelf to his left, he thumbed through the f's. "Flying Kite, Flying Shark," he read aloud to himself. "Ah, here it is. Flyswatter...sweet Lord in heaven!!"

He dropped the book on the small metal ledge in front of him and hit the intercom button.

"Bridge, radio. I need the CO down here right now!"

Barry, hearing the announcement and the distress in the man's voice, leaned forward and punched the intercom button. "On my way!"

Reaching the communications area, Delaney didn't have to ask what was up, as the radio operator was holding up the code book with his finger pointing to 'Flyswatter'. Barry took one look and reached down for the intercom button.

"Helm! Bring us right zero three zero degrees, maintain speed!" He wanted to steer away from the interception area but couldn't go too far off the track or they'd be hours longer picking up the downed aviators.

The acknowledgement immediately came through the speaker above him and he felt the ship heel over and come around onto the new course. Looking down at the radio operator who was still clutching the code book in his hand, he tried to reassure him.

"Don't worry, 'Sparker'," he said in a loud enough voice to be heard throughout CCR. "They'll take 'em down and that'll be the end of it. No one's going to war over a bunch of flying sheet metal." He did not really believe that for a moment, but he also didn't want his crew panicking.

"Yes, sir." The man didn't sound very convinced.

Neither was Flying Officer Camille Leblanc, strapped into the back cockpit of the CF-101. He had just picked up the intruding aircraft on his radar scope.

"Bogies! At two o'clock – low!" He glanced up as if to see an acknowledgement from the pilot. "Range twenty-three miles."

"India Two, do you have them?" Ben instinctively looked over at the second aircraft which had pulled away far enough that he couldn't see the pilot's head.

"Roger that leader."

"India Two, hook approach. We'll try for a distraction pass and see if they come about. If not we'll be turning in full AB and conducting Genie launch manoeuvre," Ben instructed, surprised at how calmly he was ordering the use of nuclear weapons.

"Roger leader – hook approach – if no joy, zoom AB for Genie launch." Flight Lieutenant Jeff Talbot was thinking the same thing about his own apparent calmness.

Endless research had shown most men were fine in the period leading up to the use of nuclear weapons as there was seldom time to contemplate the ramifications. After 'pulling the trigger' however, no one could predict which of many ways a man would react.

Meanwhile, blissfully unaware of the drama unfolding in the skies south of them, the downed airmen slumped against the sides of the life rafts riding the swells. They were trying to pass the time with word games, made more interesting by the participation of the Soviets who argued in jest, that the Canadians were clearly cheating.

* * *

The pilot of the lead TU-95 roaring low over the water had just completed a smooth turn to starboard and was now leading his squadron on a slight north easterly heading, away from the Canadian coast. He had been surprised and even a little disappointed at the lack of interceptors which he and his camera armed crew had expected to come chasing after them.

"Radio operator," the squadron leader queried. "Are you picking up anything on the intercept frequencies?"

"Nothing much, sir," the young man sitting before a bank of radio receivers at the very rear of the fuselage replied. "There was some communications in the VHF and UHF channels far to the south, but they were too weak for me to understand. Probably from a ship."

The radio operator had a good command of the english language, a necessary requirement for dealing with international air traffic control. It was also convenient to have someone able to monitor the military UHF frequencies during the regular intercepts by NORAD fighters.

The Russian pilot adjusted his seat to a more comfortable position and throttled the engines back to their most efficient cruising speed. He was still uneasy about the lack of attention his squadron had received but as they settled into the routine of the long flight ahead, he focused instead on his plans for that evening. There was a celebration planned for one of the pilots who was retiring and he...the thought was broken by a persistent nagging that something was wrong. They should have been intercepted by now. Perhaps the other flight had taken all the attention of the Canadian Voodoo's. They would probably be going home with incredible photographs and bragging about them all over the base.

"Good!" the aircraft commander said aloud, causing his co-pilot to look over. He'd just brag back that his group's prowess and skill had prevented them from being intercepted at all! Surely that made HIS squadron the more successful one!

PART III

CONFLICT IN THE NORTH

Looking through the Voodoo's windscreen, Ben imagined for a moment that he could see the squadron of Russian Bears far below him, skimming low over the waves. The sun would be glinting off their bare metal fuselages, marked only with the red star of the Soviet Air Force and large blue identification numbers on the forward fuselage.

You had to hand it to the Russians. They didn't bother much with superfluous markings or paint on their aircraft. Unlike his CF-101, which was adorned with a lightning bolt down the length of the fuselage as well as the new Four Sixteen Squadron logo on the vertical stabilizer ahead of the newer still Canadian flag. He still found the flag a bit hard to get used to, but it certainly left no doubt as to what nationality the aircraft was.

"Bogies dead ahead – five miles," Cam announced. "Looks like they've turned north."

"India Two, pull in tight. I'm going right through the formation."

Ben noted the other Voodoo sliding in closer as he pushed down slightly on the stick and brought the big interceptor down to a thousand feet over the waves. This, he thought, was far from the aircraft's usual element. Moving the throttle forward, he watched the airspeed indicator slowly climb.

"Cam, how's our distance?"

"Four miles, sir. You should see them shortly." Cam's eyes were glued to the radar scope and reaching down with his gloved hand, he flicked the armament selector to 'Special Weapons'.

"Got them! India Two do you have visual?" Ben wanted to make sure both pilots could see the Russians at this rate of closure.

"Affirmative. India Two has visual!"

"I'm taking us through to our right of the lead aircraft. Keep close!" Ben did not want to join the other airmen in the drink and needed the second

Voodoo flying as close as possible to his in order to present a small cross section of metal to squeeze between the Soviet bombers. Nudging the stick slightly he brought the nose of his aircraft slightly to the right until it lined up with the opening between the lead Bear and his wingman on the port side.

The two groups of aircraft were closing at almost eight hundred miles per hour and had come within a mile of each other when the navigator in the clear nose of the lead Bear noticed the incoming fighters and yelled a warning into the intercom. The Canadian radar had been picked up by the Bear's ECM and there had been almost a feeling of relief at the appearance of the interceptors.

Ben watched the oncoming aircraft closely in case the Russian pilot tried to perform an evasive manoeuvre with the big bomber. He needn't have worried though as the Bears maintained their altitude and heading.

The Russian pilot upon seeing the Canadian's intention to pass through his formation held a steady course and prepared for the turbulence which would come from the passing Voodoo's. In the TU-95's nose, the navigator had his camera ready as he tracked the pair of interceptors which seemed headed straight for him.

He quickly snapped a couple of photos as Ben's aircraft tore by only a few feet away, then froze in fear as he caught a flash of white below the Voodoo's fuselage. The previous year he had been to Moscow for a special course on foreign airforce weapons and tactics and recognized the markings on the large rockets hanging below the fighters.

"Commander!" he screamed into the intercom.

"Yaakov, please do not shout into the intercom," the pilot admonished, fighting to hold his aircraft level in the severe wake turbulence from the passing interceptors.

"Sir!" the navigator spoke again, his voice under control, "the Canadian aircraft are carrying live nuclear weapons!"

It took a few moments for this information to register with the pilot. He knew the NORAD interceptors would not normally be armed with nuclear rockets. Something was very wrong.

"Are you sure?!"

"Yes sir," the navigator replied, his brow breaking out in a cold sweat. "I clearly remember studying that rocket during my weapons training. The Genie is distinctive. Only the live ones are painted all white."

Shouting a warning over the radio, the pilot turned the control wheel to starboard, bringing the huge silver aircraft into a sharp turn. The crew of the Bear on his right barely had time to react and turn as well, causing the bomber formation to fragment before the pilots formed up once again on the leader.

"Leader to Flight 2, maintain new course."

In the lead Voodoo, Ben watched intently as the sky suddenly seemed filled with huge silver aircraft heading in all directions.

"Damn!" Ben exclaimed, "Look at that!"

"Looks like we spooked them, sir," Cam responded watching the group of Russian aircraft complete their sudden turn and fly off to the east.

"Must have been your flying skills, sir." They both laughed, more from relief, than Cam's comment.

"India Two, One is climbing to angels five but let's hang around for a few minutes and make sure they don't turn around and come back."

"Roger that One. I was sure glad to see that turn."

"Me too," Ben replied. "Me too."

Five minutes later, the Russian aircraft had all but disappeared from the Voodoo's radar screens and Ben called cancellation of 'Flyswatter', much to Cam's relief. Reaching out, he flicked the 'lock' key over hard, disarming the nuclear weapons sitting only a few feet below his seat. Climbing rapidly, the flight of CF-101 Voodoo's made a long port turn and headed south west back to Chatham. Cam contacted Sunflower and informed them that it appeared the intruders had been off course and after seeing the Voodoo's streaking at them, realized their mistake and headed back to sea.

* * *

Breaking from their standard procedure, the Russian pilot ordered his radio operator to report the incident and the nuclear armed Canadian fighters. Passed along various radio channels, the message finally reached the headquarters of Soviet Naval Aviation where the unauthorized actions of the TU-95 squadron were causing more alarm than the appearance of Canadian nuclear weapons.

An aide delivered the report to the admiral commanding the Northern Fleet area at his winter home just outside Moscow. The admiral immediately picked up the phone and demanded to know what idiot in GRU headquarters had foolishly authorized such a large force of aircraft to operate so close to Canadian territory! Unable to get an immediate answer, he yelled for his aide and ordered his car brought around. Striding quickly down the stairs to where his driver waited, he climbed into the passenger seat. A long association with the admiral had accustomed the driver to the fact that, unlike most of those he had served, this man did not pompously stand or sit waiting to have the car doors opened for him.

"Kremlin!"

The driver noted the admiral's rigid posture and grim expression, and forwent the usual small talk they shared during their drives through the city.

Fortunately the Moscow traffic was light this time of day and the man expertly manoeuvred the Gaz-13 limousine around the narrow streets before picking up speed as they roared across the expanse of Red Square, a privilege reserved only for the elite of the Soviet hierarchy – and their drivers.

Slowing to a stop outside the Kremlin entrance closest to the admiral's office, the driver had barely turned to ask when the car would be needed again, when the admiral threw open the door and without a word, slammed it shut behind him. Yes, the driver surmised while pulling ahead to the parking area reserved for the Soviet Union's military leaders and shutting off the motor, something big was up. Reaching under the dash for a magazine he kept hidden in a small compartment below the steering wheel post, and finding a comfortable position, he awaited the admiral's return.

Admiral Victor Sominski forced himself to walk at a normal pace to the entrance of the historic building. He didn't dare rush – that would show he was in a hurry and there were far too many western spies constantly watching the Kremlin to risk that. Slowing his pace further as he reached the entrance, he tried to appear nonchalant as he saluted the guard holding the door open and exchanged pleasantries. Once inside, he broke into a fast jog as he hurried down the hallway on the left which led to his office. Alerted of his arrival by a phone call from the security guard at the admiral's home, his aides were busily going through reports from the TU-95 Squadrons, trying to determine what operation the aircraft had been part of, and why Northern Fleet had not been notified.

They had been unable to find any written orders pertaining to the squadron's mission, but had come across an unusual request for a submarine sortie from the army. The appeal, labelled Sector 2, alerted the aides that it was highly classified and it had taken half a dozen phone calls before they'd been able to track down the source of the order. Invoking the admiral's name had finally frightened a lower rank into explaining that the mission had initiated with Spetsnaz but had been routed through the airforce. The admiral's aide had commanded the man not to mention the phone call to anyone before hanging up on him abruptly. He had no fear the man would disobey him. In the Soviet Union, keeping one's mouth shut was the primary means of survival.

The admiral burst into the room like a tornado, throwing his uniform jacket on a chair by the door.

"What have you got?" he commanded, knowing his aides would have managed to find out something in the short time since departing his home. They were good people and exceptionally talented when it came to ferreting out information – an invaluable talent in any military organization and doubly so within the Soviet military hierarchy.

"Nothing on the squadron orders," the older and more senior of the aides responded. "However, we have found a Sector 2 request for *K-32* to assist a Spetsnaz operation."

"*K-32*? I approved no such order!" The admiral's voice reverberated around the room.

"It came through the airforce, sir."

"The airforce!?" The voice was considerably more powerful this time.

"Yes, sir," one of the younger aides responded in a meek voice. "I am awaiting a call from Spetsnaz Group Four as to where their men went."

"Are you telling me," the admiral's face turned scarlet, "that one of MY submarines is on an operation ordered by the airforce that did not clear through this office!?"

Sominski was furious. Buried within the heat of his anger was a fear of what kind of danger the submarine's crew was involved in. Underlying that fear further still was the nagging question of whether the unauthorized mission would bring his highly successful career to an abrupt end.

"It appears so, sir," the senior aide responded. The admiral was startled for a moment, thinking the man had read his mind. Recognizing the look on his admirals face, the aide broke into a conspiratorial smile and continued. "It is not a concern however. *K-32's* captain accepted the orders without receipt and therefore is in violation of standing doctrine." He knew this would set the admiral's mind at ease.

"Good work, comrades! When the call comes in from Group Four, I will take it in my office." Damn airforce, he growled to himself. What the hell did they think they were doing? He headed for his private inner office and then stopped, turning towards the aides.

"Where is *K-32* right now?"

"His orders are to wait off the Labrador coast – that's on the east coast of northern Canada - until a pre-designated time. I would suspect they are going to rendezvous with a team from Group Four, sir."

"Fine! Let their orders stand! Anything from the Western forces in regards to the TU-95 excursion?"

"Nothing at all, sir," replied the younger man this time. "I have checked and they have lowered all alert levels. Air Defence reports that an earlier alert by the American B-52 bombers appears to be concluded and the aircraft have returned to their bases. Only the usual number of bombers are currently patrolling their Fail Safe points"

"Damn! I need to find out what is going on!" The admiral continued into his office and slammed the door shut behind him. The aides looked at one another and relaxed. Both were relieved that nothing could be blamed on them. Never the less, they pitied whoever was responsible and what would happen when the admiral was through with them.

Sominski's wrath was legendary, and more than a few high ranking officers had paid a heavy price for daring to cross him. The admiral was slowly tearing out the 'old boy's club' from the navy and turning the Soviet blue water fleet into a force which would make the Motherland proud. His goal was made all the more difficult by the many roadblocks politically motivated officers under him seemed intent on placing in his path.

The admiral knew the American navy was recovering quickly from its own post-war cut backs and would soon once again be spreading out over the world's oceans in huge numbers. The focus of this growth was currently the dreaded American nuclear submarine fleet which seemed to be growing at an alarming rate. Recent KGB intelligence had also uncovered US Navy plans for more nuclear powered aircraft carriers. The Soviet Union could not possibly hope to keep up with the massive industrial might of America, nor did he think they should try. On the other hand, they could not afford to fall too far behind either.

* * *

"All quiet, sir."

It had been four hours and the operators monitoring *USS Shark's* acoustic sensors had been unable to detect anything other than a few frisky whales. Earlier, Captain Dan Hetherington had ordered all stop, and let the boat drift aimlessly two hundred feet below the surface. The stress on the crew during the extended quiet routine was starting to show and after three hours, the captain had sent off duty personnel to their bunks rather than risk a distracted sailor making a noise.

Crammed into the tight confines of the torpedo room, the SEALs were growing increasingly restless and claustrophobic, more from inactivity than anything else. The commandos kept gazing at their weapons. Normally, they would be dismantling, cleaning and reassembling them during this time, but the captain had ordered that stopped – not wanting to risk someone dropping a gun barrel onto the deck.

Dan was convinced they had not been detected by the Canadian patrol planes flying overhead and expecting that they were searching for him, had ordered the boat deeper. *Shark's* captain was also unaware of the search and rescue operation for the downed Argus crew and the presence of *HMCS Margaree* steaming close by on her way to pick them up.

"Helm, make turns for five knots. Maintain this course."

"Make turns for five knots – maintaining course, aye sir." Relief flooded the control room as the submarine began to move. The crew had previously shut down all unnecessary equipment striving for silence and now they were bringing the boat back to life.

Shark slowly picked up speed and slithered silently through the depths. The SEAL's mission schedule had been thrown off but Dan was hoping they could make up some of the lost time with a speed dash to the insertion point, arriving after darkness fell over the area. There would be an increased risk of detection with the increased speed, but he needed to land the SEALs before the Russians had evacuated.

There had still been no information from Norfolk as to what the Russian mission might be but the SEALs seemed unconcerned with that detail. Their orders were very clear. Take the Soviets out – period! No prisoners were to be brought back aboard the submarine.

* * *

Deep below the city of Ottawa, raucous cheers broke out in the shelter's control room. Officers and enlisted men alike slapped each other on the back as the large screens showed the Soviet aircraft, now positively identified as TU-95 Bears, turning away from the Canadian coast.

The Prime Minister looked up at the screen and wondered silently if anyone would ever know how close they had come to using nuclear weapons. It was hard to say how the Soviets would have reacted to their aircraft being taken down by atomic warheads, but now this event would join many others; never to be spoken of again.

The RCAF commander was beside himself over the job performed by his interceptor pilots, especially considering the difficulties with the Pinetree sites.

"Prime Minister, I think we can all head back 'upstairs' now," the Minister of Defence announced. Now that the mission of the Soviet commandos in Labrador was known, he didn't think there would be any serious repercussions from the Communists should there be casualties among them.

"You're right Ted," the man smiled in return, then paused a moment before continuing. "But I think I prefer to stay here until all our men are safe."

He was thinking of the Rangers about to take on the Spetsnaz commandos. Nothing further had been heard from them in the past hour and he could only guess at what they were going through. All of the commotion with the unidentified aircraft and the possible use of nuclear weapons, had momentarily distracted everyone from the situation on the ground in Labrador. He knew the odds were not great for the Canadians facing the Soviet troops and he felt he should be in the command center in case things went badly and reinforcements had to be called in.

The Prime Minister desperately wanted this mission handled with as little fanfare as possible, but if the Rangers failed, he knew he would have to send in a much larger force and that would be all over the news. The soldier turned politician wondered what was going through that army sergeant's mind right now. He knew the worse part of any battle were the long minutes leading up to it.

* * *

Sergeant Ashe took one more look at the men around him before the onslaught began. He and the Rangers had managed to crawl within a few hundred feet of the Russian camp and he knew there was little likelihood they would get much further without being spotted. Fortunately, it seemed, the Russians were so engrossed in packing up their equipment, they had lowered their guard.

Brian decided the best approach would be for his group to lay down a solid barrage of fire on the Russian camp and hope the intruders would mistake them for a much larger force and decide to surrender. He didn't have a lot of faith in that last part of the plan, but there was no other alternative and a full frontal assault would quickly show the Soviets how small his force really was.

He glanced up to where he could just make out Church on the higher ground to his right. The Ranger was nestled into a rock crevice and was barely visible and from that position he would have a commanding field of fire over the Russian encampment. Hopefully Church had internalized Brian's instructions to aim carefully at the soldier who appeared to be the leader and take him down first.

Ashe brought up his FN and took careful aim at the only commando currently in his line of sight. The Rangers had orders to fire on his first shot. Carefully wrapping his finger around the trigger, he squeezed and felt a solid kick against his shoulder as the hammer struck the shell's primer and a 7.62mm round exploded down the barrel of the rifle. The soldier in his sites spun around as the full metal jacket slug caught his right shoulder, partially shattering his collar bone and sending him flailing to the ground.

The man was badly wounded, but still alive and the Russian's training immediately kicked in. Ignoring the intense pain, the Spetsnaz flicked the safety lever on his AK-47 while trying to bring the assault rifle up to bear in the direction the round had come from before squeezing off a long burst.

Two more bullets ricocheted off the rock he was using for cover and the man had just started to swing his rifle in the direction they had come from when a single .303 bullet caught him squarely in the forehead, dropping him to the ground.

Grandfather did not pause to consider his shot, which had found its mark cleanly, and smoothly cycled the Lee Enfield's bolt, bringing the rifle back to his shoulder, firing, and placing a well aimed shot on one of the tent supports, causing it to collapse. From the moving bulge that appeared in the canvas he knew that at least one man was trapped inside, struggling to escape the folds of heavy canvas.

Seeing what had happened with the tent, Church placed a round right into the middle of the bulge. The 'bump' continued to move slowly a moment longer before collapsing and laying still.

More rounds fired from the Canadian positions ricocheted off rocks, electronic equipment which had been brought outside to be packed up, and parts of the now fully collapsed tent. Two of the Russians had managed to crawl behind a nearby rock outcropping and were now pinned down by the accurate barrage thrown at them by the Canadians.

Carefully rising to return fire, one of the commandos' head exploded as two bullets simultaneously tore into it. His body fell back on top of another commando who in a moment of panic ran to the left only to be hit by well aimed rounds, dropping him dead in his tracks.

Crouching behind a rock alongside the dismantled antennae, Senior Lieutenant Kristoff Nikolev was shouting commands to his men, although his words were continually drowned out in the constant crash of bullets against the now mangled equipment. The delicate electronics they had so carefully brought up from the submarine, popped and exploded as they were shredded by the fusillade of fire which seemed to be coming from all directions at once.

"You must go around to their right flank!" Kristoff shouted to the man behind the rock next to him during a break in the firing. He had heard no further response from anyone else and had to assume the rest were either dead or badly injured. This unit attacking them must be a trained sniper force, he thought. There was little automatic weapons fire which would have been expected from regular soldiers.

"You will cover me?" It was a question from a man who in spite of his exceptional training, was facing death for the first time.

"I will. Now go, Nikolai! And do not drop your rifle!" Kristoff momentarily forced a grin, bringing a look of relief to the younger man's face.

Nikolai scurried quickly around the rocks and managed to half crawl and roll to another smaller pile of boulders which offered him limited cover.

He paused there for a moment catching his breath, hearing the distinctive sound of Kristoff's AK-47 firing at the enemy. He briefly wondered again who was shooting at them but there was no time for that right now. Regaining his breath, he crawled further along the ground, keeping the rocks between himself and where he surmised the attackers to be. Looking ahead, slightly to the left, he noted an especially large, flat boulder where he would be able to get a good shot at the men firing at them.

Dashing in a low crouch, he jumped for cover behind a rock sitting on a patch of open ground, halfway to the flat boulder. Dropping to one knee, again keeping the rock between himself and the direction of fire, he paused for a moment before moving on. In a brief moment of silence, he heard the sound of a rifle bolt being worked only a few feet away.

"That's about far enough, comrade," hissed Ranger Ted Brown, leaning over the rock and poking the barrel of his Lee Enfield under Nikolai's nose.

Nikolai saw the determined look in the other man's eyes and knew if he made one wrong move his life would be over. Carefully stooping down, he lay his AK-47 on the ground, placing it as he had been trained, in a way that would allow him to grab it quickly by the pistol grip should the opportunity present itself..

That wasn't going to happen however as a second man appeared and quickly picked up the rifle, examining it with the delight of a child. For the first time, Nikolai noticed that these men were not wearing regular uniforms. They were dressed in simple, ragged civilian clothing which went along with their unkempt appearance. One of them looked to be very old and their rifles were of the kind his father had used in the Great Patriotic War.

"This way," the old man commanded while carefully slinging the AK-47 over his shoulder and pointing. Nikolai understood english well, as many of the Spetsnaz commandos did and simply shrugged before moving off in the direction indicated.

Fifty yards away, still ducking stray rounds which were now landing too close by, Kristoff realized he was in a very dangerous position. He was fully aware of how this was going to play out since no fire from the direction Nikolai had gone meant that he too was either dead or captured. With only two magazines remaining in his ammo bandolier, Kristoff would soon be joining him.

Senior Lieutenant Nikolev had switched his rifle to semi-auto in order to conserve ammunition, knowing that his attackers would note the change and realize what it meant. The massive barrage of fire from the soldiers beyond the rocks had died down and he could tell now that there were fewer of them than he had first thought. Not that it mattered now. A vision of his mother and the troubled expression on her face the last time he had seen her came to mind. The image was interrupted by the security devices, on the other side of the rock he was using for cover, exploding, as a stray bullet found the trip wire which had been set up to protect them from intruders. With that went any chance of the commando's escape.

"No mother, this is NOT the day your son will die," he said aloud in Russian. Throwing his AK-47 over the rock, he waited until the firing stopped fully before yelling 'Surrender' as clearly as he could in english.

Slumping down, he waited. What seemed like an eternity went by before he heard noises beyond the rock and finally the clink of a magazine being slid into a rifle followed by a hoarse shout.

"Stand up! Facing the water!"

The man was smart Kristoff realized. He knew they would shoot him dead if he tried to turn quickly. He stretched out one leg and stood slowly, feeling naked.

"Turn around," the voice commanded. "Very slowly."

It didn't sound like an angry voice, he thought. Almost soft. Kristoff slowly turned, facing his enemy for the first time.

"Who are you?" Brian asked, not really expecting an answer from the rugged looking warrior standing in front of him. He was momentarily surprised by the man's red hair; uncommon in Russians.

"I am Senior Lieutenant Kristoff Nikolev of the Soviet Army…and I am your prisoner."

The man holding the weapon on him appeared young, Kristoff noted. He wore a look of stern determination on his face however and he carried himself well. The three stripes on his sleeves marked him as a sergeant in the Canadian army. The other men were not wearing uniforms of any kind. Perhaps they were a special Canadian commando group he had not been informed about.

"You are that!" Sergeant Ashe responded. "Over here," he motioned with the FN.

With two Rangers covering Kristoff, Brian carefully searched the man. Removing the pistol belt the Russian wore, he handed it over to one of the Rangers. Finding no other weapons, Brian stood back and saluted the Soviet officer.

"Sergeant Brian Ashe. Canadian army. You will follow these men to our encampment and be warned," he added firmly. "If you try to escape, you will be shot."

Returning the proffered salute, Kristoff nodded and followed the two men. He was surprised at the sorry state of their clothing and was shocked to see what they were carrying for weapons. Was Canada so poor they were arming their soldiers with ancient rifles and making them wear rags or were they some new unit of the Canadian army? Certainly their marksmanship was beyond that of an ordinary soldier. This would be valuable intelligence to bring back to the Motherland when he managed to escape. It had never occurred to him that he might not make it back to Russia.

A commotion to his right caught his attention and he looked over to see Nikolai being led in his direction by another pair of men in similarly tattered clothing. The young Spetsnaz was not being very cooperative and his captors were shoving him along as best they could. The look on his face when he saw that Kristoff had also been captured however, turned from insolence to resignation.

"I tried comrade. I…"

"I know you did Nikolai," Kristoff consoled the soldier in Russian. "We did the best we could."

"Please speak english, gentleman," Brian ordered. "Or keep quiet!"

He did not want the two captives conspiring to escape. Especially now that they knew the composition of the force which had captured them. He had noted the look of disbelief on the Soviet officer's face earlier and he had no doubt in his mind that the two Spetsnaz saw the probability of escape to be in their favour.

Sergeant Ashe knew he had to get word back to the encampment where a report could be sent to Goose Bay that they had secured the intruder's base and taken a pair of prisoners. Taking Horton aside, he ordered the Ranger to get back to camp as fast as he could and get a radio message out updating their situation. Brian didn't relish losing one of his men, but he knew it was crucial that word make it back to Ottawa as soon as possible that the threat had been dealt with.

Before leaving the area, the Rangers carried the bodies of the two dead Russians to the collapsed tent to join the other dead commando who was still covered by the canvas where he had fallen. Ranger Jimmy Karnes carefully covered them with a layer of the heavy material, before placing a half dozen heavy rocks upon it to keep any wild animals at bay. There was no time to carry the bodies with them and the ground was far too hard to allow for a burial. Besides, he thought as he put the last rock in place, the unfamiliar tent material would keep a wolf at bay much longer than a simple mound of dirt. When he had completed the task, all of them had stood sombrely while one of the Rangers gave a short prayer.

"I'm sorry we cannot do better for your men, sir," Brian explained to Kristoff.

Nikolev gave a simple shrug. It was more than he would have done in the sergeant's place.

"Okay, let's get going," Ashe ordered. "I want to reach camp before dark."

The sergeant formed the men into a line with the two prisoners each followed by a pair of Rangers and began the journey back the way they had come. Brian took the point and the odd assemblage moved gingerly across the rugged terrain. He noticed that the men spoke very little. As he walked at the head of the column, Ashe felt the adrenalin leave his body and the full realization of what had just taken place hit him hard. He experienced a brief wave of nausea which washed over him and just as quickly left. Concerned for his men, he signalled the group to stop and rest for a few minutes.

Glancing back at the rag tag parade coming to a halt behind him, he wondered how the Rangers were handling their first brush with combat and the killing of the three Russians. Brian examined their faces one by one but saw no sign of strain beyond what he would have expected to see from men marching over a rugged landscape.

Seeing the sergeant studying him, Grandfather adjusted his hold on the AK-47 he had liberated from one of the Russians and spoke. "We did a good job here today."

"Yes Grandfather," Brian answered smiling. "We did good."

The Rangers would be fine.

* * *

"It will be dark in three hours, lieutenant," Captain Dan Hetherington announced to the man standing in front of him. "We'll be kicking you and your boys off then."

"Thank you, sir," Hansen replied. The SEALs had run a final check over their equipment and then cross checked – each going over a team mate's weapon in case through familiarity, the first man missed something.

"With the tides where they're at, we'll be able to bring you in pretty close," Dan smiled. "Won't be too far a swim for you guys."

"Thanks, captain," the SEAL lieutenant grinned. "We were kind of looking forward to a nice long swim. I hear the water's pretty warm up here this time of year."

Dan laughed at the bad joke. "I'll see you before you egress. Carry on."

The SEALs were anxious to escape the confines of *Shark's* torpedo room and get to work. They had been stuck inside the sub far longer than normal and even though they were carrying a small load out, there was little room amongst the torpedoes and machinery surrounding them to allow for much in the way of exercise.

The men were contemplating the upcoming mission in different ways. Most of them had been on special ops before and were familiar with the tensions that built up in their body over the coming unknown. Those on their first op – there were two in this group – sat and stared vacantly into space. Their minds running over endless scenarios from the plans they had gone over so carefully.

The mission was simple, the lieutenant had explained; land, scale a medium cliff, locate and eliminate the enemy, return to the sub. There were no 'house-cleaning' orders – directions on how to dispose of bodies and equipment - attached to the mission profile, so it would be relatively quick. It was assumed the 'enemy' were Spetsnaz and therefore well trained and motivated. One of the 'veteran' SEALs had earlier commented that it was a good thing they were here. The Canadian army would have never been able to handle the tough Russian commandos on their own.

Petty Officer Tanner, a student of military history had tried to explain that the average Canadian soldier was in fact very well trained and how during the two World Wars and Korea they had fought hard and had earned the respect of their allies.

"Sure man," Ensign Donaldson had laughed. "Like super soldiers you mean, EH?" He had added the emphasis to the 'eh' as a jab at the young man.

* * *

Two hundred and twenty miles north of *USS Shark's* position, *K-32* rested silently on the ocean bottom. The water was relatively shallow at this point and the boat's captain had ordered the submarine submerged slowly until it had settled into the soft silt. Glaciers over the centuries had scraped the ocean floor in this area clean, leaving the bottom relatively flat and covered with a fine sand.

The submarine's captain, Gregory Cherenkov, casually leaned against the periscope mount. He patterned himself after his heroes from the Great Patriotic War. Men who had taken on the German navy in a small number of old submarines and had still given a good account of themselves. His uniform did indeed look like something from decades earlier. Gregory claimed it brought him luck, although inside, he knew luck had little to do with a submariner's success – or failure.

As the boat struck the bottom, it rolled slowly until finally settling at an eight degree list to port with no apparent damage to his hull. He had ordered the crew through various drills to keep their minds sharp during the wait and there had been the usual grumbling from some of the submariners over how they were being used as a taxi service by the self important army commandos. He had quickly identified the malcontents amongst his crew and had his political officer deal with them. One crewman in particular, who had been especially antagonistic to the officers, had been made an example of and ordered confined to his bunk area for two days with only bread and water for rations. Gregory had quickly learned that some of the crew were sneaking food to the man, but had overlooked the indiscretions.

Glancing around the control area, he could see written on the crew's faces that they realized it was coming close to the time when they would again approach the Canadian coast.

During the two week transit from the submarine base at Murmansk, the commandos had not divulged anything to the captain about their mission and the equipment they had brought aboard remained sealed and closely guarded; one of the commandos always sitting over it with an AK-47 resting upon his knees. Gregory had been tempted more than once to explain to the soldier on guard exactly what would happen if he should fire his rifle and the bullet hit the pressure hull while they were submerged. Something told him however, that the man would prefer that outcome over allowing someone to examine the contents of the crates.

After the recent confrontation with the Canadian destroyer, the Soviet captain was not about to risk causing any more damage to his submarine. Luckily for him and his crew, the *Victor Lewinsky* had been close by and able to take him under tow. Reaching a thick fog bank, a rarity this far north, the large ocean going trawler had stopped and brought the crippled *K-32* alongside.

Under the concealment of the fog, the true nature of the 'trawler' was disclosed. The sides of a large boxlike structure on her deck folded down to reveal a heavy lift crane. Huge spotlights, cleverly hidden by various pieces of the ship's gear, slid out on extended rails to bath the submarine in bright light.

While making sure the lines fastened to the submarine were made fast, *K-32's* captain had looked up as a sudden noise emanated from the ship's stern. Moments later, a motor launch appeared from a hidden well in the hull of the 'fishing trawler' and sputtered quickly over to the submarine. He was able to make out divers standing on the small boat's deck preparing to go over the side.

Communicating with the 'trawler's' captain through a telephone line which had been rigged along the tow cable, Gregory had learned that the ship was carrying replacement propellers and his divers would attempt to replace the damaged one, allowing *K-32* to continue his mission.

Lewinsky's captain, looking down at the small black vessel alongside, had not known the true mission of the submarine tied to his ship, nor would he have asked. It was his mission to sail this quadrant of the ocean waiting to rush to the aid of any Soviet submarine in distress, and not to ask questions of its crew.

Surely the submariners led a glamorous life compared to his own crew, but since one or more of the deadly craft failed to make it back to base every year, he preferred to serve on ships that stayed ON the water. A crackle on the radio had taken him away from his reverie.

"Repeat that?" he'd asked.

"The shaft is fine and we have almost finished installing the new screw." The civilian engineer standing on the deck of the submarine had given him a wave as he made the announcement, obviously pleased with himself and his work party.

"Good work, comrade. Let me know when you are finished." The captain of *Lewinsky* had turned away and given orders that fresh food be transferred to the submarine. He had already determined that the newest of the Soviet Union's nuclear warships did not require torpedoes as he was already fully armed. The ship's captain had been surprised to learn that they were carrying one of the navy's new 'nuclear fish' as the submarine's commander had called it.

"Yes," the 'trawler' captain had spoken out loud to himself. "The sooner we get rid of this customer, the better."

Two hours later, the fog had gently lifted to show a Russian fishing trawler slowly dragging a net behind in its wake. The rusty ship looked like any one of the hundreds of large, sea going trawlers that plied the Atlantic waters and on her deck, men dressed in the same fishing gear worn for a hundred years appeared hard at work while the captain stood on a bridge wing yelling down at them.

One hundred and fifty feet below, *K-32* had been moving slowly through the water with the crew testing the newly installed propeller. The sonar crew meanwhile, listened diligently for any sign of noise or vibration from the repairs. No unusual sounds had emanated from the new propeller and Captain Second Rank Cherenkov was soon able to order his submarine brought to where it now sat motionless, quietly awaiting the time to retrieve the Spetsnaz team.

"Captain, it is almost time," a junior lieutenant whispered to him, interrupting his thoughts.

"Thank you Micah. We will go pick up our guests now." He smiled wryly as he added, "Let us hope their mission was more routine than ours."

* * *

Approximately one hundred miles to the south of *K-32's* position, *HMCS Margaree* was just coming upon the location given by a Royal Canadian Air Force Dakota circling slowly above the downed airmen. The aviators were weakened from sitting in the rafts for so many hours and their earlier high morale had given way to exhaustion and frustration at how long it was taking anyone to come for them.

The air temperature had dropped as the day wore on and the sun started to settle lower in the western sky. Worse, a sharp breeze had picked up and was continually spraying sheets of fine spray over the rafts, keeping the men soaked. At one point an argument had broken out when one of the airmen spilled his water ration and a few of the others had demanded that he be refused another one.

"Look guys. Someone will get here before nightfall," Cormier had yelled, bringing the argument to an end. He prayed that his prediction was correct. It was becoming hard to stay conscious as his body, wracked with exhaustion, became more cramped from the cold and lack of movement. The radar operator was also finding it difficult to move his legs without a sharp pain shooting through them.

Based on the survival training he'd taken, Pudgy was trying to figure out how much longer it would be before the weaker men in the rafts would start passing out. One of the Soviets looked especially exhausted and Cormier could see that he would not last the night without aid. The earlier enthusiasm amongst the men at spotting the aircraft circling above, had waned as hours passed and no ship appeared over the horizon to pick them up. The crew in the circling Dakota had been working hard to encourage the survivors over the small emergency radio which had been dropped to the rafts, but the batteries had long since died and another one would not be dropped to them until just before dark if they were still in the water by then.

Looking up at the aircraft, almost willing it to land on the water to pick them up, Cormier noticed the pilot was wagging the transport's wings violently. He thought something must have gone wrong with the plane when it suddenly descended and appeared to lose control, heading straight for the rafts. Shoving the man next to him, Pudgy shouted a warning to the others in the raft as it looked as if they might have to jump into the water as the aircraft descended lower and continued to fly straight at them.

"What the hell is he doing!?" yelled the Argus's navigator, preparing to dive into the ocean as the Dakota roared over them. It never dawned on any of them that they themselves routinely flew at the same altitude. Turning

147

to watch the aircraft fly on, Pudgy watched as the pilot again wagged his wings.

"Asshole must be… SHIT! Look!" He had nearly jumped up, which would have dumped them all into the water but at that moment his legs would not move. Pointing and shouting, he yelled at the top of his lungs as he finally saw what the Dakota pilot had been trying to bring to their attention. *HMCS Margaree* was just visible on the horizon, throwing up a bow wave so huge the spray obscured her most of the time as she crashed through the waves toward them.

A cheer went up from the airmen as they yelled and slapped each other on the back. Those with the energy hugged the man next to him and laughed loudly – their eyes filled with tears of relief at the knowledge that they would soon be rescued.

On *Margaree's* bridge, a cheer had also gone up at the first sighting of the men by one of the ship's radar technicians. The petty officer had risked life and limb to climb nearly to the top of the ship's mast where he had tied himself to the steel supports to keep from falling while searching the sea for any sign of the survivors.

"All hands! Prepare to bring wounded aboard. Boat crew stand by for launch!" Barry replaced the microphone and ordered the ship slowed to ten knots as they approached the rafts.

"Keep a tight grip on that wheel, petty officer," he commanded. "We need to bring them into our lee and I don't want to come closer than two hundred feet from them."

"Ay sir," the petty officer replied. Then almost smiling, he added, "they won't even know we're here, sir."

Barry chuckled silently at the remark from the usually stoic sailor.

In the rafts, the men were shifting between hysterical laughter and tears, exhaustion giving free reign to their emotions. At one point the aircraft commander had to warn them to calm down as it would still be an hour or so before they were brought aboard the destroyer and they'd need their energy to climb the ship's ladder. He knew the destroyer crew would launch a boat to pick them up and they'd be hoisted to the deck in the craft, but he was afraid that if his men didn't calm down, someone would fall into the water. There was little doubt in his mind that none of them had enough energy left to haul anyone back in.

Margaree's boat crew unfastened the tie downs and prepared to lower the large motor launch into the water the moment the destroyer slowed enough.

Pudgy watched as the ship, which to him had grown incredibly huge, slowed and pulled slightly away, coming around to place them on the lee side where they bobbed slightly on the relatively calm water. The launch had barely hit the water when another cheer went up from the airmen. To Cormier it appeared as though the entire ship's company must be leaning over the rails watching the rescue operation. Orders to various parts of the ship wafted clearly over the water to them from the address system.

"Which raft has the most seriously wounded?" shouted a rating from *Margaree's* boat.

"We're all fine!" replied the aircraft commander. "Frostbitten and tired, but fine!"

Again a cheer went up from the men and the sailor, seeing no obvious priorities, directed the other two men in the launch to start bringing the airmen in the closest raft aboard. One of the sailors started for a moment upon recognizing the insignia on the Russian pilot's uniform, but quickly recovered and gently brought the man into the boat.

"Spahseebah…thank…you," the Russian managed through chattering teeth.

"You're welcome, Ivan," smiled the rating, who couldn't help but laugh when the Russian tried to explained that his name was not Ivan.

In less than fifteen minutes, the sailors had transferred all the men from the first raft onto the launch. Promising the remaining survivors that they would return as quickly as possible, the sailor manning the wheel spun it over hard and sped back to the destroyer, where the launch was quickly hoisted aboard and the airmen carefully moved onto the ship. Once safely on deck, they were immediately bundled up in thick blankets and brought into the mess area which had been converted into a makeshift hospital. After a brief examination, they were all fed a bowl of lukewarm soup as directed by the ship's medical officer. A couple of medics chatted with the survivors while watching for signs that any of the men might be having difficulties or suffering from shock.

Returning quickly to the second raft, the boat crew brought the freezing men aboard the launch. The aircraft commander was the last to leave the raft. Looking back at it from the relative comfort of the motor launch, he marvelled at how such a small craft had held so many men for such a long period of time.

"Thanks guys," he spoke in a hoarse whisper turning to the man who had helped him into the launch. His strength was all but gone.

"Don't mention it, sir. You're almost navy to us," joked one of the boat's crew, patting the man's shoulder while indicating where he should sit. In moments, the launch was again approaching the lines hanging from the boat davits. Quickly making the launch fast, a sailor gave a thumbs up to the operator above and caught his breath as the boat was hauled up level with the ship's deck. Hands reached out to the airmen to help them aboard as waiting sailors quickly bundled the survivors into warm blankets and brought them inside to be examined.

Commander Delaney, noting the rank insignia on the aircraft commander's uniform followed behind and sat alongside as the medical officer examined the man.

"You're fine sir," announced the ship's medical officer, "but I'd avoid swims in the ocean for a few days."

"Thank you," the pilot managed a weak smile. "I'll take that advice, doc."

"Good to see you're okay, captain," Barry said holding out his hand. "Commander Barry Delaney. Welcome aboard *HMCS Margaree.*"

"It's really good to be here sir," the airman answered. "The moment I stop shivering, I'll salute."

"No need. You can owe me one," Barry laughed.

"I'm sure glad you guys…" The address system cut him off.

"Captain to CCR immediately!" There was no need to add the 'immediately'. Commander Delany could hear the anxiety in the mans voice, even distorted as it was by the tinny sounding address system.

"I'll catch up with you later," Barry yelled as he turned and hurriedly rushed out. Moving quickly down the passageway and ducking through the dark curtains to CCR, he saw the sonar operator waving him over with one hand and holding his headphones in place with the other.

"Submerged contact, sir. Real close!" O'Hanlon whispered loudly as though fearful the submarine crew might hear him.

"Do you pull these things out of your butt every time you go on watch O'Hanlon?" Barry asked, frowning in jest at the man.

"I try not to, sir. I'd swear it's the same Russian we ran into before."

"Can't be, son. He should still be under tow to Murmansk," Barry replied. A strange feeling deep inside however suggested that might not necessarily be true.

"I know, sir. But if it's not, it's that boat's twin sister."

Brent listened again for a few seconds before adding, "He's really close. I picked him up the moment we slowed to pick up the survivors."

"How clo…" A quick hand signal from O'Hanlon cut him off.

"Shit! I've got another one! Bearing two three seven – three thousand yards!" O'Hanlon was staring into the scope, oblivious of his commanding officer hanging over his shoulder.

"The Russian's at zero seven zero, no more than a thousand yards. We're almost right in between them."

"Any sign they know we're here?" Barry asked quietly.

"They must. We came crashing in at twenty-five knots, but they're both ignoring us, sir." He paused a moment. "They're on a collision course with each other and – Active sonar!! American! He's got Ivan! Russian's gone active as well!"

Barry straightened up quickly. This was definitely not a good place for his ship. Seeing Lieutenant Learner moving towards him, he called out.

"Learner! Action stations!" Looking back down at the scope, he patted Brent's back. "Keep on 'em, O'Hanlon!"

Turning quickly, he made his way up the short ladder onto the bridge, locking the blackout curtain open behind him. If things got hot, he wanted to hear any warnings without having to use the intercom.

"Helm, get us moving, this course all ahead!"

"Yes, sir," the sailor on the wheel answered smartly.

"Lieutenant, sonar has two subs, a Russian and an American and we're right in the middle. I want to put some space between us and them in case someone gets a little antsy. O'Hanlon is sure the Russian is the same one we dealt with earlier," he added.

"That's impossible," the officer retorted.

"I know, but maybe they had a service vessel up here or something. O'Hanlon's got good ears."

As if on cue, the speaker above his head came to life.

"Bridge, sonar. Russian contact has turned into the American. They're both pinging like crazy."

Lieutenant Learner reached for the intercom. "Thank you sonar. Keep us informed." He looked back to Barry. "Damn!" was all he could say.

*　*　*

Kristoff walked slowly in front of the old man who kept an AK-47 pointed at his back, at least when he wasn't busily admiring some feature of the compact rifle.

The Rangers, along with their two prisoners, had been marching through the wilderness for almost an hour. It was slow going for the column as the terrain was extremely rough in places and jagged rocks stuck out of the half frozen ground at all angles while sharp branches of vegetation grew from what few patches of earth existed. The Rangers moved slowly while diligently watching over their captives.

Sergeant Ashe still had the point and was checking his map and compass carefully to make sure they were headed in the right direction. The possibility that the group might not make it back to camp before darkness concerned him. He wanted to avoid stopping for the night but admitted to himself that traveling over this terrain in the dark would not be the smart thing to do. Seeing how quickly night was falling, he realized they had little choice.

"Alright men, hold up," he announced, holding up his left arm. "We're going to stop here for the night. Church! You have the first watch. Keep a good lookout and if you think you're getting tired, wake someone to relieve you."

"Will do, sarge," he replied. Glen was impressed with how the skirmish had played out and he gave the two Russians a fierce look of disdain. The older one simply looked away in disgust.

"You Russians don't seem so tough," Church verbally prodded Kristoff, wanting to make sure the man knew who was in charge.

"Perhaps you would like to place your weapon on the ground and find out young man," Kristoff replied calmly, looking Church straight in the eyes.

"I don't think so, man."

"Why do you add 'man' to everything you say?" Kristoff threw back at him. "Yes, I am a man."

Glen moved forward, his Lee Enfield almost touching the commando's chest. With a quick practiced move, Kristoff grabbed the barrel of the old rifle and pointed it off to the side but made no attempt to take it from the Ranger.

"Never point your rifle at someone unless you are going to kill him," he spat out. "Perhaps," the Spetsnaz officer spoke softly, staring hard into Church's eyes, "you need more training on how to properly guard prisoners." Lowering his voice, he added in a threatening tone, "If I wished it, you would already be dead."

Glen backed away a few steps being careful to keep his rifle barrel a good distance from the Russian. Slowly seating himself on a rock, he watched the commando as he too sat down trying to find a comfortable spot. Kristoff looked up at the stars which peppered the clear sky, contemplating the hand that fate had dealt him this day.

Not far away, Brian had watched the exchange closely, his FN ready with the safety off. Seeing that the pissing match between the two men appeared to be over, he found a flat rock and opened the map, examining it with his flashlight in the gathering darkness.

Ted Brown and Grandfather returned from a short search with some brush and a few rare pieces of wood to start a fire. It would give them some warmth as well as enough light to keep an eye on their captives. Sergeant Ashe was amazed that the two Rangers had been able to find anything flammable amongst the rocks.

Grandfather made himself comfortable and began cleaning the AK-47, making sure every part of the assault rifle was spotless before applying a thin coat of oil to it from his kit. Completing the task, he slung the rifle over his shoulder and strolled over to where Kristoff was attempting to keep warm by the now roaring fire.

"Nice rifle." Deniigi patting the barrel over his shoulder.

"It is yours now," Kristoff replied with a genuine smile, again amazed that a man so old would be out in the wilderness with these young men, let alone on a combat mission.

"You think they will let me keep it?"

He saw the look in the aged man's eyes and was reminded of his grandfather. He would travel by horse and sleigh to visit him and his parents during the winter months when work on the state owned farms slowed. At Christmas, his grandfather had always brought him a wooden toy he had carefully carved from a block of wood over the previous months.

Kristoff averted the man's eyes for a moment, wondering once again what he was doing in this foreign land and for the first time in his military career, it bothered him that he didn't really have an answer.

"They should," he answered, looking again at the man who had sat down in front of him. "You are a brave soldier. You captured us and the rifle should be yours."

"Yes, we were brave Rangers today."

The old man appeared to be thinking what to say next before he went on. "But you are brave also," and standing up he walked over to the Russian commando and held out his hand. Kristoff shook it and looked into the man's eyes. In the light of the fire he saw a youthful glow that belied the man's years. He also noticed something else for the first time - pain perhaps.

"Who are you and these men," Kristoff asked, sensing a need to change the subject.

"We are Rangers. We protect Canada. That man," he pointed over to Brian who was intently studying the map, "he is a sergeant of the Canadian army."

"Rangers?" Nikolev was curious now. He had not been informed of these 'Rangers' and although they wore no uniform and the weapons they carried looked like they had been made in another century (not withstanding their deadly accuracy), the men were clearly at home in the wilderness.

He also noted they carried no rations and yet not one of them had commented or complained. His own men he knew, on being told of a surprise encampment without rations, would have protested immediately. His own men... The words haunted him. The thought struck him for the first time that this mission would not end in the usual wild party back in Barracks M. Looking over at Nikolai, the full force of losing so many of his team struck him fully for the first time.

Kristoff rubbed his chin and again looked up at the stars. Where did they go, he wondered. Maybe there really was some place to go after death. Maybe his men were there now. Maybe you are getting too old for this Nikolev, he thought with a cynical smile. If he ever returned to Russia, he'd go home and take care of his mother like a good son should. They had enough land to farm and in a few years the government would give him some animals so he could...

"Nice watch," Grandfather noted, ignoring the commando's question.

Kristoff looked up at the old man who he saw was staring at his father's watch.

"Yes. It was my fathers."

"Can I see it?"

This old man was like a crow, thought the Russian as he removed the watch and handed it over to Grandfather. He had caught on that these Rangers called him Grandfather. He wondered if it was possible that he was related to all of them.

"Nice. Your father gave you a nice gift."

"He didn't give it to me."

Deniigi studied him. For a moment he considered that perhaps this Russian had stolen the watch from his father, but recognizing the look of sadness in the younger man's eyes, he realized the truth.

"Your father is dead?"

"Yes, Grandfather," Kristoff replied. "My father is dead."

Making himself as comfortable as possible, Nikolev relaxed and shared the story of his father with the old Ranger. As the fire warmed their faces he told of how heroic the young navy officer had been and how he had saved so many of his own men, only to die himself on the sinking destroyer. He told of the hated German U-boats and how one of them had hunted his father's ship down that night.

Grandfather's expression changed and his face took on a cold, hard look as he listened. Kristoff paused, thinking perhaps he had said something to offend the old man.

"I am sorry," the Ranger said, seeing the concerned look on the commando's face. "Go on with your story."

He did not really hear the rest, however. His mind again drifted to that day so many years ago when he had returned to his small house to find his wife. These men who work in submarines, he thought. They are cruel men with no hearts.

* * *

"Active sonar! Four thousand yards! Russian!"

"General quarters! Helm, bring us right to zero five zero degrees! Sonar what's their depth?" Captain Dan Hetherington realised at this range the other boat had to have been in his baffles for them to miss him.

"No depth at this time, sir," reported the sonar operator.

"Flood tubes five and six!" The sound would hopefully be heard aboard the Russian submarine and it would warn them not to come any closer.

Aboard *K-32*, the captain had just given the order to flood his own boat's torpedo tubes. He was gravely concerned that the American submarine was going to interfere with the pick up of the commandos who would already be rowing out to the rendezvous point by now. He could feel the stress growing in the tight confines of the control room and looking down at his weapons officer, he ordered him to open outer doors on tube number two.

"Sir," the weapons officer spoke slowly. "Tube number two contains the…"

"Don't you dare question my orders!!" The shout froze everyone in place.

"Opening outer door on tube number two." There was no hesitation this time.

"Sir! He's opening outer doors!" exclaimed the sonar operator aboard *USS Shark*.

"Open outer doors on tubes five and six!" Dan commanded, hoping the move would make it clear to the Russians that they were not playing around. He had to get the SEAL team off the boat and this Russian happening upon them at this time was a real problem. It had occurred to him that the Soviet submarine may very well be here waiting to pick up the commandos and there was no way he was about to let that happen.

"Sonar," he ordered. "Hit him again! Hard!"

"Yes, sir." The ping reverberated through the hull as the full power sound wave raced from the active sonar transducer through the water, slamming into the Soviet boat. Within seconds the answering echo reached *Shark*.

"Range to target, three five seven zero yards and closing." The sonar operator reported. "He's turned into us, sir."

"Damn!"

The captain of *K-32* was holding tightly onto the periscope mount as the submarine came about and headed directly for the Americans. They would hopefully scare the Western boat away and then he would be free to finish his mission. The thought of using his special torpedo brought a smile to his face but he knew firing it would be an act of suicide. Assuredly, his own boat would be destroyed in the blast. Besides, his government would not want to go to war over a few Spetsnaz.

"Sir!" came a shout from the Russian sonar operator. "Active sonar! New Contact! Bearing two eight zero! Surface ship! He's almost right on top of us!"

"Surface ship?" Captain Cherenkov leaned into the periscope. It had to be an American destroyer. A surface ship would spot the Russian commandos in the bright moonlight. The question of what idiot had planned such an operation during a full moon flew through his mind.

In one of the strange anomalies of sonar, neither submarine had heard *HMCS Margaree* arrive in the area in spite of her high speed. Once the destroyer had stopped to pick up the aviators, neither the Soviet or American sonar operators would have picked her up so close to the coast where the sound of the surf made for a steady background roar, masking almost everything.

The Soviet captain's mind raced but no answers came to him. The cursed American submarine was heading right at him and now this destroyer would harass him as well. Perhaps he would use the special torpedo after all.

"Helm! Come right to zero eight zero! Full speed!" he ordered. He would head away from the coast and draw the destroyer and submarine after him. If he was lucky, he would lose them and then circle back quietly to pick up the commandos. The soldiers would be angry with him for being late but that was too bad for them. He was growing tired of their arrogance.

"Contact has turned and is heading away," *Shark's* sonar operator reported. "Sonar is identified as a Canadian warship – range twenty-eight hundred yards."

"Canadian?" Dan didn't like the sound of that. Surely, he thought, the Canadians didn't know about the Soviet commandos and it was imperative they not learn of the SEALs!

* * *

Fifty-five miles to the west, the two surviving Spetsnaz commandos were trying to sleep on the cold, hard ground, lying against each other for protection against the dropping temperatures. They had watched in disbelief as the Rangers who were not on watch simply leaned against a rock and fell asleep, as though in bed.

"Sir?" Nikolai had asked. "Do they not feel the cold?"

"They do starshina," Kristoff answered. "They just choose to ignore it."

"I wish I could ignore it," the young man commented, trying to make himself comfortable again.

"Yes. I as well."

Kristoff lay looking up at the bright, full moon which was bathing the landscape in an eerie ghoulish glow. These Rangers, he thought, must be a militia of sorts. Now that he had observed them, it did not appear that they possessed much in the way of military training. Grunting, he rolled over on his side and found what was probably the most comfortable spot he would on this night. He imagined what these men could do WITH proper training.

Glancing up at the moon again, he thought about what his mother would say when they came and told her that her son would not be returning home. Guilt filled his mind as he pictured her standing on that same old door step where so many years before, someone had come to her with news about his father. Finally, he fell into a fitful sleep, but his sleep did not bring escape, for in his dreams he saw his mother on her knees crying. Only this time his father was standing over her, comforting her at the loss of her son.

* * *

"Sir?"

"What!...I'm sorry. What is it?" He had fallen asleep at his desk. Embarrassed for a moment, the Prime Minister tried to remember how long it had been since he had slept. It seemed like days now. A couple of hours earlier, word had come in that the Rangers had skirmished with the Russians and were returning with two prisoners.

The news had overwhelmed him with relief. He had ordered the captives whisked to Ottawa the moment the Rangers returned where they would be interrogated by specialists from the RCMP's espionage unit. He had little doubt they would be able to retrieve only basic information from the commandos but that was all he would need before he called the Russian Premier. Then he would be taking an unpublicized flight to Washington where he would lay it on the line to the President that Canada was NOT a play ground to be used by the two superpowers as some other countries had recently become.

You would think they would learn their lesson with the blood bath going on in Vietnam, he thought. The ex-soldier in him knew there was no such thing as a 'good war', but surely anyone could see the folly of that one. Either fish or cut bait, as his MP's from the Maritimes liked to say. The aide who suddenly appeared in front of him looked down sheepishly. The Prime Minister wished it was the one who had been there earlier – the one who had brought hot coffee.

"We have a report from Halifax sir. It seems that *HMCS Margaree* has come across two submarines while picking up the downed air crew." He saw the look on his leaders face and added, "Sorry sir."

"Let me guess. One American and one Russian." It wasn't a question. He knew the answer.

"Err...yes sir. That is right."

"Thank you." The Prime Minister stood. His knees cracked and he made a promise that he would get back to walking downtown again. He loved the Byward Market and 'most' of the people he met there were quite courteous to him.

Walking stiffly over to the desk occupied by the navy officers, he noticed there was now a full contingent of them milling around. Seeing Ted standing with a cup of coffee, he walked over and held his hand out.

"Oh, sorry sir. I thought you could use the rest." He handed over his cup of coffee and watched as the Prime Minister took a long drink, finishing it.

"Not yet, Ted. What have we got?"

"*Margaree* had stopped to pick up the survivors and her sonar operator picked up two submarines. The Russian was almost directly below him and the American sub was a few thousand yards off. *Margaree* didn't detect them earlier because of the speed they were traveling to get to the downed flyers," he explained.

"What does Barry do anyway? Sail around looking for trouble to get into?" The men around him broke into laughter and when it had died down, the admiral went over the current situation pointing to the wall display.

"The Russian boat has broken to the east and Barry is chasing after it. We think it was coming in to pick up the commandos, so he's watching for it to try and slip around in an end run. Delany is aware of the situation and he's going to act as though they lost contact with it and then try to tail them back into Canadian waters where we'll have him dead to rights."

"Planning on sinking the Soviets, admiral?" The Prime Minister was only half kidding with the question.

"Hell no! Sorry sir." He blushed. "We'll go through the standard drill. Drop some grenades and try to force him to surface. There's not much else we can do, sir. After that I would suspect you'll call the Kremlin and give 'em hell! Sorry again, sir."

The Prime Minister laughed again.

"Admiral. You hit the nail right on the head!"

* * *

USS Shark had slowed and with her sonar operator calling out the growing distance between themselves and the racing Canadian destroyer and Russian submarine, Dan began to relax. Now the coast was clear, literally, for him to get the SEALs on their way.

Ordering the boat back to the designated drop off point, he went forward to the torpedo spaces and wished the SEALs luck with their mission. Just a damned weird coincidence that Canadian destroyer being here, he assured them.

The SEALs checked over their equipment one last time and headed for the hatch where they would egress quickly when the submarine surfaced. The commandos would be swimming in, carrying their weapons in waterproof 'socks'. Once they reached the beach, the SEALs would complete their mission quickly and return to this same spot.

"We'll see you in three hours then," Dan confirmed. "Then we'll be here every hour after that for four more hours. After that, you're on your own."

It was SOP. The submarine was far more valuable an asset than the SEALs and if they couldn't make the pick up point by then, they would have to find their own way back. It wouldn't be the first time. Ensign Donaldson had enjoyed a European tour last year, including France and England, after barely escaping with his life from East Germany.

Dan shoved the intercom button on the bulkhead behind him.

"Con, this is the captain. Surface the boat!"

Eleven miles to the east and growing further away by the minute, *K-32* was running at flank speed at a depth of one hundred and fifty feet. That shallow, her propellers were cavitating madly, making an immense noise as bubbles broke behind the fast turning blades of her twin screws. At a greater depth the bubbles would not have formed at all because of the water pressure, but with the submarine being so shallow, they added to the roar in the speeding boat's wake. Her captain knew this and it was part of his plan to keep luring the destroyer and American submarine after him. He had pondered what the two warships were doing there in the first place and surmised they must be part of an exercise that the Kremlin had been unaware of.

It would not matter, he thought. He would continue to lure them further out to sea and then run quietly around them, heading back to the coast. It never occurred to him that both warships might not in fact be chasing after him and with the noise created by his own propellers, he had no way to know for certain.

Aboard *Margaree*, Brent O'Hanlon was trying to visualize what the submarine's captain was thinking. The man had to know that at the depth he was running his props were cavitating like crazy. Ivan wanted them to keep chasing after him and apparently the Canadians were going to accommodate him. The commander had so far held back on sending up the Sea King to hunt down the Russian sub, but Brent figured Commander Delaney must have other plans for the helicopter.

He had lost contact with the American boat shortly after the chase began and had no idea whether the US sub was pursuing along after them or not.

With all the noise generated at this speed and *Margaree's* active sonar pinging like mad, a battleship could sail by them and he would never hear it.

Two hours later, the first rays of dawn were noticeable on the eastern horizon ahead of the ship, when Brent, about to go off watch, noticed a change in the sounds from the submarine. The range to the Soviet boat seemed to suddenly decrease and he was about to notify the bridge of that fact, when the echoes returning from the submarine stopped altogether.

"Bridge, Sonar!" he called into the intercom. "We've lost contact with Ivan!"

Barry was behind him in seconds.

"What was his last location?"

"Right in front of us, about two thousand yards. Then it dropped to about eighteen hundred yards and fell right off the scope, sir."

"Air! Get the Sea King up!"

"Aye, sir!" answered the leading seaman at the aviation console.

On the helicopter deck, the Sea King's rotors had already been unfolded and locked in place. The pre-flight checklist had been completed and Flight Lieutenant Phillip Barkus was casually browsing through one of the service manuals, bringing himself up to date on the latest upgrades to the helicopter's systems.

"Hey Phil!" Sub Lieutenant Kevin Long called out as he sprinted across the deck. "Start 'er up! We're being kicked off!"

"Swell!" Barkus answered, reaching for the power switches. He noticed the rest of the crew pouring out of the hatch leading to their ready room dubbed 'The Palace' due to the furnishings the air crew had brought aboard. Well-padded lounge chairs and their own bar filled the space allocated to the Sea King crew members and maintenance staff.

"They'd been tracking a Ruskie sub a few thousand feet ahead of us and lost her," Kevin explained while strapping in.

"Probably dropped below a thermal layer," Phil yelled back to be heard above the increasing whine from the engines. He called over the intercom, confirming that everyone was strapped in before engaging the rotors. Then looking over to Kevin again, continued. "We'll find him."

The rotors slowly began to turn and as usual, a large number of the ship's crew had turned out to watch the helicopter take off. It was still quite a novelty to them, seeing the large, noisy machine lift into the air and characteristically slide over to one side of the destroyer before dropping its nose and moving away quickly while picking up speed.

A few of them noticed the pair of torpedoes mounted to brackets on the Sea King's sides and wondered if they were going to have a repeat of last month's adventure.

"*Flapjack*, this is *Buttersquare*, we are airborne," announced Barkus swinging the Sea King along the ship's starboard side and heading to the last known position of the submarine.

"Roger that, *Buttersquare*," came the response from the air control officer. "Ship's sonar still has no contact with the submarine."

Barkus looked down and noted the ship swinging away from its course, to stay clear of the area where they would be using the Sea King's dipping sonar to try and locate the Russian sub. In less than three minutes they had reached the point of last contact and Phil brought the helicopter to a hover over the spot while descending to fifty feet above the water's surface.

"Okay guys! She's all yours!"

"Sonar head is dropping," Ted announced as the dipping sonar began to unreel from its well in the bottom of the fuselage. The sonar head struck the water and continued down through the depths. The crewmen at the sonar console carefully watched the depth readout and halted the cable as soon as it reached one hundred feet.

"*Flapjack*, this is *Buttersquare* – going active."

"Roger, you're going active," Brent replied, now in direct communications with the helicopter. He slid the headphones off his ears, still leaving them on his head. He waited for the loud ping which would come from the Sea King's sonar.

The sound waves emanating from the transducer at the end of the dipping sonar pulsed through the water, some of them reflecting off a thermal layer at one hundred and twenty feet. Aboard the Sea King, the sonar operators noted no echo from the pings. Ted reached for the depth control and dropped the head another fifty feet before locking it in place again.

"Sending ping," Ted announced again before hitting the button. This time there was a distinct but weak echo.

"Contact bearing...two five zero degrees..." He let the sentence run off as they were expecting the submarine to be further east when in fact it was now behind them.

"Are you sure?" Phil asked.

"No question, sir. Looks like he's made a U turn."

Phil pushed the radio button on the control leaver in his right hand and called out to the destroyer.

"*Flapjack*, this is *Buttersquare*. Contact is bearing two five zero..."

"Sir, contact is moving west – approximately five knots," Ted cut in, knowing the information was critical.

"Roger that *Buttersquare*. Captain orders you to return to the ship."

"Roger. Returning to ship," Barkus replied. "Well boys," he noted through the intercom, "looks like this was a short hop."

Phillip brought the Sea King back over *Margaree's* stern and engaged the 'Bear Trap', letting it haul the aircraft to the deck before shutting down the engines. Crewmembers quickly secured the folding blades of the helicopter, before guiding it into the hanger.

Hopping down from the aircraft, Barkus scooted up to CCR where he found the flight controller chatting with one of the ship's sonar crew.

"So did you gentlemen feel we couldn't track the sub or what?" It was more of a statement than a question.

"Aww, you know how these sailor boys are, sir," the flight controller joked. "They don't want us getting all the glory!"

"That's it exactly, sir," Brent quipped. "We know how deadly you and that contraption are and I think the cap's afraid if he turns you loose, you'll sink the whole Soviet navy."

"Very funny O'Hanlon." Barkus appreciated the good natured ribbing which flowed between the two branches. It was great for moral. "So, now tell me what's really going on?"

"They think the sub is on its way back to pick up some commandos and they want to catch it red-handed so to speak," Brent replied, smiling at his pun.

"Petty officer, with quick thinking like that, I expect you'll be an admiral some day," Phillip laughed. "Commandos? In Labrador? What are they supposed to be doing? Stealing our permafrost?"

On *Margaree's* bridge, Barry and a few of his officers, were pouring over a large chart of the Canadian coast. They surmised where the submarine was most likely headed and wanted to make sure they moved into the area quietly. The destroyer at any speed above five knots would be easily picked up by the Soviets unless there was a thermal layer between them. Especially if the sub was sitting still, waiting to rendezvous with the soldiers.

"Okay," Lieutenant Learner continued his brief, "sonar reports they have no trace of the American submarine so we can assume it is either still patrolling along the coast ahead of us or has moved on to another patrol zone."

"I don't know," Barry responded. "I have a feeling we'll be running into them again."

"They may have been tracking the Soviet boat and weren't aware that it was heading in to pick up the commandos," Lieutenant Jim Craven offered.

"You may be right Jim, but I don't want to assume anything at this point." Barry knew there was more than a slim chance the Americans were aware of the Russian expedition. They had excellent resources and he would be surprised if their boat being in the area was a mere coincidence.

"Okay boys," he announced, "let's wrap this up. We'll follow this track at seven knots. They shouldn't pick us up while we're astern of them and Jim, make sure the crew keeps it quiet for the next couple of hours. I don't want anyone banging their head against the hull and alerting the Russians that they have a 'tail'," he added with a smile.

"I'll make sure they understand, sir. Head banging will only be permitted against interior frames."

"Thanks Jim. Helm, make our course two eight zero degrees and maintain seven knots."

The helmsman repeated the order properly and nudged the wheel over slightly, bringing the destroyer to the new course.

Twenty-three miles ahead of *HMCS Margaree*, two hundred and sixty feet below the surface, *K-32* moved quietly through the water on almost the same course. Her captain was relaxing in his cabin, writing the more recent events of the day into the submarine's log book. This mission would bring great honour to the Soviet navy, he expected. Having escaped from the Canadian destroyer, repaired the damage to his boat and yet again evaded not only an American destroyer but a submarine as well, would look very good on his record. Perhaps after successfully completing this mission, he dared hope that he might be rewarded the red star insignia of Hero of the Soviet Union for his bravery and perseverance. He'd known other officers who had received the award for doing much less.

The Soviet captain had been generous with his praise of the crew upon learning from his sonar operator that they had successfully evaded the pursuing destroyer. Now they were safe to continue the mission and retrieve the Spetsnaz. The commandos would be angry for the delay in being picked up, but when they heard of the ordeal he and his crew had been through, even they in their great arrogance would surely have to appreciate the diligence shown by *K-32's* men. Yes, he thought, standing up and gazing into the small mirror above his bed. The medal would not only further his career but would also be an attraction to the women who lived around his base.

* * *

Walking along behind the Canadian sergeant, who was no longer on the point, medals were the furthest thing from Senior Lieutenant Kristoff Nikolev's mind. He was however pondering how long the submarine captain would wait for them before finally giving up and heading home. Looking at his watch, he realized they had been due at the rendezvous half an hour ago. He imagined the frantic scene in Moscow, when the submarine captain reported that Nikolev and his men had failed to return from their mission.

Kristoff knew there would be no rescue or reinforcements sent. They would simply be removed from the active list and their records placed in the ever growing file of 'unknowns'. His mother would be notified that her son had died as the result of a 'training accident' and she would receive a few extra Rubles every month, the value the State placed on her son's life.

"It is a nice morning."

Turning at the sound, Kristoff realized Grandfather had joined him. The old man moved very quietly, he noted.

"Yes Grandfather. It is a beautiful morning," he replied, noticing for the first time since they had continued their trek this morning that it was indeed going to be a clear day.

"We reach camp in four hours."

"That will be good. Then what will you do?" Kristoff found himself curiously interested in the old man.

"I will go back to my village and hunt."

"How large is your village?"

"Not big," Grandfather replied. "A hundred people."

"Much like the village I come from, north of Moscow." The commando went on, ignoring the security breech the information represented. "My mother still lives there - alone now."

"Your father was a good man. He is a hero. Your country will take good care of her, will it not?" Grandfather looked into the man's eyes and noted the softness and sorrow that filled them. He imagined this man's mother grieving, having lost the person she so loved as he had so long ago.

It had been wartime of course, and Grandfather knew from experience that there really were no good men or bad men on the battlefield. Only those who survived and those who did not. The winners were called victorious and heroes. The losers were the vanquished and evil.

"Yes grandfather, they will take care of her."

Deniigi again looked into the man's eyes and clearly saw the lie. He slowed his pace and fell back in behind the commando, walking quietly in thought. Again he imagined this man's mother and how she would react to being told that now her son would also not be coming home.

Kristoff wondered what the Canadians would do with him. He presumed they would eventually release him and send him back to his country. Almost better they killed him, the commando considered. He would never be trusted on another mission and his military career would be over. Perhaps it was time for him to find something less 'interesting', he thought. Something he could do close to home.

There had been little real information shared about the Canadians during his training for the mission, but he had read that they were a fair people. The large country had always acted as a buffer state between the two powerful adversaries but everyone knew Canada was a Western ally, part of NATO and now the new alliance; NORAD, as well.

During their intelligence briefing by the 'Canada expert', one of his men had asked why they were trying to anger this country of peace keepers. The bespectacled man standing in front of them had warned them not to be complacent – that these 'peace keepers' had a valiant military history. In fact, Canadian soldiers had proven in both major wars that they could complete tasks larger armies had failed at.

When questioned by Nikolai that perhaps they had been a country of warriors in the past but they were obviously focused on peace keeping, he had been abruptly cut off by the 'expert'. The instructor brought up an image on the projector of Canada's current weaponry. Nikolai had fallen silent and slumped back into his chair as he saw clearly that most of this 'peace keeper' nation's weapons were nuclear.

Kristoff smiled to himself. Perhaps the 'expert' should have studied a little harder and learned of this group of men who wore old clothing, carried older rifles and fought like mad men. If he ever made it back, he'd enjoy sitting with the instructor and explaining about Grandfather although he doubted anyone in the Soviet Union would believe him.

"Close it up!" Sergeant Ashe ordered. He didn't want anyone getting lost or one of the prisoners slipping away into the rugged countryside. Brian stopped and let the parade of men pass him. He noted that the two groups of Rangers were following a safe distance from the captives, but still close enough to make sure they didn't bolt and disappear.

Nodding at Grandfather as he passed by, he noticed how the old man was holding the AK-47 taken from the Russian leader. There was no question that particular rifle would not be going back to Gagetown with him.

*　*　*

"Sir, contact bearing zero seven three degrees."

Captain Dan Hetherington moved over to *USS Shark's* sonar console and looked at the display. How anyone could make anything out of the mess of static showing on the screens was a mystery to him. Years earlier when he had first stepped aboard a submarine and watched the sonar operators at work it had been all about the sounds. Now they not only listened but also watched a video display which his sonar operator assured him was the visual equivalent of what they heard through the headsets.

"What have you got?"

"Very faint contact, sir. I'm sure I have pumps though. It's probably the Russian boat coming back."

They had been sitting still for what seemed like hours after listening to the Russian submarine move off with the Canadian destroyer giving chase.

"Any sign of the destroyer," Dan asked.

"No sir. Just the boat."

Dan hoped it would stay that way. The SEAL team had been instructed to head south along the coast a mile to make sure they wouldn't be meeting *Shark* anywhere near the Russian pick up point. He pictured the SEALs mistakenly swimming up to the Soviet submarine and their surprise when they realized their error. No, Dan thought. That would not be funny!

Not far to the west of where Dan was contemplating the situation, the SEAL team had reached the rocky shores of Labrador after their long swim. Relaxing for a few minutes, they had carefully hid their flippers amongst the rocks and began the slow climb up the small cliff to the ground above, where they knew the Russians were camped.

None of the men spoke, being careful to avoid making any sound as they scaled the ragged cliff. Years of Atlantic storms had pounded natural hand and foot holds into the stone, and the climb was easier than they had anticipated.

Reaching the top, Lieutenant Gary Land gingerly pulled himself up to look over the cliff, expecting to see the Russians working around the tent, and the equipment the SEALs had studied in the photographs taken by the SR-71 over-flights. He could see the tent which appeared to be taken down but there was no sign of human activity.

Quietly lifting himself up to the ground, he lay still for a moment, his CAR-15 snug against his body to present as small a profile as possible. Slowly moving forward he could make out the wrecked remains of some kind of antennae close by the collapsed tent, but there was no sign of the commandos.

Backtracking a few feet, he leaned over the cliff's edge and signalled for the rest of the men to come up before crawling slowly over towards the tent. There were pieces of damaged equipment strewn over the ground and it appeared as though the Russians might have left in a hurry.

Seeing no sign of life, he stood and walked over to the collapsed tent.

"Shit!" He didn't have to nudge the canvas material to confirm what the shapes below the folds in the material were.

"Shit!" he said again. Louder this time.

"What is it LT?"

"Somebody beat us to it, gentleman," Gary remarked, pointing with his CAR-15 towards the lumps under the tent.

"How the hell…"

"Doesn't matter now Johnson! We have to get out of here – PRONTO!"

After erasing any sign of their presence, the SEALs lowered themselves over the cliff edge and descended to the rocky coast. Sliding their flippers on, they swam furiously until they were well to the south of the Russian camp before finally slowing their pace. Gary spoke for the first time.

"It had to be the Canadians. They must have gotten wind of what was going on and sent a unit to take them out."

"Hard to believe they had the gonads to try that, LT."

"Yeah, well remember what that guy on the sub said about them. Maybe they're tougher than we think."

"I doubt it," the young SEAL responded. "Probably had a couple a' platoons go in there, man."

Not speaking any more, the men swam slowly on to the rendezvous point. They would be a little early but only by minutes as the plan had been to kill the Russians quickly and get out immediately. The cold water did not concern them as they wore special diving suits which locked in their body heat, capable of protecting them from the numbing cold of the Atlantic Ocean for hours. Gary's mind was pondering the question none of his men had thought to ask. If the Canadians had taken out the commandos, why were they ignoring the Russian sub they had to know would be coming in to pick the commandos up?

* * *

"You still have him O'Hanlon?"

"I do, sir," Brent answered while listening to the sound of the reactor pumps aboard the Soviet submarine. Commander Delaney, monitoring through an extra headset, had to admit that he couldn't hear anything other than strange unidentifiable noises coming through the earpiece.

"Don't lose him!"

"I won't, sir," Brent replied. He wished the captain would leave and stop breaking his concentration. At one point, he thought he had picked up a second mechanical sound but it hadn't reappeared, so he returned his focus to the Soviet submarine. Without warning, the sound of the reactor pumps grew louder.

"He's slowing!"

"Helm," Barry barked into the intercom. "All stop – let her drift."

The propellers beneath the stern of the destroyer stopped turning and *Margaree* quickly lost headway, starting to wallow in the moderate seas. As the ship came to a stop, the rolling motion became more pronounced, and in the PO's mess, the rescued airmen, who moments before had been cheerfully sharing their adventure to anyone who would listen, suddenly found themselves unable to hold down their food.

"Oh man," Cormier groaned. "How do you guys stand this?"

"We don't," a sailor answered. "The ship almost never sits still like this. I wonder what's going on?"

"I don't know, but that life raft suddenly seems like…" The rest of the sentence never made it out as Robert rushed to the head to lose the first real meal he had enjoyed since being rescued.

With water no longer rushing past the sonar dome beneath the ship's bow, Brent immediately picked up the other contact he had heard and lost earlier.

"Active sonar! Submerged contact! US submarine! Two three zero degrees! Distance to contact is unknown."

Well that's just great, Barry thought. Three hours later and here they all were – together again.

"The Russian boat just started moving again," Brent announced. "He's just gone active!"

Barry and a few other officers crowded around the sonar console.

"Does he have the American?" Delaney asked. He surmised that the Russians might be well past their pick up time and were checking the area before leaving.

"Can't tell yet. He's starting to move. Pump noise increasing."

Barry hated not knowing what was going on. Not wanting to take any chances, he turned to the officer next to him.

"Get Barkus and his noisy machine back in the air. Make sure they have a full load out," he ordered. "O'Hanlon, any chance they have us?"

"No, sir. They haven't indicated that."

"Good. Let me know the second anyone farts over there!"

Commander Delaney headed for the open bridge. If the shit was about to fly he wanted to be where the captain of a warship belonged – on the bridge – the REAL bridge.

To the south west, the captain of *USS Shark* would have enjoyed the fresh air a 'real' bridge afforded right now.

"Sonar, anything?"

"No, sir. But he had to hear us."

"Okay, target him again. Let's make sure they know we're awake over here."

Aboard *K-32*, the crew did not have to be told that another warship had targeted them. The pings were clearly audible within the hull and for a moment, no one dared speak.

"Okay comrades! Now we have a toy to play with," the Russian captain announced with enthusiasm. It was a good act. The last thing in the world they needed right now was another submarine chancing upon them, and where, he wondered, were those damned Spetsnaz!? The prearranged grenade explosion the commandos were supposed to use every thirty minutes had not been detected and with an American submarine just outside his hull, he wasn't about to stay in this area for very long.

* * *

Sergeant Ashe was unhappy with the terrain. It would have been an easy trek for him and the Rangers, but with a couple of prisoners in tow, the journey was becoming more difficult with every passing minute.

"Keep it tight men!" he called back for the second time in ten minutes. Standing on a large rock he could see the Rangers climbing over the rough ground, prodding the two prisoners ahead of them. One moment they were climbing over a steep rock face and the next they were breaking through a clump of dense brush.

"Brown!"

"Yes sergeant," the Ranger called out from the tail end of the group.

"Keep an eye out for the man in front of you and don't fall behind!"

Ashe was concerned the Russians might use the terrain to their advantage and try to escape. They had been warned that the Rangers would shoot to kill if they attempted it, but Brian knew these were not run-of-the-mill Russian soldiers. The commandos had probably spent a good part of their training in escape and evasion tactics and in spite of their success to this point, he wasn't sure the Rangers would be able to do much if one of the captives made a run for it in the scraggly brush.

He did note that the Rangers had paired up, with two men closely watching each prisoner. That would certainly lessen the chances of an escape. Climbing down from his perch on the rock, he checked his compass again and followed after the men. If all went well, they'd hit camp in a few hours and be able to turn the Russians over. Then it would be another exciting jeep ride back to Goose Bay and a quick flight home. He couldn't wait to tell his wife about this adventure, certain he would be ordered not to mention it to anyone else.

Ahead of Sergeant Ashe, the men continued to traverse the rough ground with difficulty and although he was in very good shape for his age, Deniigi had started to slow down, adding to Brian's concerns. The man should not even be out here, he thought watching him climb over a rock with obvious difficulty. Grandfather's progress continued to slow, and it was apparent he was encountering some difficulty climbing the rock outcroppings which often blocked their path.

At one point, Deniigi stumbled on a particularly steep rock and looking up, saw the Russian he was guarding reaching down to help him.

"Thank you," Grandfather managed.

"You are welcome, sir. Perhaps we should stop to rest."

"No, not here," replied the Ranger. "Not the right place."

Kristoff looked at him, confused by the answer. Looking back, he saw the old man scamper across the rock, causing the Russian to suspect his apparent difficulties. Shrugging his shoulders, the Spetsnaz continued walking, but listened carefully behind for any sign that the old man was having further difficulty.

Grandfather watched the commando move ahead and easily kept up, cradling the AK-47 in his arms. He had earlier pretended to trip over a rock and stumble to his knees, hoping it would appeared to the others that he was tiring. The Ranger knew this area well and he was aware of a particular spot ahead which would be perfect for what he planned.

Kristoff looked back and saw that Grandfather no longer appeared to be having any problems making his way over the rough ground. As they rounded a corner, he could again see ahead to the front of the group and once again, he heard the man behind him trip and stumble to his knees.

"Sergeant!" he hollered ahead while turning to help the man up. Reaching down and leaning forward, he grasped the old Ranger's hand and was surprised when Grandfather brought him close with a firm grip on his arm.

"When we rest," Deniigi whispered into the Russian's ear. "Sit on the rock right across from me."

"Why..."

"Quiet!" the Ranger whispered hoarsely.

"Grandfather! Are you alright?" Church asked, his voice showing concern, as he rushed to the man's side.

"I am..." he panted. "I am okay."

"Sergeant!" Glen called out. "We need to rest!"

Brian turned and walked back to where Grandfather was sitting on the ground, wincing in pain and gingerly rubbing his right leg.

"Hold up!" Ashe called out. "We'll rest here."

The Rangers sat down, catching their breath while still keeping a close eye on their captives. Deniigi limped over to a rock and sat, again massaging his leg. Kristoff, unsure of what the man was up to sat across from him on another rock.

"Are you okay?" he asked, genuinely concerned for this old man who reminded him of his grandfather and yet possessed the energy of a man half his age.

"Yes," Grandfather answered, looking to see if anyone else was watching them. From his perch on a boulder about twenty feet away, Glen watched the Russian commando, but he was also intent on examining the AK-47 he had confiscated from their other prisoner.

"When I signal, you will drop down behind the rock. Go in that direction," Grandfather whispered to Kristoff, pointing to the west.

"But why? And your camp is that way." Kristoff replied.

"You go home and take care of your mother," Deniigi said quietly. The commando could see the compassion in the man's eyes. "They will not look for you that way."

"Thank you," Kristoff replied, meaning it.

Deniigi smiled at the Russian before suddenly falling from the rock he was sitting on. He lay on the ground not moving. Having seen him fall, Church rushed over.

"Sarge!!"

In the moment of confusion, Kristoff slid backwards off the rock he sat upon and quickly getting to his feet headed west, crouching low in the thick brush as he ran.

Brian turned, saw a couple of the Rangers kneeling over Grandfather and rushed over to find them loosening his collar.

"Is he…"

"No, he's breathing," answered Glen. "I think he's out cold though. He was just sitting there and collapsed."

"Where's the other Russian?!"

"Oh shit!" Church jumped up to a high rock and looked around. There was no sign of the commando.

"Alright, Church, Karnes - grab the 47's and head east. He must be trying to get back to the coast," Sergeant Ashe ordered the men. "We'll get Grandfather and the other prisoner back to camp."

"On the way sergeant," Church responded, quickly grabbing the AK-47.

Brian watched as the two men disappeared back the way they'd come. He honestly didn't think they would catch the commando but they had to try. He'd send reinforcements out after them once he reached the camp with the rest of the group. Leaning down next to Grandfather, Brian checked his pulse. It was fine.

"Are you able to get up Grandfather?"

"Yes."

"Do you feel dizzy? Are you in pain?" Brian asked, making sure the man wasn't having a heart attack.

"No, I am fine. Just move slow."

Sergeant Ashe looked over at Nikolai and noted his expression; one of pure anger.

"I don't want any trouble from you!" Brian got right in his face. "One wrong move and we'll tie you up and leave you here until someone comes back for you. Of course by then the wolves will have been around to visit and..."

Nikolai was too angry to care about the veiled threat. His pride was devastated that he would be the only one of his group captured alive. Until Senior Lieutenant Nikolev had escaped his own situation hadn't seemed so bad. Now he resigned himself to his fate, feeling he had let down not only the Spetsnaz, but the Motherland as well.

"I will not be any trouble," he responded, the anger visibly leaving his face.

Brian helped Deniigi to his feet and noted that the Ranger still clutched onto his rifle. Odd, that in passing out, the Ranger hadn't dropped the weapon. Picking up the FN, Brian pointed ahead with it.

"You!" he commanded, looking at the Russian. "That way!"

Slower this time, the men continued their march. Brian kept a close eye on Grandfather for any sign that the man might be having a relapse. Surprisingly, he seemed fine now and appeared to have no problem negotiating the terrain. Two hours later, they reached the camp and Brian immediately encoded a message, radioing the results of their excursion to Goose Bay where the information would be relayed to Ottawa and Gagetown.

* * *

"Sounds like they're having quite a pissing match right now, sir." In the excitement, Brent had spoken without thinking.

"Good! That means neither of them know we're here," Commander Barry Delaney replied through the intercom from the open bridge. He knew the Russians were waiting for what he presumed was a Spetsnaz team. They would be flustered at the presence of the American submarine – much more so if they knew that *Margaree* was sitting almost on top of them.

"Sir, message from Halifax." A sailor appeared at the top of the ladder from the deck below. Walking over to the sailor, Barry grabbed the folded note and read the short message. His face broke into a grin.

"Thank you son. No reply."

"Aye sir," the man replied before disappearing below.

"Lieutenant! Good news. The army got the Russian commandos."

Lieutenant Learner smiled.

"Should I raise the Sea King, sir?"

"Hell yes, Lieutenant! It's time to throw both of these assholes out of our swimming pool!"

A few minutes later, the Sea King which had been hovering just above the water a mile away swooped in fast, barely clearing the wave tops, heading for the last known position of the US sub. Arriving at the spot, Flight Lieutenant Barkus slowed the large helicopter into a hover and waited as his sonar operator lowered the dipping sonar into the water. One active ping was all it took to lock in both the American and Soviet submarines.

"Got 'em both, sir!" Sergeant Bob Turner shouted into his helmet headset. "The Ruskie is right below us and the Yank is about fifteen hundred yards bearing three one zero."

Barkus passed the information on to *Margaree* where Barry pondered it. He had a dilemma. He didn't want to spook the Russians too badly as they were trying to recover their men who of course would not be coming. History had shown time and again that too many adversaries in too close a proximity was a deadly situation at best. He didn't want to push someone into a rash or dangerous move. His concerns were validated at O'Hanlon's announcement over the ship's intercom.

"This is sonar! Russian has gone active again and opened his torpedo tube doors!"

Damn! Barry thought.

"Lieutenant! Sound Action stations!"

As the horns sounded throughout the ship, Barry could hear the clang of watertight doors being battened down.

"Sonar, what's his heading?"

"Approximately three three zero degrees, sir," Brent replied almost immediately. "He's heading for the US boat. US boat has opened torpedo doors!"

"Oh hell! Helm! Make your heading zero nine zero!" Barry wanted to put some distance between *Margaree* and whatever was about to happen below the surface in case a torpedo decided the destroyer appeared to be a much juicier target than the sub it had been fired at.

"Coms! Have the Sea King return to the ship but instruct him to remain airborne." And as an after thought he added, "Have them prepare to pick up possible survivors."

A short distance away, approximately two hundred feet below the ocean's surface, a professional bearing had blanketed the usually casual atmosphere throughout *USS Shark*. The officers and crew were meticulously going about their duties calmly in spite of the tension in the air.

"Sonar, hit him again!" Dan ordered.

"Yes sir!" A mid frequency sound wave flowed out from *Shark*, striking the Russian submarine and reflecting back.

"Bearing unchanged! Range fourteen hundred yards and closing!" There was a slight pause and… "Active sonar!! Close aboard! Dipping sonar! Canadian!"

"Shit! – Ignore it!"

Dan's mind quickly calculated the range and time it would take a torpedo to reach them.

"Ready tubes five and six!" The order echoed back to him, repeated correctly as his weapon's crew double checked that all indicators relating to the torpedo tubes were in order. The weapons officer had his hand poised over the uncovered firing switch. Seconds could make the difference in this scenario. Everyone aboard the boat was aware that in most of the simulations run at the Naval War College in Newport, Rhode Island, both submarines had been sunk ninety percent of the time in this underwater version of an old west shoot-out.

The more sensitive sonar on *Shark* had picked up *K-32* a few minutes before the Russian captain realized the American boat was there waiting. Dan knew that if he waited for the Russians to fire first, it might be too late for him to save his own command, and besides, the Russian being here in Canadian waters was provocation enough for him to act.

"Fire five! Fire six! Helm! Right turn to one eight zero! Make your depth three hundred and fifty feet!" From the bottom pair of tubes in the round bow of the submarine, two MK-37's emerged. Their electric motors enabled them to swim out from the torpedo tubes rather than being ejected with a blast of compressed air. This left the enemy with no tell tale sound signature to indicate that they had been fired at until their sonar picked up the torpedo's speeding props.

"Depth below keel is three hundred and sixty eight feet, captain," the helmsman announced, in case with all the excitement, his captain had forgotten how close they were to shore.

"Thanks Carey." He hadn't. "Make your speed twenty knots."

The crew hung on to the nearest object as the submarine twisted in a hard turn to starboard and dove sharply to the ordered depth. Their only chance to evade a counter strike was to turn away and hope the Russians would be too busy trying to avoid the MK-37 torpedoes to fire any fish at them.

Aboard *K-32* things were happening far too fast for the captain's liking. The sonar operator had just reported an active sonar from behind them and had barely finished speaking when the second operator had turned from his console shouting.

"Captain! Torpedoes! Same bearing as the other submarine!"

"Dive to forty metres! Turn to port! Make course zero two zero!" The submarine dove and turned quickly as her large rudder moved to the right.

"Torpedoes on same bearing!" Called out the Russian sonar operator.

"Release counter measures!"

"Counter measures released, sir!"

From small tubes in the back of *K-32's* sail, a pair of cylindrical shaped objects, 35 inches long, propelled themselves away from the submarine. A vibrator built into the nose of the devices caused a distortion in the water to hopefully distract the torpedoes' sonar. One of the MK-37's immediately turned to chase after the decoys and lost contact with the boat.

The second torpedo continued to bore in on its target and quickly caught up to the submarine, exploding against the hull on the starboard side, just behind the control room. Something in the warhead of the torpedo malfunctioned however, and the explosion was far below the force that 330 pounds of HBX-3 should have released.

Inside *K-32*, the crew were slowly picking themselves up off the deck. The captain held his hand tightly against his forehead, stemming the flow of blood from a gash he had received when he was thrown violently against the dive panel.

"Damage report!" he ordered, while the zampolit attempted to wrap a bandage around his head.

"Propulsion room reports no damage to the reactors, sir, but there is a leak in the galley. They request we surface to make repairs."

"Nyet!"

The last thing he could to do right now was to surface with the American submarine so close. It would be tantamount to surrendering. Grabbing the microphone, he contacted the mess area.

"This is the captain. How bad is the leak?"

"Comrade captain!" He didn't need to hear more. The shouting in the background and the sound of water hitting a nearby bulkhead was enough. "We are doing everything we can but the water is rising!"

"Thank you comrade," his voice lowered as he replaced the microphone. He knew there was no choice.

"Dimitry, bring us to the surface. Quickly!"

"Yes comrade captain!" The sailor was thankful they weren't going to try and save the submarine while submerged. Pulling the levers which activated the emergency blow of the ballast tanks, the sailor was rewarded with his ears popping, as high pressure air blowing water from the submarine's ballast tanks, also leaked into the pressure hull. Instead of the usual push on his feet as the boat began to surface however, the submarine wallowed, not appearing to change depth.

"Captain," he looked over at Cherenkov, "nothing is happening."

"We have taken on too much water. Engineering! Give me maximum power on the reactors!" He knew their only chance was to drive the submarine to the surface using forward motion and the diving planes. Once there, they'd hopefully be able to pump out enough water to keep *K-32* afloat.

"Reactors at one hundred and three percent, captain," announced the chief engineer from his console.

"Helm! All up on the planes. Let us leave this place!"

"Yes, comrade captain!"

The sailor manning the boat's wheel yanked back hard on the control column, causing the planes on the submarine's bow and stern to turn up. Slowly at first, the depth gauge indicator started to climb. All eyes in the control room were focused on the needle as it moved hesitantly up the linear display. It crept further as they watched and then began to move more quickly as it passed the thirty meter mark, continuing even faster towards the black line that indicated the submarine was on the surface.

"Hang on," the executive officer yelled as the boat rose quickly. The *November* class submarine broke the surface in a huge cloud of spray, water cascading in waves from her hull.

A short distance away, the crew above deck aboard *HMCS Margaree*, looked on in shock as the vessel popped to the surface like a cork.

Aboard *USS Shark*, the sound of *K-32's* ballast tanks being blown had been picked up through the turbulence in the water caused by the exploded torpedoes.

"I have her sir!" The sonar operator had announced. "She's blown tanks and is surfacing!"

Dan had been surprised at the news. The two explosions heard so close together had surely signalled a pair of hits and there was no submarine which could stand the power of one MK-37 torpedo's warhead, let alone two. His mind had been a torment of second guesses at his decision to fire on the Russians. No submarine captain would expect anything less caught flat footed in another country's territorial waters, but he was concerned that he may have jumped the gun since they were within Canada's limits and not the United States'. He felt a flood of relief wash over him at the news the other submarine had survived.

"COB, periscope depth. Let's see what we've got."

Aboard *HMCS Margaree*, Brent O'Hanlon had picked up the explosions and reported them to the bridge where Barry made a quick decision to turn back towards the Soviet submarine's last known location.

Lieutenant Commander Delaney was concerned that he might be taking his ship into dangerous waters, but someone had been hit and there might be survivors. He had radioed Halifax with the news but there had been no reply as of yet. Small wonder, they probably had no idea what to tell him. This wouldn't be playing well in Ottawa either, he thought just as *K-32* exploded to the surface ahead of them.

* * *

"Yes, comrade Premier," Admiral Victor Sominski agreed, "It is best that this information not be released. I will inform you immediately upon the submarine's return. The crew will know better than to speak of this incident."

After saying good bye, the admiral slowly replaced the receiver on the telephone, his mind churning over the events of the day. The Soviet Premier had understandably been angry at the news of the unauthorized mission and had immediately ordered the arrest of general Ustinov. The admiral momentarily wondered if the man would be allowed to live. Probably not, he surmised. The Politburo did not like to leave loose ends laying around which might come back and haunt them. Brushing the thought aside, he focused on solving the current dilemma - their not being able to reach *K-32* over any of the navy communications systems.

* * *

"Unbelievable!"

The Canadian Prime Minister was exhausted from the long night of waiting but this latest news brought him fully alert. With the Russian commandos disposed of he had hoped this misadventure was over but had decided to wait in the bunker until the Rangers reported back to their camp.

"...and *Margaree's* captain is certain the torpedoes were fired by the American submarine...?" the Admiral stopped as an aide handed him a note. Reading it quickly, he continued. "This is interesting; it appears the Russian submarine survived and has surfaced. Commander Delaney is heading for them to render assistance."

"He'd better tread carefully, admiral. It sounds like there are some mighty itchy trigger fingers out there today."

"He's one of our best sir – he'll be okay," the officer replied, hoping he was right.

* * *

"Bridge, radar," came the report from *HMCS Margaree's* CCR. "Small target dead ahead!"

The announcement came only seconds after the men on the bridge witnessed the Soviet submarine surfacing. Ignoring the intercom for the moment, Barry yelled into the voice tube, "All stop!" Then realizing what he'd done, punched the intercom button and repeated, "All stop! Medical on deck!"

Within moments a group of sailors appeared alongside the three inch gun mount, laying out stretchers and medic bags on the deck around them. Barry watched as the Russian submarine settled into the waves and began to flounder, water cascading off the casing and down the rounded sides of the warship's hull. He immediately recognized the pennant number on the side of the sail and pointed it out to Lieutenant Learner.

"Look familiar?"

"I'll be damned."

"Better hope not, Henry. I'm not sure getting this close is a smart move. Their reactor better be intact."

"Bridge, sonar. The American submarine is closing on us sir." The message came through the intercom speaker behind the officers.

"I hope that asshole isn't stupid enough to try and sink them right under our noses!" Delaney roared. He was furious. Like the Prime Minister, he was outraged with all this foreign traffic in HIS part of the ocean.

"Air!" Barry spoke into the intercom. "Have Mr. Barkus sweep that US boat out of here!"

The message was echoed back to him and a few minutes later, Delaney watched as the Sea King roared over the ship and headed west. He noticed the dipping sonar starting to unreel from beneath the helicopter as it sped away and muttered under his breath, "I wouldn't think they'd want to lower the sonar while they're moving that fast."

Aboard the Sea King, there was agreement with the commander.

"Head is dropping sir! I still don't think this is a good idea!"

"Noted sergeant!" Phillip yelled into the headpiece. "I just want to make sure those yanks don't sink our deck!"

Within minutes Barkus had the helicopter over the location of the American boat and quickly lost altitude, lowering the sonar head into the ocean. A moment later, the active sonar had the submarine.

"Good aim sir! He's almost right below us."

"Keep hitting him! I don't care if you burn out the transducers," Phillip ordered. "Just make sure he realizes we're here!"

Aboard *USS Shark* the sonar operator had removed his headset to keep from being deafened. He didn't need it anyway as the pings were clearly audible throughout the boat.

"Dipping sonar sir. Definitely Canadian," the petty officer reported. "I think his send button is broken. He's just pinging away and he knows where we are."

"Thank you." Dan had figured out what was going on. Obviously the Canadian destroyer had quietly tailed the Soviets back and that meant they were aware of the shot he'd taken. If it wasn't for the SEALs he would have simply run, but leaving them behind to be picked up by the Canadians wouldn't play well back home.

"Cob," he hesitantly ordered. "Surface the boat."

"Surfacing the boat, aye sir," he acknowledged, while looking back at the captain with a questioning gaze.

Aboard the Sea King, the sound of ballast tanks being blown was immediately picked up.

"Sir!" Hollered Sergeant Turner, seated at the sonar position in the Sea King's tightly packed fuselage. "He's blowing ballast!"

"Far out!" Barkus smiled broadly. "Damned yankees! That'll teach 'em!"

Looking down to his left, he saw the sleek sail of the *Skipjack* class submarine break the surface followed by her rounded, whale shaped hull. The boat remained motionless as Phillip brought the Sea King around in a lazy circle over the sub.

"Get lots of pictures guys! We're gonna want proof of this!" He laughed aloud, enjoying the obvious frustration on the faces of the men who had appeared on the sub's bridge as he buzzed the sail.

Half a mile away, the Russian submarine lay still while Barry brought *Margaree* close alongside, placing *K-32* in her lee. There was no refusal of assistance this time as the Soviet captain was not sure he'd be able to save his command from sinking. Although he'd never let the submarine fall into the hands of the Canadians or anyone else, losing his crew was another matter.

"Ahoy!" Barry hollered over to the sub using a megaphone. "Does anyone speak English?"

The look of confusion on the faces of the officers visible aboard the Russian boat was answer enough. Reaching for the intercom button, Barry called down to the bridge.

"Lieutenant Jenson, get one of those Russian airmen up here! On the double!"

Three minutes later, Asimov, the co-pilot of the TU-95 Bear was standing on the open bridge looking with a stunned expression at the Soviet submarine floating only a few hundred feet away from the destroyer.

"I understand you speak pretty good english," Barry asked.

"Yes comrade captain. What is it you wish me to do?"

"Captain will do fine." Barry handed him the megaphone. "Would you ask your friends over there if they require any assistance?"

"Yes com…captain."

Speaking into the megaphone, Asimov first identified himself to make it known he had survived the plane crash as he wasn't sure if the Canadians would ever let him return home again. He then inquired as to whether the sailors needed any assistance. Unlike the last time the two warships had met, *K-32's* crew needed help and desperately.

"Tell him we need pumps immediately!" the Soviet captain hollered in Russian from the boat's control room to the men on the bridge. He was trying to conduct damage control operations while at the same time compiling a list of injured crew members and which of them were in serious condition. It had not occurred to him at the moment that none of the bridge crew spoke english and yet they were communicating with the Canadian destroyer.

He despised asking the Westerners for help, but saving his crew was much more important than his pride. The leak in the galley was almost dogged but there was still water entering from somewhere and the small onboard pumps were not able to keep up. A yell from the bridge above relieved him of that fear.

"They say they will send over two portable pumps for us to use right away, comrade captain. They are asking now if we require any medical assistance."

The captain looked over at his medical officer who's grim expression confirmed what he already knew.

"Ask the Canadians if they have a surgeon on board. We have two men who are gravely wounded and require immediate help."

The request would probably end his career he thought, even though the zampolit had readily agreed to it. Bringing foreign sailors aboard any Soviet submarine, let alone a nuclear one, would surely result in his immediate court martial upon returning home, but better that than losing two good men who might have been saved.

Aboard *Margaree*, Barry was torn with the decision of sending ANY of his men aboard the crippled boat. There was not only the obvious danger of the submarine sinking with them aboard but also the chance that the Soviets might attempt to take them hostage. Not to mention the known instability of their nuclear reactors.

The strong bond amongst all mariners prevailed however and he ordered his medical officer and an assistant into the ship's boat to be taken across to the submarine. Lieutenant Commander Delaney needn't have worried as less than an hour later his men reappeared on the submarine's deck, making their way back into the boat tied alongside.

Minutes later they were both on *Margaree's* bridge giving their report.

"They have two men who were badly injured when the torpedo hit, sir, but I believe we have stabilized them well enough for their trip home. The pumps are coping with the leaks and they seem to have the damage contained. I doubt they'll be submerging any time soon however."

"Just as well," Barry noted. "I want them sailing out of here on the surface so no one else takes a shot at them." He paused. "Learner, make to Halifax that we'll be escorting the Russian boat out of Canadian waters."

"Right away sir."

"Okay, you two get back to the airmen. How are they doing anyway?"

"The Canadians are fine, sir. They're eating our stores down to nothing. The Soviets were shocked at the quality of the food we fed them," he added with a laugh. "I get the impression their food back home is not up to our cook's standards."

That's great," Barry replied and turned to Asimov with a smile.

"Asimov, I'm glad you liked the food, but I'm afraid it's time for you to rejoin your countrymen." He reached out a hand and the Russian shook it firmly. "Thank you for your help. Please go down and inform your... comrade...that we will be sending you both over to the submarine, so you may return home with them."

"Thank you sir!" The bear hug he gave Barry and the huge smile on the airman's face was understandable in any language.

"Now, let's see what our American friend is up to," Barry murmured to himself while heading down the ladder. Reaching the 'air' control position, he leaned against the radar scope.

"So what's Barkus doing to the Americans?"

"They've surfaced and it appears that Bar...err Flight Lieutenant Barkus is 'pestering' them sir."

"Good!" Barry had a good idea what 'pestering' entailed in the pilot's mind. "Have we established communications with the yanks yet?"

"We have sir. They've made a rather strong protest and demanded that we stop badgering them and I might add the language used was rather strong."

"I bet it was!"

Barry moved over to the radio room, actually an alcove on the starboard side. "Okay petty officer, put me through to the American boat."

"Here you are sir. We have them up now."

"American submarine, this is Canadian warship *HMCS Margaree*. Do you read me?"

The sailor at the radio console aboard *Shark* recognized the authority in the voice coming through his headset and called over to Dan.

"Captain, I think this is someone you'll want to talk to."

"Thanks," Dan replied, reaching for the microphone and headset.

"This is the American warship, we read you *Margaree*. We request that you call off the helo."

No doubt you do, Barry muttered under his breath, amused at the American officer refusing to identify his submarine. Silent service indeed!

"*USS Shark*, this is *Margaree*. We thought we'd stand by in case you have problems locating your SEAL team."

Barry laughed out loud knowing that would hit home hard. There was a pause of several seconds before an answer came back over the headset. He could picture the sub's captain trying to figure out if it was a lucky guess or if his government had notified the Canadians as to what was going on.

"We appreciate that and thank you but do not require assistance at this time, *Margaree*."

"Yeah, I'll bet," Barry said to the petty officer sitting in front of him. "Get me the Sea King, John. I want to rattle this guy's chain some more."

"*Buttersquare* is on channel three", the young man replied, switching frequencies.

"*Buttersquare*, this is *Flapjack One*, climb a few hundred feet and see if you can spot some men treading water over there."

"Roger that," Phillip replied, confused at the order as there had been no report of anyone in trouble or falling overboard. Pulling back on the controls he slowly brought the aircraft higher, until a few minutes later he had a panoramic view of the area and the submarine below was shrunk to the size of a toy.

Setting the auto pilot, he grabbed the worn binoculars that hung from a hook on his left.

"Well I'll be damned," he muttered after searching the water's surface for a few minutes.

The SEAL team, oblivious to everything that had taken place around them were quite surprised to see a helicopter suddenly swooping down on them from the east. As the large, noisy aircraft came closer, the SEALs identified it as a Sea King and waved up at it, thinking for a moment they were being picked up by one of their surface ships due to some change in plans.

As Phillip swung the helicopter's tail around and the bright roundel with the red maple leaf in its center came into view, the SEALs stopped waving.

"Shit!" Ensign Grant Donaldson screamed, his shout drowned out by the rotors. "Shit! Shit! Shit!"

"Yeah," Lieutenant Hansen sighed. "That pretty much says it."

"You guys want a lift?!" Sub Lieutenant Kevin Long hollered out the open window on the co-pilot's side of the Sea King. "Your sub's over that way!" He pointed to a spot just over the horizon.

"Why not!" Hansen hollered back up at the helicopter, wondering if they could even hear him over the rotors. "This mission has been fubared since we started!"

Phillip brought the Sea King down slowly until it was almost floating on the surface and the SEALs were helped aboard. After making sure the new passengers were securely strapped in, Barkus climbed the aircraft and roared low over the surface towards the submarine.

On the sail of *USS Shark* Captain Dan Hetherington watched the helicopter approach and grimaced at the sight of one of the SEALs waving at him through the open door in the aircraft's side.

"There is going to be hell to pay in Washington when this hits the fan," he noted unhappily.

*   *   *

An hour and a half after the last SEAL had been lowered to *Shark's* deck, the Prime Minister was back in his office on the phone.

"Yes, I will find out who authorized this mission and you can count on my foot up his ass, Mr. Prime Minister."

The President of the United States wasn't used to having another leader speak to him as the irate Prime Minister had for the past five minutes, but the Canadian leader hadn't given him much opportunity to protest during the call to this point. It was clear the man was livid. He had even suggested that his destroyer could very well have sunk *USS Shark* and been well within their right to do so (the President had been shocked when the Prime Minister threw the identity of the submarine at him as though he were discussing the weather)!

"Well you'd better! Next time, I'll order my men to drag your SEALs to Ottawa and they can damn well walk home from here!" With that, he slammed the phone down, not for one moment believing the President was unaware who had ordered the SEAL mission and that he hadn't signed off on it himself.

"That's one, Suzanne. Now get me the Kremlin!"

The Prime Minister's personal secretary had never seen the man like this. She had heard him clearly through the thick office door and in the two years at her desk had never heard him use language like that before.

"Right away Prime Minister."

The Prime Minister of Canada sat back in his overstuffed chair. Damn, he thought. The men of the Canadian Armed Forces had pulled it off. They and a little known group of civilians far to the north, called the Canadian Rangers.

* * *

Far to the north, Grandfather slowly opened the door of the little house he had lived in with his wife. Again, the same feeling of emptiness greeted him, but this time there was a difference. The anger he had felt for so many years was gone, replaced with a peace he had not felt in years.

* * *

A black staff car pulled away from the headquarters building of the Soviet army offices and rapidly picked up speed. Shackled in handcuffs in the back seat, General Ustinov sat silently, watching the sights of Moscow rush by his window for what he knew would be the last time.

He hadn't spoken a word to the three men who had literally dragged him from his office and out the main entrance of the headquarters building. The very public scene was to make sure any western spies who might be watching, of which there were several, would report that the Soviet government had made good on its promise to the Canadian Prime Minister.

Watching from his office window, Admiral Sominski felt a moment of pity for the officer, but only for a moment. His submarine was limping back to its base and not only had the new vessel been damaged by the Americans, but a serious breach of security had occurred when two Canadian sailors had been brought on board to treat the injured crew members.

He had already sent a message to *K-32's* captain informing him that his presence was required immediately upon his return. Admiral Sominski chuckled to himself. The man was probably sure he would be executed for the treasonous act and the admiral would let him ponder that thought all the way home. When Captain Cherenkov showed up in his office, he planned to give him a severe dressing down for almost losing his command. Then he would slowly reach into his desk while staring the man straight in the eye. While the man sweated, wondering if he was to be shot right there in the admiral's office, he would pull out a bottle of his best vodka, pour the man a drink, and toast him for putting his crew's safety above that of his boat.

After the incident aboard *K-19*, the Soviet navy had begun to reinvent itself. Yes, Sominski surmised, it would take a great deal of time, but men like Cherenkov were just the kind needed to fill the posts currently held by old die hard Soviets. Returning to his desk, the admiral looked disdainfully at the thick pile of papers neatly arranged on one corner. An army may march on its stomach he reflected, but a navy sails on paper.

* * *

Aboard *USS Shark*, the SEALs were re-establishing themselves into the cramped confines of the torpedo spaces. To a man, they were disgusted with the way the mission had played out and were dreading their return to Little Creek. After being unceremoniously dropped on *Shark's* deck by the Canadian Sea King, they had all watched in humiliation as the men aboard the chopper had given the submarine's crew a jaunty salute. The Canadians had been a bit taken aback when the submarine's captain had returned the salute from atop the sail, followed by a grinning thumbs up.

Shortly after *Shark's* last hatch had been secured, Dan ordered the chief of the boat to dive the submarine and head east to international waters. He was not looking forward to ComSub Atlantic's reaction to this cruise. In the torpedo room, the silence was broken only by the submarine's crew going about their duties. They gave the SEALs as wide a berth as possible, the news of their retrieval by the Canadians having spread throughout the boat.

"Man," Petty Officer Tanner spoke, finally breaking the uneasy silence. "I heard those Canadians were tough!"

"Yeah, so you told us," Ensign Shepherd grunted. "Damn commies."

"Stow it, ensign." Lieutenant Hansen growled.

Four hours later, Lieutenant Commander Barry Delaney was again enjoying the fresh air washing over the open bridge of *HMCS Margaree* as the destroyer crashed through the waves on a southerly course towards Halifax. The Sea King was safely stowed in the hanger where the airman were recounting the tails of their adventure over and over again to the destroyer's crew.

The Russian submarine was just disappearing over the horizon, or rather the large ship towing it was. The second encounter between the Canadian and Soviet warships had been more cordial than the first time they'd met. Pleasantries had been exchanged and a few tokens found their way back and forth between the two vessels. More importantly, the Canadians had sent over two boatloads of fresh food which even the most diehard Communist aboard *K-32* had welcomed with open arms. The reality of the situation never diminished however and care was taken by the sailors on both sides to divulge nothing of their vessels capabilities.

The Argus survivors had recovered their strength and there had been a short, emotional good bye on the helicopter deck between themselves and the two Soviet airmen before they had transferred over to the submarine.

Following that, they once again settled down to their status as 'guests of honour' aboard the destroyer.

Pudgy Cormier was making a pest of himself with the Sea King crew, asking about every part of the helicopter and comparing notes on its various systems with those on the Argus. He found it amusing at first how the dipping sonar operated, but soon appreciated how advantageous the system could be, especially when dealing with shallow thermal layers. Barkus had just started to kid him about a dipping sonar for the Argus, hanging from some super strength cable, before Robert had walked away in disgust.

Over the coming days the airmen would find life on the ship boring with nothing for them to do, so Barry had them assigned to simple watches which would keep them out from underfoot until they reached Halifax. The Argus crew missed their new Soviet friends, who had amused them to no end with stories of life in the Soviet Union and the constant game of prodding each other for technical information.

The Canadians had been surprised at how many of their presumptions about the Soviet Union were incorrect. The Russians as well, had been equally surprised to learn that Canadians were not as they had been painted by their political officers, mere puppets, with their American masters pulling the strings.

On *HMCS Margaree's* bridge, Commander Delaney relaxed as the ship cut through a moderately choppy sea. The sun's rays were warm today, a sure sign of the coming summer. He was daydreaming about his leave which would be coming up soon, when the speaker behind him came to life, interrupting his thought.

"Bridge, sonar! Contact bearing zero three one degrees. Range unknown."

He recognized O'Hanlon's voice and smiled.

"Man really must pull them out of his ass!" he remarked, heading for the ladder below.

* * *

"Yes sir, we were following standard procedures," Sergeant Brian Ashe explained to the colonel sitting on the edge of his desk. He had arrived back in Gagetown half an hour earlier after a quick flight from Goose Bay, Labrador where he had enjoyed a farewell drink with the Rangers. Church had produced an unmarked bottle of clear liquid and after being assured that it would not kill or blind him, Brian had toasted the mission with the group of haggard looking but happy men.

Ashe had spent over an hour upon returning to the encampment, jotting down notes about the past week while they were fresh in his memory. Looking back, he'd found it hard to believe that such a short time had elapsed since the onslaught of the mission, but Brian knew how important it was to record his thoughts as quickly as possible, for once the adrenalin completely drained from his body, a lot of his memories of the mission would disappear with it.

Everything had been textbook – well more or less, he thought as he had continued to write down the events of the past few days. The escaped Russian would soon be rounded up. Spetsnaz or not, he had nowhere to go unless he wanted to try and make his way north across the pole. Not much chance of that this time of year. He paused in his writing and put the pen down. In the pit of his stomach he felt there was more to the Russian's escape than met the eye.

Closing the journal half an hour later and stretching to relieve the soreness in his legs, the sergeant had packed his few belongings and gone to say good by to the Rangers, only to find that they would be traveling back to Goose along with him. Upon landing there, Grandfather had shaken hands with Brian and invited him back to visit someday.

Now, back at Gagetown, New Brunswick, Ashe's commanding officer was trying to satisfy his own curiosity as to what might have happened to allow one of the prisoners to escape from a group of six armed men.

"It was just a lucky break for him", Ashe continued. "Grandfa - Ranger Deniigi had fallen and injured himself and when the rest of the men turned to assist him, the Russian slipped away. The team I sent out searched the immediate area to the east but didn't find any trace of the man.

"You don't think there were any sympathisers in the Ranger group?" The colonel looked him straight in the eye.

"Communist sympathisers?" Brian asked, unable to contain his surprise at the question. "No, not a chance sir. Most patriotic bunch I've ever seen. I think we should look at bringing a few of them down for our next exercise though. They could teach us a thing or two about tracking."

The colonel shrugged.

"Okay Ashe. Fine job! I've cleared some time off for you with the major. Go see what that wife of yours has been up to while you've been gone."

"Thank you, sir." Sergeant Ashe saluted smartly and turned to leave.

"Better make it quick, sergeant," the Colonel threw at Ashe as he left, a mischievous twinkle in his eyes. "I heard she's been to see doc a couple of times this week and she looked mighty happy when she left him the last time."

Brian stopped in his tracks and looked back at the colonel, a startled expression on his face.

"Just act surprised when she tells you," the officer smiled at him. "You'll want to stop off at the store and pick up some flowers on the way home. Might be a good idea not to just walk in and sit on your ass like you usually do."

"Thank you! Yes, sir!" Damn! Brian thought, rushing out of the building. I hope it's a boy!

* * *

Three weeks later, walking hand in hand along the main street of Chatham, New Brunswick, Squadron Leader Ben Jones and his wife Joanne were basking in the first warm day of spring. They had just enjoyed a nice lunch at one of the local restaurants and were heading back to married quarters when a man walking at a fast pace in the opposite direction nearly ran into them while looking back over his shoulder.

"Oh, I am very sorry," he apologized, speaking in a thick accent.

"That's okay," Ben answered with a smile, noting his rough clothing. He then added quietly to his wife, "Must be off one of the foreign fishing ships."

The man continued down the street and seeing that no one was following, walked onto the pier towards a large factory trawler. The ship was a regular visitor to Chatham, and her captain had docked here to allow his crew the opportunity of stocking up on fresh food and supplies before returning out to sea. They would continue fishing the rich grounds off eastern Canada until the holds were strained to capacity with the ocean's bounty. Then the rust streaked ship with the hammer and sickle insignia painted on its stack, would return to Russia with its catch.

Kristoff looked up at the faded emblem and for the first time in almost a month breathed a sigh of relief, knowing he would see his mother again. She would probably not recognize him. He had lost much of his body weight from eating only what he could forage. His Spetsnaz training had paid off however, and only while stealing a small boat to cross the St Lawrence, had someone almost seen him. While paddling away from the northern shore, a large dog had come running towards him. He ducked below the sides of the wooden boat and waited, not daring to breath, but no one appeared and the dog finally stopped barking and went away.

His exit options on this mission had been few, and the one which seemed most likely to succeed was making his way to the Miramichi River, where Soviet trawlers sometimes came to restock before heading back to their ports in Russia. Reaching his destination, he had skulked around the town of Chatham for a few days, watching the river for any ship flying the flag of the USSR. Most of the time he amused himself by hiding in the woods adjacent to a Canadian air base and watching the interceptors take off and land. Kristoff knew the military police would not find his presence amusing but he was well trained in evasion and had no intention of being spotted.

He had been walking along the main street of town late one afternoon when he had finally spotted a Russian factory ship tied up at the pier. He realized he would have to be careful as the civilian crew might not believe his story and could even threaten to turn him over to the Canadians. Glancing back before making a left turn down to the docks, he had nearly walked into a man strolling down the street with a woman. Nikolev apologized and tried to act unconcerned, but a warning from inside screamed that he was in danger.

The couple continued on however, simply smiling at him. Kristoff made his way down the road and marvelled at how there was so little security at this pier so close to a NORAD airbase. The Soviet flag fluttering from the ship's stern beckoned him and he moved closer to the dock crouching between two buildings. Taking one more careful look around he strode purposely to the gangway that led up the side of the ship to the deck. Half way up the companionway a shout from below caused him to freeze.

"Where do you think you are going?!" The yell, in Russian, had come from a man on the pier below.

Kristoff smiled and turned, looking down at him.

"Home," he replied.